ARCTIC
CIRCLES

PHYL MANNING

December, 2010
Phyl Manning

RAVEN'S WING BOOKS

Ward Hill, MA

Arctic Circles
By
Phyl Manning

ISBN: 978-0-9801004-6-4

Cover Art: Steve Ferchaud, www.steveferchaud.com

Book Design: Pam Marin-Kingsley, www.far-angel.com

Stylized "frost-circles" background taken from the ice photography of Doug Bratten.

Published in 2010
by

RAVEN'S WING BOOKS
Ward Hill, MA

Dedicated to
Kent Lee Brisby
and
Karol Lynne Brisby Saritaş
who consistently give me courage
and never disappoint

CHARACTERS

INUPIAT (Inuit)

NIK (NEEK): At the age of fourteen winters, Nik is an artist and a dreamer— but does he have what it takes to become an *Inupiat* man?

SITOK (SEE-toak):At seventeen, Nik's older brother is short on words but long on action.

KITI (KEY-TEE):Quick-tongued "grandmother" to Nik and Sitok, tale-teller, healer; more powerful than she realizes.

ARAJIK (ah-RAH-zhick): Father of Nik and Sitok, "son" of Kiti, *will* travel—even if it kills him!

MAWENA (mah-WAY-nah): Mother of Nik and Sitok, Arajik's wife, and known to hold a grudge.

URGIT (er-GEET)Twenty and ignorant, is he stupid, evil or merely untaught?

SARUNA (sah-ROO-nah): Urgit's aunt; how far must family loyalty stretch?

PAK (PAHK): Urgit's father, Saruna's brother, someone known not to have survived the summer.

POTOK (POE-tock):Once Arajik's treacherous friend and peer, he now wants everything.

MALEET (mah-LEET):Wife of Potok, she wants her *share* of everything.

ERIN (AYE-reen): Potok and Maleet's eldest daughter; she only wants Sitok.

UNIPAK (OO-nee-pahk): A talented bully who is politically connected.

ATIK (ah-TEEK):Loyal, this small man hunts, dances, sings—and patiently bides his time.

TUKLA (TUKE-lah): Dependable young harpooner who proves himself strong and true.

WUTIK (WOO-teek) Harpooner; Tukla's friend—up to a point.

POSI (POE-see): Older villager, mask dancer.

POONA (POO-nah): Newcomer; here comes the whale!

AKINI (ah-KEE-nee): Poona's young wife with infant.

KOTIL (KOE-teel): Newcomer, paddler from the north who accompanies Poona

KRINGMERK (Sled Dog)

NUKO (NEW-ko): Valiant dog that rushes headlong into trouble.

KALUNAIT ("Heavy Eyebrows": Westerners) . . . or DOG PEOPLE

CLIFFORD BELSON (PEHL-son, to villagers): Anthropologist focused on traditional *Inupiat* culture wants to discover what's not in his books.

BONNIE BELSON (PAH-nee, to villagers):Belson's 12-year-old daughter focuses on *people* . . . with no idea what's in her father's books.

PROLOGUE . . .

With sheltered spots containing ancient ice that never thaws completely, the barren Arctic land is deep permafrost which roils and twists with every changing season. Warring winds prevail. Summer is brief and blinding, sun-drenched continually around the clouds and rain throughout daytime and what in other places would be night. Thundering giant tides pound upon and rearrange coastlines, pummel glacier edges near the shore to hasten the birth of enormous calves that tumble booming to the sea. On land is rolling prairie, green with meadow grasses and sprinkled with bright flower, low bush, sour berry. Here are meandering shallow streams, bogs where a top few inches of the frozen land has melted and given up its moisture. The air is clamorous with insect drone and the quarrel of a million immigrant birds ground nesting with their eggs; for no tree is in this place, no stick of wood, no land form to use for visual reference.

Then comes winter, long and dark, storm filled with no sun showing for three months, and only a brief glow on the south horizon for weeks on either side of that Great Darkness. Sometimes comes a north-sky drape of color swirls, the aurora borealis, *flowing large and small, up, down, side to side—churning, blending hue and tint to delight any human eye which may glance in that direction. For* Inuit, *these are spirits at leisure.*

The time is 1935. In city centers to the south, east and west, people are dancing to the fashionable rumba, Alcoholics Anonymous is organized in New York City. Madame Curie has experimented with radium and died from the radiation in the year before, and Domagk of Germany is helping Bayer with developing the first sulpha drug. People are humming "Begin the Beguine" and—the Great Depression underway—are singing "I've Got Plenty of Nothing." Small aircraft are in general use, as is radar and a gradually more sophisticated submarine. Europe and America are concerned about Hitler and Nazi aggression.

And 1935 will include the last generation for Arctic Inupiat *to live within their five-thousand-year-old tradition, for* civilized *people and now whole governments to the south are encroaching, are determined to emend these primitive folk who have for so long lived in health and harmony with their land and with each other. Priests and ministers offer a new religion. These clergymen plus whalers, hunters, adventurers, traders and businessmen have brought into the Arctic devastating diseases for which the* Inuit *have no antibodies, imported bacteria and viruses which are today estimated to have destroyed ninety per cent of the Arctic people. Soon will begin a decades-long practice of forcing children to leave parents and place and go to boarding schools in city centers to the south, where as students they will be strictly prohibited from speaking their language, singing their songs, telling their stories, dancing their dances—from observing any of the Old Ways.*

In 1935, however, the Arctic People are unaware of this creeping threat, for little of what happens in the world to the south—and nearly all the rest of the planet is to the south—affects them. They are not in fact concerned with time as regards years or decades, centuries or millennia. For them, short spans are reckoned by the number of "sleeps," longer periods such as age and extended travel by the number of "winters." Rarely important, computation for fine figuring uses base twenty—all the fingers and toes on one person's body equaling one unit—one "man."

The Arctic Inuit, specifically called Inupiat, arrived on this continent to a stone age and remained in that stone age for five millennia—not because they were inept or limited in intellect but because stone was what they had. Stone plus snow, ice, water fresh and salt . . . plus animal parts. That combination was their entire world, and from these resources they built their vigorous life, a span of years which—barring accidents—equaled roughly the three score expectation of other humans on earth in 1935.

CHAPTER 1.
FACE TO FACE

Nik must not move or make a sound. He stood in icy wind atop a shallow rock cliff. He leaned on his spear while he watched a herd of musk oxen on prairie not far below. He listened to hooves strike sharply through ice. Watched broad muzzles reach down to pluck vegetation remaining from summer—all by now wind-seared, desiccated.

Strange and ancient beasts, these *oomingmak,* these "shaggy skins" his people loved less and feared more than the white sea bear. Unpredictable. The animals would stand to graze all independently. Then for no apparent reason, would sweep away like a school of hatchlings in sun-drenched summer shallows, a single billowing creature with one mind.

At the shoulder, each muskox was tall as Nik himself. Long, disheveled belly hair almost hid stem-like legs, hair which in fact might reach the ground—except that these tangled tresses always streamed out before the endless wind. One hide would make a wondrous sleep fur!

The boy dropped the bladder bag containing three big-foot hares. Not much to show for so long on the trail. Yet, more in one day than he'd ever taken before. And he had walked far, seen much—including now this wonder spread before him. . . .

He grasped his bone spear, careful not to dull the fire-hardened edge. And was the mighty hunter preparing to leap from this rocky bluff and throw himself among these fierce creatures? And did he plan to capture one? Oh, easily! He would stand before those twisting horns, look into those gale-reddened eyes and ask nicely whether the animal was willing to give itself. He couldn't butcher a musk ox here. His sled was far back where he'd left his team when patchy snow ended and the barren, wind-scoured ground—the permafrost—began. So then, after he had made the kill with *oomingmak's* kind permission, he would hoist up onto his back that carcass so much heavier than himself—not higher, but perhaps longer even than the great white sea bear *nanuk* standing on four feet.

Yes, he would balance the prize across one of his sturdy shoulders to haul it to the sled, take that carcass to the village with hide uncut so that everyone could admire the size—all that meat! And they would honor the hunter, too. Absolutely, he would do this thing!

Nik the mighty hunter . . . brave stalker—he snorted—the capturer of half-grown rabbits and scuttering lemmings. The fearless plucker up of discarded musk ox fur, of *quviut* snagged on rocks and across the skeletons of summer weeds. In fact, Nik's boots right now, his *kamik,* contained such shag stuffed all around his feet to keep them warm.

Hunter? His grandmother said not to despair because his time for success on the trail would come as daylight follows darkness. *Ananatsiak* Kiti was a wise woman, all knew. But here was Nik with fourteen winters past, and no more skillful in the chase than he had been at twelve or ten. Two differences, though: he was less patient than before and less confident with each day.

To become a man, one must be successful on the trail as well as eloquent before an audience. This was the way of his people. His stomach contracted, and an acrid lump rose in his throat. But he tightened his jaw, focused on the scene before him, counted twenty-three musk oxen—all of his fingers and toes to equal one full man plus three—more *oomingmak* in one place than he had ever seen. And closer. Downwind like this, he was safe. The herd would note him only if he made a sudden move or sound.

Still, he should not be here, not alone and certainly not so late on this darkening afternoon of winter time beginning. The sun had already made its brief arc low on the south horizon. Most assuredly, he should not be at such great distance from home. Grandmother would fret, might even send his brother Sitok out to find him—how humiliating! And Sitok angry about the needless walk. Dogs cannot pull sleds across permafrost exposed.

Nik clasped his spear tightly. Musk oxen are dangerous. How often had Sitok told him?

"Leave them alone," his brother would growl whenever they saw a cluster of the blowzy beasts. "They're smart, they're fast, they're *deadly!*" He also said they weren't all that tasty on the tongue.

But Nik had never tasted *oomingmak,* and he didn't think Sitok had, either. Nik wanted to inquire—but the custom of his people permitted only small children to ask direct questions that might invade the privacy of another. Certainly Nik must not ask something so personal. He was supposed to *observe* and *do.* All right, now he had *observed* the graze of musk oxen. But what could he *do?*

Nik heard a snort behind him, and he remembered to turn himself slowly in order to see what made the sound. A lone muskox bull was but two sled lengths away, walking up behind him from downwind. Had the creature been nearby when Nik climbed this rise to overlook the herd? But then, had the great *Inupiat* hunter paid heed to anything around him while climbing to the crest of this hill?

The big head tilted on its short, thick neck as the animal peered at the boy. Rolling eyes *observed* Nik as the creature shook his head, then lowered it to rub his blunt muzzle on first one and then the other foreleg. What would it *do?* Nik thought the beast was thinking, *How dare this puny man-thing take space the bull has chosen for himself?* That great tangle of mane and boss, broad-span horns with sharply upturned tips now raked indignantly on frozen permafrost to give a warning.

Sitok said musk oxen were fast—*how* fast? Nik guessed he might use his spear, except—in no way could he sink the ivory point within that bony head of horn. The body, yes. But with hair everyplace, where did fur leave off and flesh begin? *The secret of capturing food,* Sitok always said, *is for the hunter to pick the time and place and circumstance*—not this, with the muskox choosing everything. No.

The animal's bawl became a rumble that ended as a snort.

It would charge. Nik could not outrun it, and he had no place to hide. Still facing the creature, he dropped to his hands and knees, then backed over the edge of the bluff, grappling for handholds among loose rocks on the frozen lip. His mittens slipped. Just before he slid fully below the ledge, he saw the bull whirl toward that very place where the boy had been. All bellow and fur and pounding hooves. Sitok was right—*oomingmak* was fast.

The crag face was no sheer drop-off, more a slide, but steep enough that not even the agile muskox would try to clamber down. Nik slipped lower slowly but irretrievably, mittened hands grasping, boots swinging desperately to find support. He needed a toehold somewhere. The creatures below were now alert, alarmed. Nik must not flop helpless before them.

His flailing left boot suddenly caught a gravelly outcrop, and he stiffened his knee, then felt with both mitts

14

for some jutting rock to pull himself straight. He flattened against the wall—chest, cheeks, nose, forehead—tried to let the bluff "wear" him like some furry garment. His left mitt finally found a steady stone, and he pulled himself vertical, slowed his breathing and murmured thanks to *Tornarssuk,* that strong but capricious spirit of the land.

His eyes had been tightly closed while he focused on touch alone. Now he opened them, twisted to look down, saw another shallow ledge not far below. Would it support his weight? Was it high enough above the valley floor to protect him from the animals on the plain? He clambered down, then rotated bit by tiny bit, to finally face the musk oxen below.

The creatures were inspecting him. Disturbed, they tossed their heads as the bull above had done. They snorted their annoyance over this alien's sudden appearance. Three big males stomped the frozen ground. The scent of their anxiety came to Nik on the wind, and he lifted his chin slightly to let his nose seize more of the strange odor. A smell not unpleasant, he decided, but distinctive, something he would remember. He knew the bawl and thunder of the musk ox on the cliff crest moments ago would have alerted the herd even without his own rattling drop. Now he watched the animals form an arc that curled back as if all were players in a village drum feast, but here a strange, hypnotic dance, each seeming to know exactly where to stand.

The *oomingmak* were almost directly below him, flank to flank in their semi circle, the largest at the forward curl, alarmingly close--not a full sled-length from the base of the bluff. To divert his fear, Nik examined them closely as an unfamiliar species of the tundra. . . . All of the adults had the same menacing horns: cornua which curved down close to the head, then twisted forward into sharp spikes. Horns of the big males grew together as a thick boss across the forehead. Ferocious weapons ever ready. Here was a moss eater with a head something like the caribou but more

15

ponderous, attached by an invisible neck to a shaggy torso having no distinguishable shape. All supported by those four delicate legs. So much fur covered *oomingmak*, Nik decided, that the shape and bulk of that body would be unknown until the creature was captured and dressed down. Not by Nik, he decided. And certainly not today.

The excited beasts exhaled heavily, breath condensing to sail off like smoke stolen by impatient wind. Watching him, the creatures shook their heads, stomping, muzzles scraping forelegs, ready—no, *eager!*—to protect themselves and the juveniles sheltered behind them.

Musk oxen would rather run than fight, Nik's father Arajik had informed his sons. *They do battle only when they perceive peril.* But then the man always finished with a hook of irony delivered through dancing eyes. *But being suspicious by nature, any sudden change at all is thought to be a threat.*

Nik would always laugh when he heard that line, for he sympathized with musk oxen and with every creature of land and sea. But Sitok would listen gravely, as he did to all their father said, and—also as usual—sense no humor in the words. Nik understood and enjoyed Arajik's wit. Sitok did neither. *Yet it was Sitok who received their father's valuable instruction. Why did their father so favor his elder son?*

At first, Nik really was too young. And later, when he contrived to go along on the hunt, his father was unwilling to repeat elements already taught to Sitok. Besides, both complained that Nik was too restless and impatient, too noisy and full of questions.

"Watch and listen!" Arajik would mutter on the trail.

"Silence!" Sitok would grumble.

And their criticisms were valid. Nik *was* impatient. He *was* noisy. He needed motion—leaping, running—*jiggling,* Sitok called it. Also, Nik was a great one for talk. He was learning to speak mostly to himself—alone, out on the rolling coastal prairie where he could dart and howl at will, chant and sing as it came to him what might someday be great poetry at a drum feast or in camp beside the trail. He sang lamp tales. Some, he'd heard before, but more and more embellished by his fantasies. He liked to expand his grandmother's stories especially; for Kiti was the best storyteller in the village, probably in the whole world. And ever wilder and more active yarns came from the mind-pictures of Nik himself. He would sing and soar and—if he could sneak Kiti's small lap drum from the *igloo*—he would pound the beater on the rim and dance. *Boom-boom-BOOM!* . . . *Boom-boom-BOO-OO-OOM!*

Nik's ledge was only a man's height above the plain. Any determined muskox could clamber up the gravel face to hook him. The whole herd might with small effort surge through to overrun Nik's position on this shattered cliff. The boy suddenly spied his spear where it had fallen when he scrambled down. It lay on bare ground at the base of the cliff, an arm's length before the front arc of the threatening formation. He must collect it soon . . . if it happened that the spirits permitted him to survive this day. . . .

Well, he would do his best to give no cause for attack. Such twitchy, suspicious creatures—why? So well armed, they should not be fearful. His father Arajik had said he once saw a herd of musk oxen destroy an attacking wolf pack, saw them dash out from their defending circle to kill each individual one by one by one. Nik was glad now that he had resisted his urge to unharness his lead dog Nuko to come as his companion. *Ananatsiak* Kiti said that musk oxen will kill outright any beast resembling the wolf, its mortal enemy.

Nothing, not even caribou, can outrun or outmaneuver them, she said. "Not that a muskox would bother a caribou," she had added, with all who heard her wondering how she, a woman, knew so much about the creatures. Still, the dog Nuko would not have allowed Nik to be surprised by that lone bull up on the ridge.

The boy closed his eyes again, refused to allow himself to reach into his parka and draw out his killing knife. He must stand absolutely still. In the end, the musk oxen would lose interest and go away.

He wondered whether he could outlast their focus. He stood for a long time that seemed even longer. His face took the full bite of the northwest wind that swept along the cliff. Through eyes streaming, the tears freezing on his face, he dared not move to pull a thong and constrict his *nuilak*, the furry parka opening.

The creatures below continued to regard him from their protective curve. Muttering only, now, no longer tossing horns, no—but not breaking formation, either, not returning to their browse or better yet going away. Patient animals. And Nik must be more so. Always *im*patient Nik must teach himself to outwait the musk oxen or else he would die on this day.

A calf surged forward from behind the line occasionally, this one a miniature, that one half grown and popping out from some other place. In each instance, an adult would break rank to dart after the juvenile. But that move was just long enough to butt the youngster back to protection—and none too gently, either—before the adult resumed standing in the spot it held before.

Nik knew that the muskox children were weary of waiting. So was he.

At least for this brief time today, Nik had managed to forget that his parents were gone, that he and Sitok were orphans . . . or so Urgit said. *Urgit*—useless Urgit. How Nik disliked and mistrusted that young man. The villagers should not believe Urgit's story about their parents' death last summer when the icy flood came down the mountain stream. People should be going *right now*—especially Nik and Sitok should—to find their father Arajik and their mother Mawena.

But Sitok said *"Owka,* No. Wait for full winter." The unfamiliar tundra far inland was treacherous for a sled and team until the great expanse of low, bog-dotted interior permafrost froze solid and became furred with snow.

Nik knew with his brain that Sitok's words were sensible. But his heart commanded otherwise: *Go now! Find Arajik and Mawena before it's too late.*

Even *Ananatsiak* Kiti would not say that they should go immediately. "One must not lose children to save parents," she told him. "Sitok is the man with seventeen winters. He knows the ways of travel. He must decide."

Yet, Nik was convinced that every day they waited— every hour!—made them that much less likely ever to find their parents alive. For Urgit admitted that he had taken from the fishing camp everything needed for survival when he started back at summer's end—had packed up weapons and tools, he confessed, even the important sleeping robes . . . and then to lighten his load had gradually discarded everything bit by bit while he wandered lost upon the inland plains. Urgit! Nineteen winters of being in this life and *still* could lose his way? What a *soospuk!* A born bungler! The bitter taste which flooded Nik's mouth was an acid of hate the

19

boy had never known until Urgit appeared at summer's end. Appeared without Nik's and Sitok's parents—for that matter, also without Urgit's own father. . . .

Nik sighed quietly as he watched the herd watch him. The animal above was gone or at least silent. Did separated bulls serve as lookouts for the group? Or did that solitary male just happen today to be near the others? How Nik would like to ask a village hunter.

When he was very young and still permitted to ask direct questions, he had not known what to ask. Now he had more questions than there were stars in a cloudless winter sky—but was not *permitted* to ask . . . unfair, somehow. Still, perhaps only he of all children ever born was too dull-witted, too much *not*-a-hunter, to ask the right questions at the proper time.

So while Sitok was already a hunter who captured food, Nik wasn't. Not even close. Fourteen winters in age, and *still not a hunter!* And might never become one, either. His father Arajik had no great hope for him, that was certain. And an *Inupiat* who was not a hunter could never be a man. Here was the refrain that haunted him. . . . Again Nik felt the familiar tightening in his stomach. He must think of other matters. He must focus on the trouble here and now. How would Arajik handle this situation? Easy to answer—his father would never get himself *into* this predicament. Nor would Sitok.

Suddenly, the boy startled and nearly fell from his perch when he heard a piercing hiss come from above him. Then,

"**Brother?!**"

"Ee-ee, Yes." He tried to send sound without moving his lips. But in spite of his effort and in spite of the wind, the creatures before him heard. They tightened rank, heads tossing once again. The big males stomped the frozen earth.

"It happens, a line is coming," the voice continued, his brother Sitok's of course.

And silently eeling down before Nik came a tightly braided cable of split walrus hide. The boy twisted his hands and legs around it, rotated to face the cliff, then climbed frantically, not waiting for Sitok to pull. A charge could come at any time. The creatures needed to see that he was moving away. One moment, he was squinting impatiently at patient musk oxen. The next, he was on the lip of the ledge and scrambling up the line to safety. Never mind that Sitok would be annoyed—Nik felt only relief.

Nuko licked his face and bounced wildly, her tail a blur of movement. That's how Sitok had found Nik, then—by having the dog track in from the sleds. His brother would have used his own team to find Nik's at the edge of the snow. There, he would have unstaked Nuko and let the dog guide him, nose in the air above trackless frozen earth. The younger boy grinned. He didn't even need to ask a question, this time. He *knew*.

CHAPTER 2.
SIDE BY SIDE

The wind was still rising on that stormy afternoon, and black clouds scurried across the sky. Nik looked at Sitok walking beside him in near darkness, tried to read his face but could make out no expression at all. The older brother was not one to talk nor one to show his feelings, either. Most likely, the scolding Nik had earned with his wanderings today would come from *Ananatsiak,* from Grandmother Kiti.

He considered excuses he could give for sliding over a cliff and getting himself into a dangerous confrontation with musk oxen. He was chased over the ledge by a white bear? No, Sitok would know that no sign of *nanuk* had been on the ridge. And beside, Nuko would have picked up the scent immediately and sounded her wailing alarm. Then what about saying that the ground gave way to send him tumbling? That untruth, too, would have been evident to his brother inspecting from the top. Eh, a trail spirit chased him? He had heard others say this in serious tones. He laughed aloud. Kiti would demand that he take her to the place and introduce her to the specter.

"Someone finds the situation funny." Sitok was in a bad mood, understandably. How many times had he been interrupted in what he was doing, just to go find the younger brother?

Best to say nothing, Nik decided. Sitok with Nuko would certainly have scented the lone muskox which had been on high ground. Sitok knew what had happened without being told. Not that he would ever let such a thing happen to *him*.

Ordinarily, the younger boy would have chattered all the way home, leaping as he sang and chanted and told wild tales, Sitok grinning or grunting or ignoring each sally, according to his disposition at the moment. But Nik was absorbed with sober thoughts. Yes, he had *observed*, today— but once again, he had not *done*. How should he have acted differently as he faced the creatures below him on the cliff? Perhaps if he had at least managed to hold onto his spear? . . . *A true hunter does not drop his weapon, and certainly does not leave it behind, no matter what.* Yes, he will have to retrieve it soon or make another.

The boys said no more on the long walk back to their sleds. Nor did they speak while they unstaked and re-harnessed dogs. When they got to Potok's snowhouse in the village and were feeding their teams, though, Sitok growled, "A mere child should not hunt alone."

Nik felt his body's middle parts get heavy as stone. "The young man did not so much **hunt**," he explained, "as happen to *find* !"

Sitok's voice resumed. "And especially, a child does not hunt the savage muskox, *oomingmak.* "

Sitok was not clever with words, yet his mild reprimand managed as always to make the younger brother feel like a nitwit, a *soospuk*. Nik was no longer actually a child, and Sitok knew this. But he had been rescued from a childish dilemma. An experienced hunter would have noticed the lone bull before the bull noticed him. But Nik was no hunter. Not yet . . . perhaps not ever. Again his gut churned as if a hostile being lived independently within.

Sitok grumbled a final *"Hoo-oo"* of disapproval, then walked away to where villagers gathered on the far side of the tiny cluster of snowhouses. Nik saw him pulling food from the pocket of his tunic. Sitok loved to eat almost as much as he loved to hunt. And Sitok was usually hungry. That he did not bring out food to share with his brother during the trip home indicated the extent of his annoyance. Nik ducked into Potok's *igloo* to find something to chew on and silence his own belly. The rabbits he carried were useless as food until skinned and butchered, with precious sacs and casings as well as fur removed and cured for important use at home and on the trail. He reflected that it would be Grandmother, his *ananatsiak,* who would do this preparation, even were Nik's mother Mawena here. Why was that, he wondered idly. Hungry! Something in this place was bound to be edible.

Ah yes, Potok's untidy *igloo*—the spot where Nik with Sitok and Grandmother Kiti had been living since return to the coast from summer camp—a return missing Arajik and Mawena. But this overcrowded dwelling place would never be home.

Later, Nik crawled out from the porch tunnel wiping grease from his mouth with a parka sleeve. Outside, he noticed for the first time that a drum beat thundered insistently—*Boom-boom-**BOO-OO-OOM** !* He had forgotten about the duel today. How long had it been going? No wonder Sitok was particularly angry. Nik ran toward the sound, saw his brother standing behind the main group of spectators gathered on snow. Beyond and down a white ridge was sea ice. Nik walked up, put a hand on his brother's arm.

Sitok turned, saw Nik and, still irritated, shrugged the hand away and turned back.

Nik walked around to get between his brother and the duel. Then softly, "It happens that this child of whom Sitok spoke must learn to hunt!" His voice broke when he said the words. He hoped the older boy would think it only an adolescent crack. He could not blink away all the ready moisture in his eyes.

Sitok compressed his lips and looked at Nik for several moments. Then he walked away to find a better place to watch the combat.

Nik drew in several icy breaths. What a very cold world. . . .

CHAPTER 3.
NAKED TRUTH

With the *boom-boom-BOOMs* getting louder as he worked his way through people in order to be closer to the ring, Nik remembered other drum duels, surely two or three each winter season as far back as he could remember.

When weather permitted no hunting, village men cooped up became restless as days between sleep times grew interminably long. They might argue about past and present slights, real or imagined—if only for something to do, something besides wait for a storm to end and hope that food would hold out until they could resume the trail. Such disputes might sound bitter at the time, might even continue through several sleeps—but were mostly forgotten when the storm ended.

But a serious quarrel, where personal honor and manhood were at stake, ultimately would be drummed out in a duel like this one today. Now Nik remembered seeing men heel out a ring before the sleep last night. Two *kayaks'* lengths across the middle—they then stamped down all snow inside. The debate would be public, of course, so that the matter could be judged by village viewers. The two adversaries always took turns as they used rhythm, dance and poetic chant to state their case and later respond, back and forth until all that could be said was concluded. Those adults who watched and listened must then judge which person was right, which wrong. In addition to the merits of points brought up in debate, the decision of the people was based on a dueler's wit and grace as well as endurance in the lengthy performance.

Spectators must also decide what would happen to the loser. A mild dispute or one where guilt and dueling excellence were closely balanced might result in the loser's handing over a seal or a sleeping fur to the winner, perhaps providing servitude for half a moon. A truly grave matter where shameful acts were proven or where precious human life and death might be at stake meant that the loser could be shunned for a time—or far more seriously, banished from the group, expelled, sent forever from the village. In such a situation, this would in winter time mean death unless a friend or family member chose to accompany the one so sentenced.

How serious was this duel today? Trying to view the proceeding, Nik walked the perimeter of bystanders who watched. He found Sitok again, but decided this time against disturbing him. His brother was tall enough to look over other heads and see the ring. Nik was not. He backed away, clambered up onto a snowhouse nearby. Now he could see well the opponent who drummed and leapt within the circle. In fact, and with only moon and stars to illuminate the scene, he could see all around from his high perch.

His gaze went past the eight white domes of his village strewn across heavy coastal snow. It swept beyond the clustered people, then across fully empty and featureless plains and flat sea to the circling horizon. Even in that moonlit dark of middle afternoon, in this early winter season, what could be more beautiful? His father Arajik had traveled and described the strange places he had seen, including even the *Irkrelrete*—the fierce, tall and slender people many sleeps to the south and west. He spoke of giant plants reaching high into the sky with aid from rough brown bones which at their base stuck deep into the ground. But although Nik's father had seen much, he too believed that the greatest beauty lay

27

here, where the uninterrupted eye could see far and all around in every direction.

Shouts of laughter returned Nik's attention to the duel.

Big Unipak had been dashing, dipping, leaping, stomping to a steady beat. Now he made a fierce face as he raised the drum above his head. A moon of taut hide stretched across the circling bone frame. A handle of precious carved driftwood smoothly twirled and twisted in his grasp as if it were a living thing. Expertly, he struck the rim with a beater, more precious wood swaddled in caribou fur. *Boom, Buh-bah-BOOM! Buh-bah-boom, Buh-bah-BOOM!* Rhythms rapid and sure came forth to match the agile skips and jumps.

Unipak has great confidence, Nik thought. And why not? Tall as a seacliff boulder, the man possessed the chest of a bull walrus—and a roaring bass voice to match. Known up and down the coast for his great skill with voice, drum, and dance, he was invited by other villages to perform at their feasts. Unipak ate especially well at such times—growing ever larger, always stronger, to handle the magnificent drum with even greater ease . . . so then invited to appear all the more often. *Ai-ee!* A spiral of invitations and honor that widened endlessly. Still, Nik knew that his brother maintained distance from Unipak. Why?

Unipak and Atik had a serious conflict. Atik the Accuser said that Unipak claimed for himself the game captured by younger men and those less physically powerful. And Unipak the Accused said that Atik made the allegation to excuse himself—Atik—as a hunter who had neither skill nor luck. The controversy was not about hunger—for food taken by the group was shared. It was about honor. It was about a man's character and reputation. One of the adversaries could not be telling the truth.

Nik listened to Unipak's deep voice rumble out in song amid observers pressing in from the blackness of what was now full night. Perspiration rolled from the man's jaw even though his hood was thrown back, a rich stand of long dark hair shadowing his movements. Drum whirling, Unipak shifted his attention to Atik, the opponent who stood quietly attentive just outside the dueling ring. A great black grin sliced open the lower third of Unipak's face as he bent down to snort and wheeze at his accuser. To widen his eyes. To roll his head humorously as he drew closer and closer to Atik's face, staring insolently without blinking, drum thumping, feet busy at the beat. Nik attuned himself to the words.

> . . . Mighty hunter Atik here before us
> Whose power so frightens every creature
> Of the land and sea and air
> That each hides from him
> when they sense his coming,
> As his giant footsteps tramp the ice
> And coastal plains and tundra. . . .

A murmur of laughter passed through the crowd. Nik himself had to chuckle. Atik was such a *brief* man! He had doll-like feet. His heart was generous, but he would never make giant footsteps anywhere. This man was small. True, he was broader and stronger than the boy who watched him so fondly, for Atik had lived at least twice as many winters as Nik. When they last spoke together, their eyes were level; but Nik was still forming where Atik was fully constructed. So Unipak was a bull walrus whose adversary at this event was a sweet-fleshed earless seal. How did Atik ever have the courage to accuse this behemoth of anything?

Now came the challenger's turn. Small Atik leapt into the dueling circle, took the drum from Unipak as that man stepped out. Pride lit Unipak's features. He already counted himself the victor. Nik decided to watch the big man's face often while Atik presented his argument.

The little fellow raised the drum and gave it a twirl to get it going. He began to pound a slow rhythm. ***Boom-bah-Boom-bah-Boom-bah.*** He lacked Unipak's assurance. His movements were light, though, his dance lofty despite the drum's bulk. His tenor voice soared above crowd noise to create a startling but not unpleasant contrast to Unipak's gravelly bass. Nik listened to the taunt.

> . . . And you saw mighty Unipak
> Relieve Atik once again
> Of the burden dangling from his sea-borne float—
> Sweet *nathek,* bearded seal,
> Laced as he was on the harpoon,
> After he gave himself. . . .

> Now does Atik thank this Unipak!
> So thoughtful—inland, too—
> Carrying his load of caribou,
> The weasel taken prematurely from the trap line,
> The fish from sinew left in summer streams—
> All this, powerful Unipak hauls for him,

> Relieving even Atik's sled dogs of the labor
> In their chewing and digesting—
> Often sending their ration of fresh caribou and fish
> To the mouths of Unipak's plump and willing dogs—
> Those kringmerk appetites helping
> In this terrible task. . . .

> Atik's burdens taken over as Unipak's—
> Ah, many thanks!

Nik remembered to keep glancing at Unipak. While Atik sang, the man accused glared at snow in front of his fur boots. As Nik watched, he remembered that Unipak always seemed to hunt with the group whereas Sitok and others among the really good trackers—certainly their father Arajik—quite often went alone. But not Unipak. Nik would see him return with villagers every time, his sled piled high with caribou and seals and fish according to the season, sometimes even walrus. His dogs had glistening coats and always looked well fed.

Whose fish did Unipak transport and feed his team? Nik wondered now. *Whose* seal and walrus and caribou? Atik was saying that big Unipak was a bully who took the catch of others. And Unipak's dour expression suggested that the small man's words were true.

Laughter rippled among spectators. Approving *"Ai-ee-ee!"* came from the surprised audience as Atik stopped singing. No one had expected such a clever tale or such adroit moves. The drum whirled above him, and Atik leaped straight up like a fox that jumped for low-skimming ptarmigan. Atik's landing was balanced and graceful, his tiny feet busy as lemmings when he scurried and darted around the circle, every step accompanying the beat, each facial twist and warp with meaning. Unlike the larger man, Atik ignored his opponent and concentrated on amusing onlookers as he pleaded his case.

More "Ai-ee!" came from people to express their admiration.

Unipak's scowl deepened.

Someone's size was not supposed to matter in a duel, so long as the person could manage the drum. Wit, cunning, grace were what the villagers prized: *performance* well blended with facts showing innocence. Any dispute was abandoned by duelers after a drum duel was concluded. The issues were to be left within the ring, not to be mentioned once the circle was destroyed. But Unipak did not strike Nik as a man likely to forget being censured. Not if he won this duel, and especially not if he lost. And in Nik's estimation, Unipak *was* losing—not because he lacked skill in the ring but rather because of the circumstance reported and his response to Atik's accusations. His sullen manner conceded guilt. Would the ones who judged the duel—all adults in the village—see it so?

Nik shrugged. Here were matters to think on, but he had more urgent worries. He slid down from the *igloo,* realizing for the first time how very cold he was. He went up to Sitok, asked to meet him at Potok's place. He pointed with his nose and chin to the snow house where they stayed. Temporarily. At least, Nik *hoped* their stay was not permanent. Still sulky, the older boy finally agreed. He would be there *soon,* he said impatiently—no, he'd not go this very moment.

CHAPTER 4.
DECISIONS

As he left the dueling place, Nik's eyes slid across the ring to fasten on one particular spectator—*Urgit!* His mouth tightened. How he disliked the young man. Brooding black eyes behind slits of a permanent squint. Tall and rangy, but unmuscled. His broad forehead had no marks at all. In twenty winters, should he not have some record of life upon his brow? *Ho-oo,* not Urgit! Nik clenched his fists within his mittens.

Where are the parents, Arajik and Mawena? Are Sitok and Nik truly orphans? Did a father and mother actually drown in a giant wave, last summer? Or did a frightened rabbit peer nervously about and then hop away to leave them stranded by an inland lake? Take their tools and weapons with him as he panicked and retreated like the kussuyok, *the coward that he is?*

Eh, this today should find not Atik and Unipak but Sitok and Urgit in the dueling ring!

Nik moved slowly back toward Potok's snowhouse. He hoped everyone from there was outside watching the duel. What he disliked most about living with this family—and he disliked much—was having no privacy at all. Ever. Eight people on the sleeping ledge at night were too many. But he could say nothing, for three of the eight were his own family. Sitok and he should have built an *igloo* for themselves by now, already a dozen sleeps beyond their return here to the coast. Potok insisted that they *not* do so, and Grandmother Kiti advised quietly that they avoid offending their host, Arajik's long time friend.

"It happens," their grandmother told them in secret, "that Potok needs an extra hunter for his hungry brood."

It was true, both boys had to admit. The man had a wife and three daughters to provide for in addition to himself, and no son at all. But where Sitok had taken for granted Kiti's confirmation of his status as a valuable hunter, Nik stung sharply from her reference to but *one* hunter offered from their family.

Not that he *was* a hunter, of course. He knew that. But did everyone else, as well? And someday—surely—he *would* be! Perhaps someday soon.

Nik reached the too-small *igloo* of Potok and crawled down through the tunnel from the porch. He pushed aside the heavy hide baffle draped across the opening to discourage cold. *Hoo-oo!* What odors were here! The lamp was a mere flicker emitting much smoke. The vapory cloud mixed with other smells to sting his eyes. Potok's wife Maleet was not one to take lamp duty too seriously. As a result, the place was always smoky but hardly ever warm—something else Nik detested here.

He dragged a reeking, half-thawed seal from near the lamp over to the doorway. He held it stiff-armed, far as possible from his nostrils. The night bladder was still waiting, too, and stank of urine. At home, the job of emptying this container made from animal intestine fell to Nik, as youngest—and spirits of both land and sky needed to protect him from *Ananatsiak* Kiti if he did not take it out first thing after a sleep. But Potok blustered that no male in **his** house would do such menial work. Nor would the esteemed guest

Kiti, mother of his friend. So the two youngest girls, one hardly more than a toddler, were supposed to take it out and store the contents well beyond the village but at the ready for processing hides. The children often forgot, and no one reminded them. Yes, Nik had many objections to living in this place. . . .

When would Sitok come? Nik sat upon the sleeping ledge, the *iglerk*, among robes still rumpled from the night. He supposed he should feel grateful to have any place at all. Still, Potok knew what he was doing. Everything Sitok captured while they lived here belonged to his host. So now, *two* men fed eight instead of one feeding five—and perhaps with the possibility in Potok's mind of Nik also becoming yet another hunter. Too, the man's eldest girl Erin would someday soon be of marriageable age and had her eye on Sitok despite his youth—as did Potok's wife Maleet on behalf of her daughter. Nik and his remaining family had known from the start that Potok's insistence on their sharing his home was not based upon the man's kindly nature.

In fact, there was and always had been something Nik mistrusted about his father's friend . . . but he was not sure what it was. Strangely, it was Erin and not Potok's wife who tried to keep the lamp going in this miserable household. It was she who seemed to lead the processing of hides. Had her mother ceased to care?

All right, the housing could be worse. For example, Urgit and his Aunt Saruna slept a few nights in one place, then had to move somewhere else. No one so far had offered them permanent space or to build them quarters. No one would, either. An old widow with shallow teeth, and a useless young man who did not go out to hunt? Still, not pity but anger and helpless rage warmed Nik at the very thought of Urgit. His fury banished what for anyone else in such a predicament would surely be sympathy. Widows and orphans—even *old* orphans when unskilled—rarely had a bright future.

Nik watched the entry baffle and sighed. Still no Sitok. . . . Urgit surely knew more than he told. Last summer, that hapless young Urgit with his own father Pak had left the village camp inland, along with Nik's parents Arajik and Mawena, to find a good fishing lake in the south that Arajik thought he remembered.

They did not come back when expected. Then cold weather started early, and the tundra froze up. People became restless, eager to return to the coast for their usual winter camp. Early snow covered the ground with a fragile, undependable layer. Villagers grumbled that walking back to their home prairies located by the sea would now be treacherous and slow. The dogs were with them, but sleds had all been left at the permanent winter camp. Still they waited. Then it became necessary to fashion something to use as a sled so that teams could draw them where possible. No coastal *Inupiat* wants to be caught on unfamiliar tundra over winter.

Even so, people waited half a moon more with still no sign of the fishing party. Meanwhile, the lake fish nearly unaccessible beneath thick freshwater ice, villagers and dogs alike consumed during this unexpected delay a part of their precious supplies gathered against the coming winter. These provisions collected, dried and stored during the summer moons were meant to vary winter fare. The months of cold meant solid, fatty creatures captured on the coast: seal, walrus, perhaps a white bear—a late-migrating caribou or, even before spring thaw, an early whale. The bird eggs and herbs and freshwater fish of summer time provided variety.

Well past summer's end, Nik with Sitok and Grandmother Kiti did return to the coast along with the villagers. But it was a grave decision, to leave people inland without sled and dogs as winter time began. But *pirtok,* one

36

must work with a situation as it is, not as one might wish it. Arajik and Mawena would catch them on the way back, Nik thought at first. . . . Eh, no? Then they must be waiting on the rolling plains above the sea where the village built their igloos for winter.

But no one joined or met them anywhere. And *still* not, for half another moon. Villagers did, as they returned, find Urgit wandering on the plains, half-starved and nearly mad with the raptures of his solitude. It was five sleeps at least before he could speak sensibly . . . as sensibly as Urgit ever spoke.

Nik jumped up when his brother crawled past the baffle. With no preliminary greeting, Nik blurted, "It is necessary— Sitok must challenge Urgit to a duel!"

The older boy's eyes widened in surprise, and he stepped back involuntarily. Then with a slow smile, "It happens, such a duel is not possible."

"Sitok is no coward!" Nik knew that his brother was by now no longer annoyed with him.

"*Owka*, no, nor not a fool, either." He laughed without humor. "Someone who cannot perform must take care to avoid large quarrels." The older boy went to the seal carcass by the door, took out his hunting knife and cut off a chunk, wrinkled his nose at the rank smell as he pulled away the fist-sized piece. He grasped a section with his teeth, then used his sharp round knife, his *ulu,* to slice neatly and rapidly at his lips one single bite from the portion he still held. He chewed absently.

The two had talked before about Sitok's drum dueling with Urgit. Nik would like to duel himself. He was good at skills of entertainment—he *knew* he was! But no one would permit someone so young to enter the dueling circle. Besides, he was still too small physically to handle the big drum, even though with every moon his muscles were bulging nicely and his chest broadening.

Sitok, though, was sure that he himself could *not* beat a bright rhythm, could *not* dance or chant poetry, let alone compose shrewd words which would at once accuse and amuse. He had convinced himself further that he possessed no personal charm at all. Convinced himself wrongly, Nik believed. The older boy thought himself to be a clever hunter, which he was. But he had decided many winters past, for some reason, that he was not very smart otherwise, and certainly not witty with words. Only that last was true, Nik thought now. But his brother hardly ever *spoke!* If he practiced as Nik did, who could guess what sort of poet and singer, dancer and drummer Sitok might become? Or even a storyteller like his honored grandmother?

From the few words spoken, as now, Nik knew his brother must often brood about these shortcomings. For to be a true man, of course, *Inupiat* males needed skill in both hunting and entertaining. Nik was Sitok's opposite. Nik had the keen—at least well-practiced!—tongue and nimble feet. He had confidence in his ability to perform well when the time came. Didn't he rehearse often as possible when he was alone or with the dog team, sometimes with *Ananatsiak* and even on the trail with his brother?

Oh yes, he reflected. Nik practiced leaping and singing to a fault. *Used time when he should be learning the secrets of the trail.* Nik's private horror. Whenever he let his thoughts stay long on the subject of his hunting, he panicked. He could control the waking hours by shifting focus onto something else. But late during the sleep time, he would awaken dry mouthed, choking beneath a claw of terror that clutched his throat. For if he was not to be a hunter, then he would have to be *angakok,* a shaman healer and magician. He knew how most people—in his village, at least—felt about such persons. He knew how *he* felt.

One finger of skill and four fingers of fakery, villagers would declare. *Like the summer time louse which consumes the life blood of others and later warms itself on fur not its own.*

Grandmother Kiti, though, assured Nik that some few *angakok* were not parasites. Their great talents were bestowed as gifts for any needing help, she insisted, with no favor asked and none accepted. How did his grandmother know so much about *angakok?* She would use her thumb and forefinger to rub the scar on her right ear lobe, get a far-away look in her eyes—but never say.

No, *not* a shaman. Not Nik. Somehow, Nik had to become a hunter. But how? His father had taken him those few times, then brought him back in disgust if not actual disgrace over his ineptitude. Nik was without talent, Arajik said. The younger son had no patience whatsoever, was hopeless, so his father insisted. Nik was not worthy of his father's time upon the trail. And then Arajik would go back to training Sitok. What bothered Nik late in the sleep time was that he really might **not** have the ability to become a great hunter—not even a good one. Or worse, that he might somehow teach himself patience, that he might actually learn the skills and gain mastery through effort and practice—but then not have that special measure of good luck necessary to be successful.

When he worried aloud to *Ananatsiak,* Kiti always smiled and said the same things: *anxiety alone can disable the hunter's hand, and confidence is the headwater for luck.* So Grandmother—as always—recommended that he relax and spend some time at practice, yes—but then patiently let time pass. Patience. Commodities which Nik always found in short supply: *Practice . . . Time . . . and Patience.*

Both boys were wrapped in their own thoughts when Nik heard sound in the porch tunnel. Up into the room came Kiti. Followed by Urgit. *Urgit!* Why?

"It happens that two *Inuit* need warmth," Grandmother said. She bustled over to the lamp and adjusted the wick. The vertical tail of dark smoke ceased immediately, and a cheerful flame soon brightened the room.

Urgit. Nik looked at the recreant who stood huddled and cold by the baffle. Did Urgit's conscience bother him? Nik wondered. Did he too find it hard to sleep at night? All right, Urgit also was newly orphaned. His mother had died many winters before, and now he had returned last summer without his *own* father, Pak. Nik had been over and over Urgit's story in his own mind. Urgit's *flexible* story, never quite the same in retelling. *Hoo-oo!*

Kiti pointed to the seal Nik had rescued and Sitok had tasted. Urgit rapidly pulled out his *ulu* and helped himself, chewed noisily with a rapt expression on his face. Nik reflected that Urgit's village host of the moment must be frugal in provisioning his guests. He wondered how that timid hare Aunt Saruna was managing, then pushed back his sympathy and cleared his throat to get attention.

"Once again," he demanded, at the same time motioning their visitor to sit on the *iglerk* close to the lamp, "would someone kindly describe for the bereaved family what happened in the summer?"

Urgit shuddered. He glanced back to the entry as if to weigh intense cold outside against the unpleasantness of fulfilling Nik's request. He pursed his lips in irritation, chewed and chewed, but not quite daring to cut off another bite, then drew a long breath, stepped over to the lamp, removed his mittens, put long, bony fingers to the flame.

"So many times!" he grumped, fixing his eyes on Kiti for reprieve.

40

Ananatsiak plucked up a hide on which she had been working, put the caribou skin to her mouth, said nothing.

Nik waited. His request had been too direct, so was discourteous. But as a youngster, he could sometimes at home get away with making such demands. . . . At least, Kiti heard his words and had neither stopped nor admonished him.

Urgit saw that he was not to be rescued. He cleared his throat. "Heavy rain had fallen on the inland hills all that day and one before," he began. "The warm summer air was filled with the song of mosquitoes—"

"—*Where* were the parents when the wave washed down!?" Nik blurted, and both Sitok and Kiti reproached him with a low *"Hoo-oo!"*

Urgit blew on his frosty white fingers, returned them to the meager warmth of the lamp. "This man's father, his *atatak* Pak was fishing from the bank near the mouth of the lake. Arajik and Mawena were up on the bubbling stream before it joins the quiet lake."

"With *kayaks?*" Nik prompted. "Someone *saw* them there?"

Urgit raised his eyebrows, Yes. "They had both craft," he said, "Pak's as well as Arajik's. But the height and power in that wall of water when it washed down from the hills—eh! A *kayak* to that wave was a solitary seal to a whale."

"And someone was watching them at the time the wave came down?" Nik's dark eyes bored into Urgit's. The foolish man had answered only the first part of his question.

Urgit shrugged, bare fingers fidgeting. "Who can say he saw the exact moment of calamity? No one gazed at every move—no one knew that disaster approached."

"So it happens that Urgit last saw the parents of Sitok and Nik fishing on foot in the stream, *kayaks* tied nearby— last saw Pak at the edge of the lake—"

"—*Owka,* No!" Urgit's voice trembled with passion. "Later, the son beheld his father's body broken and spiritless on the shallow of the lake."

"Arajik and Mawena?"

Urgit stared at him, said nothing. Once before, he had admitted to Nik that although he later found many bits of *kayak* he was unable to find the bodies of Arajik and Mawena.

"And . . . ?" Nik prompted.

"And nothing! The lone survivor piled all that he could carry—"

"—Which was *everything!*" Nik declared.

Urgit sucked in breath, Yes. "It became necessary to leave the heavy lamp."

Nik snorted. "So without waiting to know with absolute certainty whether any others were alive, Urgit took every tool, every weapon, every blanket and tinder and flint—all but the stone lamp . . . and then ***got himself lost!***"

He spat out those last words and earned from Kiti another stern *"Hoo-oo!"* but he didn't care. True *Inupiat* do not get lost. Not even children, and Urgit was at least five winters past being a juvenile.

Urgit's jaw thrust forward. "Someone saw a *kayak* fly high on the wave crest and burst apart. That same someone saw his father's broken body flung onto a rock before the next surge swept it away!"

This was the first time Urgit had described such details.

"But the other two? Arajik and Mawena? Urgit saw them, too? Or did he even look?"

Urgit blinked, held his eyelids down, No. "Had Nik been there—"

"—But he was *not!* And the story of Urgit changes with each telling!" Nik growled.

Silence followed the insult. Rancid oil stank. Residual lamp smoke floated in a haze overhead. All could hear the *THUMP-et-er, THUMP-et-er-BOO-OOM!* of the dueling drum outside.

At last, Kiti coughed lightly to ease the moment. *"The stone called memory has many facets, some parts to light, some shadow: and every time one probes a recollection, light and shadow change."*

Urgit shot her a grateful glance, then put his mittens back on and left the igloo without another word. Most of the tension went with him.

Sitok finally spoke. "Before taking a trip to find parents, it happens that the family must store much food in caches—for *Ananatsiak* during the absence of her grandsons, and also for two young men to take upon their journey."

The one storage mound of perfectly rotted seal that remained to the family from last winter had been used up completely soon after they came back from summer inland. Nik remembered reluctantly helping his brother and Potok take away the protective rocks to break into the cache. Too early, he thought then and still believed. Because the carefully processed seal would keep for years, it was his family's custom to use it only for emergencies.

But because the boys and their grandmother were in Potok's household, the man had insisted that it was now their responsibility to share all that they had. All. With profound emotion, Potok explained how it was that although he himself was a highly skilled hunter, his family presently had no back-up provision from their summer hunting and gathering because they—and the rest of the village, as well, although Nik knew this to be untrue—had eaten all they had collected while they waited for the fishing party that did not come. The boys could see readily, could they not, that Potok's lack of food from summer stores was the fault of Nik and

Sitok's family? Nik wondered now whether Potok would have offered his home if Arajik's family was not known to possess provision in reserve.

But what was Sitok saying? Nik had begged since their return to go back inland and look for Arajik and Mawena. But this was the first thing definite he had heard from his brother. Now Sitok suddenly made the trip sound like an event certain to occur as soon as food could be stockpiled.

"Can the sons not hunt as they go?" Nik asked in a subdued tone. He was ashamed of his harsh exchange with Urgit.

Sitok smiled at him and Kiti laughed aloud. Nik was suddenly embarrassed. *The sons?* Both of them? Why was he including himself as a hunter? Once again, a *soospuk!*

Sitok replied gently, "Inland during winter has uncertain food supply, especially for *Inupiat* from the sea unskilled with tundra game. So Arajik has said. It happens that the two hunters will capture familiar food on familiar terrain right here. They will be far more certain to eat with regularity when provision needed is carried on their sled."

Kiti spoke thoughtfully as she looked around the filthy snowhouse. "One cannot store food separately when one lives in the home of another." She was reminding them that they were guests of Potok, a host who they knew by now was greedy.

"Then it is also necessary to build a separate *igloo!*" Sitok declared.

"Soon?" asked Nik, spirits rising. How he wanted to be away from Potok's house!

"Ee-ee, Yes," Kiti decided aloud. "And then quietly cache food from the great success to come in having two grandsons on the trail together."

"Nik also shall capture food!" the boy agreed boldly. Sitok and Kiti both looked at him, said nothing. Embarrassed once again, Nik added, "Even though Arajik himself declares his younger son lacks talent on the trail." There! He had told his fear aloud to the two people whom he loved best and who loved him. A black presence within him suddenly turned gray when he shared it.

Kiti spoke up. "Arajik has many fine qualities—" and Nik noted that she too spoke of their father as alive, "—but these have rarely included patience. It is best for the elder brother to teach the younger."

CHAPTER 5.
SEAL HUNT

Nik crawled on his stomach across snow and rocks. He must follow Sitok's boots half a *kayak* ahead of him. Their walrus hide soles were barely visible under the waning moon and fading starlight of late morning. He must be patient . . . he must think like a seal. He must remember, as they crept closer to the rocks where seals could be, to *scratch.* For seals on rocks scratch a lot—and seem to notice when forms they take to be other seals do not. Sitok had told him this. Nik could pretend that he had sleek fur infested with saltwater lice . . . . imagine that he had crawled up here from the water for an airbath and to catch a bit of sunlight when it glowed briefly in the south at mid-day.

Nik must keep his attention on what he was doing, dull and uncomfortable as it was. The thought of blubber—that good-tasting fat right under the crispy skin. . . . think *like* a seal, he reminded himself; don't think *of* a seal. . . . eh, *be* a seal! He rolled half over, tucked his mitten beneath his arm and flopped an elbow. Back and forth, a flipper movement such as Sitok had shown him yesterday.

Nik's mind shifted to plan the many questions which crowded his brain and demanded answers he would seek from his brother. Soon, these were neatly arranged in his mind, awaiting only clever terminology to make them *non*questions. *Why, for example, did the villagers name Unipak victor of the drum duel?* Everyone could sense that Atik's accusations were true. And then, when Sitok built their new snowhouse two sleeps ago—his *first igloo* without their father's leadership, Nik and Kiti working with him—*why did no one from the village offer help?* This disregard was not *peeusinga,* not the Way of Inupiat. A third question was the one always on his lips, these days: *when will the sons go to search for their parents!?*

And finally, coloring many moments of each day and half his nights besides, was the area of inquiry he wanted answers for but dared not ask in any form because his brother's answer might paralyze Nik's further effort: *how soon will Nik become a good hunter? Is there any hope at all?* He had been out on the trail with Sitok on five different days, now . . . and had himself captured nothing in that time.

Eh, he must keep his mind on seals. He paused to scratch again.

The sun was beginning its blush in the southeastern sky as they reached a bluff which afforded a view. Ahead and below them was the mostly frozen seacoast. He spied the open lead—that broad, deep channel of salt water which separates coastal ice from mighty *siku,* the treacherous, wandering islands of unanchored ice. Before him was a small inlet off that lead. Stones and flat boulders were scattered along the narrow, descending beach. Nik clutched his killing spear. Sitok barely moved. But he *had* timed their arrival perfectly—of course! Sitok was the mighty hunter!

His brother in front of him twisted his head around. He wore sun goggles, *idjak* he had carved carefully from a bit of precious driftwood. Nik took out his own less artful spectacles made of walrus ivory. Glare on snow and ice and water could be fierce when the sun peeked above the horizon however briefly. That glare could blind a person temporarily, sometimes permanently. After making himself a fine new spear with Sitok's help, Nik by himself had carved the ivory band with two tiny horizontal slits to peer through. Now, he need not be made sightless by dazzle. The spectacles limited his vision, though. Twice he bumped his head on Sitok's boots.

Don't try to go fast—be peaceful! Nik commanded himself. *Seals move slowly on land, and Nik is a seal.* The cold from ice on which he crawled flowed through him in spite of his heavy trousers and parka. Under the wondrous fur covering similar to Nik's, the boy reflected, seals wear at least three full fingers' depth of insulating blubber which no *Inuk* can possess. . . . Patience, patience—a trait he must develop. Yes, and someone *can* learn! This he was doing, was determined to do.

Once more, he ran into Sitok's *kamik.* This time, he drew back so suddenly that a chunk of ice was displaced, then grated mildly as it slid to the promontory edge and dropped into the lead. Sitok stopped and oh-so-slowly moved his head around. His mitt waggled palm down at Nik, the signal to stop. He was to stay motionless where he lay. Nik wanted to argue, but he dared not make another sound. He watched his brother get well ahead of him without seeming to move at all. Nik wanted so badly to be active on this hunt—to at least *see* the creatures they stalked. Very gradually, he raised himself to his hands and knees so that he could look over at the rocky headland above the inlet. Now he made out first one and then another featureless shadow.

Two seals! He rose to a squat and reached up automatically to adjust his goggles and loosen the string that let his hood open to provide a better view—and too late realized his mistake as both shadows bumbled across to land's end and flopped into the sea.

His brother stood up and turned, saw Nik crouching. Caution useless now, Sitok strode back noisily and his voice trembled with frustration. "A brother promised to practice patience on this day!"

"Ee-ee, Yes," Nik said miserably. How could he have done this thing?

"Come!" Sitok headed back toward sled and dogs. What had been a long cold crawl now became a short, warming walk. Darkness collected as they went, for the sun had concluded its fleeting journey. Early afternoon. In anguish over his error, Nik wondered whether Sitok would take them back home immediately, himself in disgrace. He must not ask. His brother was in no mood for bold, discourteous questions.

Yet, twice during their return, Sitok stopped to let them watch the brilliant blue and green display of lights rippling and pulsing in the northern sky. Idle spirits at sport, those waiting for a newly born body to inhabit. Nik relaxed a little. His brother was not one for admiring sights—he was halting for Nik. Sitok knew how much the younger boy loved seeing the aerial panorama where the spirits danced and feasted.

The older boy unloaded the sled when they reached the team. He upended it and drew from inside his parka a bladder of water. Nik watched as his brother expertly took liquid into his mouth, spat it onto the brittle, mud-packed runners, whisked lush bear fur back and forth, spat again, rubbed—until starlight glistened on an ice coat thick as the bone runner above its pack of frozen permafrost. Luckily, the sled had not struck raw rock in coming here. It would have taken a long time to first make a fire and then spread thawed earth onto the runners.

"It happens," Sitok told him, "that the two distinguished hunters will now go out to sea ice."

Did that mean they would not go straight home? Or did it mean they would return on the frozen surface of the sea? That route home would be longer but far smoother—more hazardous, too, so early in winter when ice depth was uncertain. More exciting for Nik, then, but what was Sitok thinking?

Eh, why did Nik always have so many questions? Because it was difficult to get answers, that's why. He would probably by now possess all the skills to be a fine hunter except that his head was continually clogged with questions no one ever answered before he had twice that many more queries waiting. If he must linger to observe and experience everything for himself—he'd have long white hair and a face wrinkled as a walrus . . . and still not be a master of the trail.

His aggravation dissipated as they crossed the tidal crack and struck smoother ice. Sitok slowed the dogs. Nik did not ask why, but he wanted to. Suddenly, lead dog Nuko stopped, put her nose to a crumple of snow off to the side. She pawed tentatively, then looked back at the brothers. Without word or sound, Sitok crouched at that place, feeling gingerly with his snow knife down into the ice. Then he buried his harpoon handle upright near the spot and left it there. He patted the dog, moved on slowly with the team, Nik following. Nuko stopped again, and Sitok motioned Nik forward, directing *him* to probe for an opening.

Sitok waited while the younger boy marked the invisible *aglu,* the seal breathing hole. He watched wordless while Nik placed a circle of bearskin from his hunting bag under his boots, then pulled it up and tied it fur side in, all around his calves, solidly enough to stay up for warmth but lightly enough to come away with a single kick. It took three tries before Sitok raised his eyebrows to endorse the effort. Next, the younger boy put his harpoon at the ready on bone crosspieces. Finally, he rummaged once more through his hunting bag to withdraw first a long sliver of driftwood and then a tuft of wolverine fur. He moistened the hide side with his tongue, then placed it onto the end of the stick, where it froze immediately and stuck. Into the hole upright went the bare end of the stick.

At last, Nik hunkered down for the wait. His fur-clad bottom was the highest point on his body. His elbows rested on his knees, and a mittened palm went into each side of his hood opening, under the pelt *nuilak* to prop against a cheek. His eyes were fixed on the dark fur bobber that was to catch his attention should it begin to move. He was comfortable and prepared to spend whatever time it took—the remainder of winter, if necessary—at watching this breathing hole not much bigger around at the surface than a thumbnail. Sitok sucked in breath to indicate approval. Nik watched from the corner of his eye as his brother returned to the first marker.

More fog swirled in, and Sitok with sled and dogs vanished completely. All but the float before him became a chill gray robe enfolding Nik. This time, the younger boy would not disappoint his brother—nor himself! He tried to clear his mind of thought, to make it bland as the ice-mist around him. But as soon as he pushed away one idea, another popped up to take its place and had to be pressed back. He tried counting hairs on the float. He must remain still, for the sharp-eared, intelligent seal could hear any movement on ice . . . and would remember. He must stay on his feet. When he at last straightened to grasp his weapon, should a seal ever arrive, the harpoon had to be sent smoothly downward. The weight of his body must power the thrust, for no second chance would come.

Ice groaned as it adjusted to a changing tide, cracked sharply somewhere near the lead, boomed in the distance where some glacier on land begot a berg and dropped it to the sea. Cold crept up through the bear pelt, up through thick walrus-hide soles, then past the musk ox shag—the *quviut*—which lined the soles of his *kamik*. Dampness from scudding snow and light precipitation came also into the hood where his mittens stretched the opening.

He let his mind soar upward like a keen-eyed spirit, to observe himself below. He became one tiny blot alone on a world of endless ice and on land and sea that reached to all horizons. Mist swirled. The float remained motionless except for water rhythm. Nik endured.

He was aware when a misty sunlight came from the south in the middle of the following day. The fog had receded, and he could see his brother far west toward land, bent like himself stationary on ice, dogs tethered well away from him to dot the surface along with the shadowy slash of sled. Now Nik must be careful that his shadow betrayed no movement. Slowly, so slowly, he took out the *idjak* for eye protection; then with equal care removed the spectacles when daylight died only minutes following its birth.

With full darkness came another spectacular northern light event. Blues, greens, purples, pinks shimmering at the hem, roiling, flowing upward, then down, sideways. Joining, separating. A *presence* in the north, all glow and form and ripples. The sounds of spirit feasting crackled in the sky—Eh, food! Nik had forgotten to eat. To put something into his belly would push away the numbing cold which pervaded every part of him. He wondered how often *Inupiat* seal hunters were found frozen on ice, hunched over a breathing hole as he was, life spirits flown long before. He had not heard of such happening—but perhaps it would be *Nanuk,* the white bear, who more often made the discovery . . . and then devoured the evidence without reporting to the village. A nearby **Boom!** of splitting ice made Nik jump. Automatically, he looked to the place where Sitok had been visible in daylight. But only blackness registered, for little light came through roiling clouds above him. His movement imperceptible as moon shadow on ice, he retrieved food from his hunting bag, then chewed silently on frozen blubber. He felt warm, and a sense of well-being spread through him with every bite he swallowed.

He was finally learning skills for finding food. He *would* be patient. He *would* become a good hunter—perhaps even a *great* hunter! A lucky one? What of that? All know that the most expert *Inuk,* a human being clever and patient and brave, is undone forever without the smile of Chance.

The boy did not see the dark shadow approach him across the ice until Sitok grasped his arm. "Anything?" he asked.

Nik straightened up slowly, achingly, stared at him without understanding while the word sank in. "Any—? Oh, no, *owka.*"

"It happens that the brothers are fortunate to have had three seals at the other hole give themselves already—one quite large. It is necessary to butcher them before—**where's the marker!?**"

Nik knelt to the breathing place. The whole stick was gone, including the fur float. "But one has been so patient!" he gasped, tears welling in his eyes, heat rising from mortification. The seal had come to its *aglu* and gone—at least once, probably more than that—and taken the stick and fur float away for good measure! Nik was distressed.

But Sitok picked up his younger brother's harpoon along with the holding stakes while Nik unfastened and folded the bearskin in trembling hands. The two started back side by side across the ice.

"One would not have thought that the youngster could stand still for so long," Sitok approved. "It happens that he did well."

Nik didn't think so. More than skill and patience— even more than *luck!*—were involved in hunting, he was realizing. One also had to *focus!* After they finished dressing out Sitok's seals—which Sitok would report to Kiti and the village as the catch of both brothers—and after feeding the dogs, the two sat on the sled for their own fresh meal. Sitok was garrulous, for once. Nik thought he might even be able to ask his most pressing questions, if only the mood would last.

Said Sitok, "On one's own first seal hunt through ice, Arajik found his elder son asleep—hunched over properly, face pointed to the float . . . but with eyes closed and spirits scattered absolutely."

"Sitok speaks truly?" Nik was astonished. *Sitok* asleep at the *aglu?* Surely not!

The older boy laughed. "The father was very angry— said an *Inupiat* who sleeps at the breathing hole is soon frozen."

Then a seal hunter *was* sometimes found frozen. And Nik had not even had to ask the question.

"And one could tell other tales of the older brother's errors as he tried to gain skill on the trail."

Nik waited, but Sitok only sat chewing thoughtfully. He *could* tell other tales, but apparently was not going to. . . .

The younger boy broke the silence to change subjects. "Someone was bewildered at the decision of the villagers."

"—Eh?" Sitok stopped mid-chew, mystified.

"—When they named Unipak victor of the drum duel," Nik said.

Sitok shrugged, raised his eyebrows, Yes.

"An older brother was surprised, as well?"

"Owka," No.

At the *aglu,* Nik had devised clever ways to get the answers he needed without actually asking questions. Perhaps with Kiti, the stratagems might work—mostly because she approved his curiosity in the first place. With Sitok, though Nik tried once again. "Unipak must have been taking creatures captured by other hunters for quite a long time."

"Ee-ee," Yes.

Nik waited, but his brother cut off more bites of seal meat, chewed contentedly without expanding on the earlier response.

"And it may be that Unipak took from Sitok," Nik finally declared.

No answer . . . indicating that he had.

"And now?"

"Aagii!" An emphatic No. An impassioned response from mild Sitok. Strong feeling here, Nik thought.

Unipak had stolen from Nik's brother, but no longer. Sitok was big, strong . . . still, Unipak was bigger! He was aggressive as a sea bear. How could his brother stop him? The problem with getting one answer was that it seemed always to give rise to more questions.

For once, though, Sitok continued without being urged. "Unipak now understands that a harpoon can go wild in the heat of a hunt. Who can say what direction the wayward weapon will take? Someone is surprised that Atik has not already demonstrated this for him." Sitok smiled. "That small man has extremely accurate aim."

Nik could not imagine Sitok or Atik or anyone he knew harpooning a human. But still, if someone were responsible for feeding a family, as Sitok now was. . . . "One cannot help wondering that the villagers did not believe Atik."

"They believed," Sitok assured him.

"And still they favored Unipak."

"Mm-mm. Someone recalls that Atik received no punishment? But all know that Unipak with his drum and song has an important place at feast times and makes this village well respected."

A finality in Sitok's words let Nik know not to explore further. But it was not *fitting* to make a decision based on convenience for the village rather than what was right and fair. Unipak surely would not dare again to steal what was captured by others. Not now that his offense was public knowledge. Therefore, the duel had accomplished something . . . but what of Atik? How must he feel?

55

Nik launched himself into another question plaguing him. "When Sitok built the new snowhouse," he said using his best non-questioning technique, "it was of interest that villagers did not help."

Sitok laughed explosively. Nik studied him open-mouthed, and the dogs stopped gnawing their dinner bones in order to observe him. "These days without Arajik, it is Potok who leads them," Sitok said finally. Then he kept on chewing and chuckling.

As if those words and that laughter explained everything. No village had a chief or formal leader. Every husband was master of his own family—although wives prevailed in quiet ways regarding many matters. But unofficially, a village honored and sought advice from its strongest hunter, its usually oldest, certainly wisest man. People now deferred to Potok, Nik believed, only because he had been a close companion of well-respected Arajik.

Nik sighed. "By chinking cracks if nothing else, others always help those who build."

"*Peeusinga,*" Sitok agreed, "it is The *Inuit* Way."

"But on that day the villagers came to watch the construction, then walked off."

Sitok's chuckle had a bitter edge, this time. Then, "It happens that Potok did not want Kiti and her grandsons to leave his shelter."

Nik knew that. "Because of Erin?" he wondered aloud. She was at least sixteen winters old, broad-cheeked and wide-hipped, comfortable. She viewed Sitok favorably as a possible husband, but who could say where that would go? Nik's brother was still too young for marriage—and although he had several times brought her to their *iglerk* for the night, Sitok still showed no interest in taking a wife from among those he brought to the *igloo* for frolic.

"*Owka,* No," his brother said presently, "or at least not *only* Erin."

"A man who can take in *two* orphans and a widow demonstrates himself to be very impor—"

"—Perhaps!" Sitok cut him off. "But Nik knows well that Potok mainly wanted a second hunter capturing food for his many women—yes, and perhaps a third hunter developing as well."

Nik knew that Sitok added Nik to the list as an afterthought, but he was pleased just the same. "Then someone believes that Potok told the villagers to stay away—"

"—Someone *knows* he did. . . . Atik and Tukla felt remorseful, knowing that Sitok and his brother had never before built more than trail *igloo*. They came later, quietly in the darkness, when the younger brother slept on the *iglerk*."

"But too late to help—"

"—They came to give advice and then labor on building the entry and porch. Too, they dug that fine pit for storage—all when no one else from the village was around. They came also to apologize to *Ananatsiak* for not daring to come sooner."

"A boy wonders," Nik said in sudden annoyance, "why the person who surely has the most curiosity is always last to receive information."

Sitok laughed again, for he was in an expansive mood. Now he stood up and strapped the load tight to the sled. "Here is fresh news," he said. "After the sleep, two young hunters will take all this extra food onto the plains and start storing for a journey soon to come."

Ee-ee-ee! Yes, yes, yes! But how could they do so without Potok's knowing? And subsequently, somehow *claiming?* And *how* soon could they go? Feeling light as mist and fast as wind in his delight over Sitok's words, Nik helped unstake and harness the dogs while he waited for more information.

"And?" he asked finally.

"Eh?" Sitok looked startled. Then, grinning, "Tomorrow the younger brother soon to become a fine hunter will help to build a *secret* cache."

CHAPTER 6.
STORM AND HUNGER

The third cache! Nik grunted as he rolled a big stone over toward his brother, who lifted it onto the mound. How many more of these, Nik wondered. When would they have enough food? How he wanted to get started on their trip! But Sitok said, "The proper time will make itself known." Did his brother await some signal from the spirits?

As if to emphasize Nik's thought, Sitok stood motionless at the rocky mound which protected their food. He gazed northeast across the empty plains into a rising wind. The blasts were rearranging ground snow as long, low mounds in radiating streaks. Each continuing hillock looked as if it were made by a burrowing creature that rapidly traveled south and west.

"It happens, a storm will come soon," Sitok shouted above the roar. He with Nik placed the final stone on top of the rockpile. These were security against marauding bear or wolverine. No Inupiat would touch another's cache—except in desperation. And if in dire difficulty, any would then be welcome. As everyone knew, food so taken by a stranger must be replaced rapidly as possible.

Halfway back to the village, pellets of snow and ice blew horizontally with such force that the boys could see nothing, and they dared not risk their eyes by straining to discern the trail. Sitok slowed the dogs but gave Nuko her head to lead them home. Each boy clung to a side of the handle on the sled and stumbled along blindly. The temperature plunged.

The gale would take breath from their mouths unless they inhaled away from the wind. Nik could feel the hairs in his nose stiffening from cold. He like all of his people knew to breathe *only* through the nose in such cold. To inhale through the mouth would freeze the lungs. Ice crystals scoured his face through the small opening he had left when he tightened the face opening in his hood. Eyes useless, now, he might as well draw the hood strings tight and let the rich *nuilak* cover his face fully. But he was too miserable to make the effort.

The tempest slashed across the empty land, a spirit howling in deep torment. Gusts smashed against them. Nik felt his boots go light on the ice when he was close to being blown off his feet. The dogs would stop at such times and hunch down in their traces, then go on when the blast let up for a moment or two as if to catch its enormous breath. Nik wanted to ask Sitok if they should not dig into drifts to shelter dogs and themselves. It did not matter that they must by now be close to home. Each stride required much effort. His lungs bellowed for warmer air, for *more* air. He was, in fact, getting dizzy, his head whirling, when a solid arm came across his back. Then Sitok's mitten tucked under his right arm, and he felt himself half-lifted and pushed forward the final steps before they stopped. Nik released his frozen grasp on the sled crossbar and lurched as Sitok thrust him forward to come up flat against the arc of their snowhouse.

Good! He was on the side sheltered from direct wind. He could at last draw as much air as he liked, so long as he remembered to breathe through the unfrosted wolverine fur on his hood by now protecting most of his face.

They fed the dogs well with fish and scraps. To do this they pulled out everything but two halves of a split seal from their new storage cavity—the tunneled excavation hacked out of ice and permafrost with such effort and skill by Tukla and Atik with Sitok after finishing the *igloo* during the sleep time. Hard work, getting into that permanently frozen soil below the few fingers' depth of top skim which thawed each year in summer sun. And how difficult it must have been to protect even the existence of their project by first building a small *igloo* over what would become the entry. Now, though, much from that fine cellar had been taken out earlier today to one of the secret prairie caches. This morning, when they decided what to take and what to leave, the two brothers had expected to hunt after the next sleep. Now inside the storage shelter and out of the wind, Sitok wondered aloud whether they might have run themselves too short on food. Dear Sitok, Nik thought, always worrying! And always anticipating the visit of his great enemy, Hunger. Kiti certainly had food inside the snowhouse. No need for anxiety.

During what should have been sleep time, the storm winds increased. Nik lay wide-eyed in darkness. Sometimes, lying awake on the sleeping shelf, on the *iglerk*, with furs tucked snugly around him, he felt alone and alarmed by such violent weather. Other times, especially when Kiti turned over in her sleep robes to trim the lamp wick and replenish oil for renewed glow and a bit of warmth, he felt snug in the tight little *igloo* they had built. Nik was beloved on this night by two strong *Inuit.* But the later musings were never as pleasant. . . . After Kiti's breaths came evenly to indicate her return to slumber, Nik would find himself imagining what his parents Arajik and Mawena might be experiencing inland *right now.* His imagination pictured them in despair. Were they too surrounded by this same miserable storm? And were they somehow able to keep themselves warm and fed? An urgency would come over him often at night, and especially on this night with a blizzard raging. *He and Sitok must go very soon to find their parents.*

Nik still refused to believe the desolate news brought by Urgit when he claimed to be the only survivor of that summer tragedy. Eh, Urgit! . . . *Ur-r-r-GEET!* Weasel-faced,

61

pinch-jawed, pebble-eyed Urgit. All right—Pak, whose lifeless body Urgit claimed actually to have seen, was Urgit's only parent. So Nik knew that Urgit, too, had suffered terrible loss. His mind knew. But his spirit refused the information. His brain reminded him that Urgit and his old Aunt Saruna were now dependent on villagers. If food got scarce, those two would feel famine first. If this or any great storm sent the temperature plummeting and a shortage of robes existed, Urgit and Saruna would be first to be uncovered and left to freeze.

Nik still had his brother, a skillful hunter, even with their parents gone. And he also had Grandmother Kiti with her amazing assortment of skills—and her wisdom, besides! But Nik's life spirit was a selfish one and could not get beyond his own family loss. His father, his *atatak* Arajik—strong, droll, always the great traveler full of knowledge about other places, other people, other ways to think and do. And his mother, his *ananak* Mawena—what did he know of her? Loving, often bubbling like the beach froth of a summer tide. But sometimes silent, brooding, particularly after Kiti scolded her for letting the lamp go out. Or for not chewing with sufficient vigor as the two women prepared hide for clothing. Or for sewing such big stitches with her bone needle that the apparel and especially the *kamik* she made would not be proof against water.

"A fatal flaw!" And Nik's grandmother would insist that every stitch come out to be done again—Mawena complaining throughout.

Nik knew that *Ananatsiak* was right. Careless sewing could mean that someone who dipped a foot into the lead during the moons of winter would freeze before he or she reached any source of warmth. No dangerous loose seam would be in boots or other clothing that came from this household. Kiti would see to that, the boy knew. The thing was, though, that Mawena *also* knew—and depended on her mother-in-law to insure quality.

Mawena. He realized now that he did not know his mother well. One thing was certain: she adored Arajik. She trusted him completely . . . to keep the family fed and well protected, to train their two sturdy sons in the manly skill of hunting and the *Inuit* art for both men *and* women of entertaining through poetry, story, song and dance. Her husband would teach their boys all they needed to know, so she thought. Mawena was certain that Arajik knew everything about everything—was absolutely wise in each decision. And Nik's *atatik*, his father, of course relished his wife's judgment.

Following sleep on the day after the storm began, the three came from the sleeping ledge into blackness with wind howling harder than ever.

His grandmother's voice came through the dark. "It happens that perhaps a family will dress more warmly to conserve oil."

Chattering, they added outdoor garments, the *silapak* of heavy fur trousers and parka over their soft pelt undergarments, their *illupak*. Even inside the *igloo,* cold was a defiant giant of increasing size.

"Plenty of food is here?" Sitok asked *Ananatsiak* Kiti.

She pointed to the doorway baffle in the arching wall where a half-cured caribou hide nearly hid three small seals frozen stiff and upright. Nik warmed with pride. Two of those had given themselves to *him!* As a hunter, he was improving.

"Plus the big split seal in storage," Nik added, "along with everything out there in caches."

"It may happen," Sitok said then, "that no one can reach the caches for a time." The boys had built them fairly far from the village in secluded places well away from Potok.

Kiti sucked in breath, agreeing.

At the doorway, a sound which they took at first for wind startled them. Then the baffle was pulled to the side and Potok came through, followed by his wife Maleet and their eldest daughter Erin. Potok grinned in his familiar way, reminiscent of times when Arajik was here. They exchanged greetings. Perhaps Potok had sulked long enough. Now that he had come, others in the village would dare to visit openly—not furtively as Atik and Tukla and even Erin were doing up to now. Nik thought that Erin would be a fine catch for his brother. Why did Sitok show so little interest?

Potok pulled from his parka a fair-sized piece of prized *muktuk,* whale skin with blubber attached. He handed it to Kiti as woman of the household, but grinned at Nik. He knew that this was the boy's favorite food. A peace offering. Did he think none of this family knew what he had been doing among the people of the village?

Kiti brought out more food to accompany the whale meat, but conversation was cautious at first, carefully courteous.

"A new *igloo* is strong and handsome," Potok complimented Sitok.

"And with much space!" Maleet added wistfully.

"Also good smells," Erin put in, her large eyes fastened on Sitok.

Nik held back a grin. This *igloo* was much smaller than Potok's. But it seemed larger because everything was in place. Kiti had no patience with disorder. See how Erin's eyes danced. She appreciated cleanliness.

Sitok responded to Potok's compliment in the traditional manner. "Here stands a poor hovel, lopsided to look at and miserable to live in."

"*Owka,* No," Potok protested. "Here is a place fit to host a village feast."

Nik knew that his brother understood the older man's veiled suggestion, that the family should invite others in the village for a feed. Potok certainly had learned of the extra provision being stored, and to him this accumulation would seem gluttonous. In his eyes, prudence was foolish and saving back was overcautious, a display of small faith and even discourtesy to others who might enjoy some extra food. But Nik remembered that even Arajik had said of his friend that Potok was short-sighted, slow to consider the needs of a later day.

Sitok ignored the man's innuendo and answered smoothly. "Perhaps the ignorant builder will do better when he constructs once again."

"No wind at all comes through the chinks," Maleet observed.

So then of course Kiti recounted made-up flaws. Here was a social game played with relish when she was in the mood. The roof arch was too low. The entry porch was too long. The whole place was too small even for three. Sitok of course did not take offense. He sat on a bearskin placed on the ice floor and nodded agreement.

Nik was just thinking that he might risk a trip outside to leave the babble behind when Potok ended all formalities with a statement that stopped the talk. "It happens, a guest will soon visit."

Everyone stared at him. Visitors announced in advance? Unheard of!

"A dog-person, a *kalunait*—Arajik called him *scientist.*"

"*Arajik!?*" everyone exclaimed.

Potok raised his eyebrows, held them up for an emphatic *Yes*. He enjoyed attention. "Arajik was in a village far to the south when a priest brought a *kalunait* to him."

Nik looked to Sitok for clarification, but his older brother had his eyes fastened on Kiti. She raised her fur-clad shoulders, left them there, frowned. She evidently knew nothing or at least very little of this matter. Was Potok inventing a tale to serve his need for power? Nik decided not, for pure fiction would reveal itself, soon or late.

"A clever *kalunait*," Arajik said, "who spoke *Inupiaq* better than the holy man."

Kiti said quietly, "This message about a visitor was learned from Arajik." She did not ask a question, but her statement required an answer, nonetheless.

Potok's eyebrows shot up, Yes. He grinned. She did not know? Loss of face for the family meant greater status for him.

"It happens that Arajik was saving the information," Sitok said finally. "He mentioned several times a possible surprise to come."

Nik recalled when his father had last taken a long trek alone. "Remember when he took those fox furs to the southwest late in the last winter season?"

"*Ee-ee,* Yes," Kiti said. "To a village so big it has a name."

Nik and Sitok's eyebrows lifted. Yes, they remembered. One could only imagine such a large place.

Potok's face fell as Sitok took up the tale. "The *scientist* was there. But Arajik did not think the dog-person would find his way to *this* place."

Nik marveled at such a speech from his brother. Almost a confrontation. Sitok implied that Potok was spreading as truth something which was unlikely to happen.

Potok said nothing, his small eyes fixed on Sitok's face, his lips pressing each other as anger drew down the

66

corners. Not for the first time, certainly, Nik reflected that Potok was an unpleasant man. Was he also *dangerous?* he wondered. But then again, might there be the possibility that they could get to see a real *kalunait,* a dog man descended from one of Sedna's litters, one of those heavy-eyebrowed persons described in tales?

"Why would such a one take the trouble to come?" Kiti asked.

Hoping to earn once more the center of attention, Potok answered. "He is to *study* us, so Arajik said. To *study* the way in which the people of this village hunt and eat and live."

"Ai-ee?" Surprise came from Potok's women as well as Nik's family. A dog-man would come to hunt and eat and live with them?

Kiti gave her low *"Hoo-oo!"* of disapproval. "Scientist? Study? What do such words mean?"

"A *scientist* is a dog-person who **studies**, observes in order to learn," Potok explained importantly, "or so Arajik said. As a hunter might *study* tracks along a trail."

Nik visualized Nuko, a sled dog very much *like* a person, who could find *aglu*—invisible seal holes—as well as lead a team home through a blizzard. What wonders might this dog-person who *studies* be able to perform?

"**Study** means observing and listening to, then thinking about certain matters," Potok continued importantly. "Arajik said that's how this scientist knows the Inupiat language, by his *study*." Potok had a smug lilt in his tone, proud to be giving such weighty information.

In the snow house was silence broken only by storm sounds outside as people considered the man's words. At last, Kiti spoke up. "It is unlikely that any dog-person will get here," she said, "but if he does, then the Inupiat shall study *him.*"

Everyone laughed. No one but Kiti among those present had actually ever *seen* a *kalunait*—the heavy-eyebrowed dog-persons who come from the south.

Gentle Erin finally spoke. "A descendant of Sedna, to visit here! Do tell us the story, Kiti! Storm time is for tales!"

Nik could have hugged the girl. Why did Sitok pay her so little attention?

Everyone clamored agreement, and Kiti hesitated for only a few moments. Then the wrinkled woman with teeth worn down from years of chewing hides came off the robes by the lamp looking alert and youthful. She placed each foot with assurance as people moved back to give her space. She pranced about the ice floor darting a step this way and that. Her voice when it came was in the tone of a whiny girl.

"No—no, my father! Not this suitor, nor yet that one! Agh, Oodlvak is too heavy!" And displeasure was in the slant of Kiti's head, in the stiffness of her body, in the angle of her feet.

Next she clawed at her nose and shivered. "Litunik smells bad!"

Spectators laughed.

Now came the father's deep voice. "But a girl must choose *some*one!" His patience was gone. "Two younger daughters are in this household, and each of the three must wed in turn."

The girl's voice became falsely meek. "Panituk? Eh, *namunilunga!*" This young woman is not good enough for him! He deserves someone more important."

And so it went with Sedna until at last her father's angry voice shouted: "Ah, then here! Wed this, the lead dog of a parent's team!" And more mildly, "He's handsome and he's willing. Having earned his place before the sled, it happens he is more intelligent than most of the suitors."

The listeners giggled, nudged each other, hushed. Echoing from the icy curved dome all around them came sounds of spirits wailing in different voices. Nik looked about him. He was always dazzled by Kiti's vocal effects. The woman seized a small drum from the wall and now added irregular, jarring **thu-thu-THUMP**s to the jumble of sound produced by her voice. She danced wildly, then sank to sit on the floor robe as spirit cries faded.

Softly, "*Kringmerk* the dog who was Sedna's husband seemed at the wedding feast to be pleasant and funny. He appeared to care for his bride. He gobbled his food without first cutting it—but everyone forgave him. After all, what does a dog know about meal manners? And how can a dog's great paw handle an *ulu?*"

Again the audience laughed.

"But then he took his bride far away to an ice island. And there, he threw off all aspect of human grace. He became a tyrant who made impossible demands—then punished Sedna brutally when she was unable to fulfill them."

Kiti stopped so that all could imagine the plight of a human ruled by a dog.

"The babes were born, as babies *are*—but these in litters, eight and ten at a time, all to be nurtured and trained before the next birthing."

"*Hoo-oo,*" gasped the two other women in the group.

"Too many!" Kiti announced. "Little dog-children everywhere! The island was small. . . . *Ho-oo!*" sadly.

"'Get rid of them!' commanded Kringmerk. 'One hunter cannot feed so many.'

"'But they are the children of this marriage,' Sedna objected, for like all *Inuit* she loved her babies.

"'*Hoo-oo!* They are worthless. . . . True, they are somewhat hairy like their father, so beautiful. But they take their mother's form—slow running with but *two* legs! And they stand upright. How can a fine hunter like your husband teach trail skills to such awkward creatures? Yet they eat more and more as they grow larger.'

"'It is necessary for a husband to reconsider. The spirits will be angry.'

"'Then let the spirits feed them! These children must go!'

"Sedna could not bring herself to harm them—no, she would not use her sharp bone skinning knife, and *no,* she could not use a rock or poison herbs. She tried to reason, offered to take the hunting trail herself, do whatever she could to save her sons and daughters.

"But Kringmerk was adamant: 'Get rid of them!'

"So with tears falling like summer rain, she placed them in a giant boot, three and four litters at a time, to go south with the tide and pushed by *ooangniktook,* the north wind. How could any mother bid farewell forever to her children?

"Remember," Kiti instructed her listeners, "these were dog-children, not *Inuit,* not real people. And Sedna was by now a mature Inupiat woman, life having left its painful marks upon her."

The listeners relaxed, raised their eyebrows, sucked in breath. Yes, yes! They would try to remember.

The life left Kiti's voice. It became a monotone to signal the passage of many sad seasons. "Sedna sent messages to her parents, telling them her dog husband was not as he appeared, begging them to come and rescue her.

"But every message was destroyed before delivery. Her husband had done special services for land creatures and for birds in order to bind and obligate them, should he ever need their help. In time of famine, he had shared freshwater fish and herbs with them according to their species. He had cleaned and tended painful wounds, for his tongue—like that of wolves—had special healing powers.

"So now, even had they wanted to, the animals of land and air were powerless to help the wretched woman. You must remember that the cold ocean waters of the northern world were all empty in those days, that nothing moved within the sea.

"And Sedna's parents did not hear from her, not for moons and moons, seasons and seasons, winter after winter. At last, they decided on their own to make a visit. After they saw their daughter's tragic condition, they of course agreed to take her home. But the dog-husband said 'No.'

"Nevertheless, they waited for him to take the trail for food, then smuggled Sedna into their ocean-worthy boat, the very *umiak* in which they had arrived. They got out to sea and headed for home.

"When the husband found Sedna missing, he knew what had happened. He called in favors frantically. He sent the creatures most savage and unfeeling—the birds—to fly out and attack the craft.

"'Make them turn around and bring her back,' he ordered."

Kiti left her drum on the floor and got up quickly. She became a wave-tossed boat in open sea, peering wildly at the dome of the snow house—first here, then there.

"'Turn—tur-rr-rrn!' the snow geese demanded. But the parents refused. And when the creatures swooped to batter them with wings, the three in the boat at first fended off the strikes.

"'Go back! Go now! Go hastily!' shrieked the gulls. But the boat kept moving homeward to southeast.

"'Im-mee-dee-ately!' yodeled the loons; and jaegers folded their wings and plunged to slash defenseless heads below.

"Sedna's parents eyed each other fearfully, not knowing what to do. Any of the large sea-birds could split a skull in one dive—and *would*, if the people did not obey.

"'*Ananak! Atatak!* Mother! Father! Please, **no***!'* Sedna begged as her parents turned the boat about. But they did not heed her entreaty, anxious only to appease the threatening fowl above. As they went back, Sedna pleaded with them until at last the ice island where Sedna had lived so unhappily for so long came back into view. By then, she was desperate and threw herself over the side of the boat into the icy sea."

Kiti treaded water, her legs churning there in the igloo, her arms over her head, fingers clinging to the *umiak*. The old woman's furs rippled in the waves, and she raised up her chin to keep her nose above the water. Every member of the audience was holding breath, eyes wide with alarm.

"When the parents saw their daughter's terror, when they realized how determined she was, they hesitated. They stopped the boat."

"*Hoo-oo!*" breathed the rapt listeners in the igloo, anticipating horror to come.

Kiti's voice became low and ominous as she resumed her seat on the robe. "And the very moment that they stopped, the birds attacked," she said as a hollow ***BOOM! Thump-er-BOOM!*** emphasized the dangerous assault. She swung the drumstick over her head, then the drum itself, to ward off the onslaught.

"In panic, both parents tried to pry loose Sedna's fingers from the gunwale of the boat. But they could not." ***TAP-a-Boom—BOOM!*** "Years of toil and strain from a difficult survival made Sedna stronger than both her parents together. Wings beat all about them, sharp beaks tore at human flesh, and bloody terror knew no boundary.

"'Get back into the boat!' Sedna's father demanded. 'It is possible to find some other way!' But Sedna would not let herself be hauled aboard.

"'Then drop away!' her father said. 'If death is the woman's choice, at least she must not condemn her parents as well!'"

Kiti quietly put down the drum and beater. Her voice mellow with sympathy. "Between the cold of the water and her great dismay over returning to a hated existence on the island, Sedna was no longer rational. She felt and heard nothing, only clung to the boat.

"The parents, too, were beyond reason in their panic." Kiti fumbled in her robes and drew out the little knife for eating, the *ulu*. Rocking as she rode the waves, she lifted the round blade high into the air, grasped the handle at the top by both hands, and brought it down to stop mid-air with a jerk.

"**Off** went finger-tips of both hands, to the first knuckles. And these fell into the churning water. There, they became instantly the many fish of the vast ocean.

"Sedna felt no pain, though. She had learned during ghastly seasons as wife of a sled dog to accomplish what she must with whatever she had. So now, she automatically clung to the boat with the parts of her fingers that remained."

Down came Kiti's knife once more, jerking to a stop as if an invisible barrier existed. "This time, the fingers to the second joint were chopped away," she said, "and these larger pieces became immediately the seals and walruses of the salty sea."

"Hoo-oo!" Spectators sucked in breath, but no eye left Kiti's form in their midst.

"Now Sedna clung with only the last segment of her fingers. And again, without mercy—" Kiti's knife made a final dive, as spectators drew back and uttered low gasps.

"Thus slashed away was the third and last bit of each finger, into the knuckle. These fragments, swirling in salt water, became the largest sea creatures, the sharks and bottom-dwelling squid and all the mighty whales."

73

Now Kiti picked up the drum again, a quiet rhythm rising. Sadly, "Unable to hold onto the boat, Sedna slowly sank into the waves and down . . . until she reached the bottom of the ocean. And there she lives today. She still has courage and strength gained in her sad lifetime on land. And gradually, she has developed great wisdom.

"Now it is Queen Sedna who reigns over all creatures of the sea, over all those *puyee.* Which among her subjects shall come to the surface and give itself for *Inuit* use? Where is the patient hunter? Where the most deserving fisherman? Who among *Inuk* have obeyed Sedna's laws to honor the spirits of those creatures taken from the water?"

For several minutes, silence was complete in the little snow house after Kiti finished, and the only sound was wild wind that wailed outside. Then, everyone at once gave her their compliments and expressed appreciation: *Nakorami, Ananatsiak!* Thank you, Grandmother!

"It happens," Potok said as he stood up, "that certain persons need to find their sleep robes." He shrugged into his parka, and Maleet along with Erin followed his lead. "And these fine seals," he said to Sitok as he pulled back the walrus hide at the door to the entry porch, "are among those captured together twelve sleeps ago? Before the two boys built their own igloo?"

They were not, and Potok knew this fact. Kiti and the two boys had left Potok's *igloo* with no food offered and none taken—an indefensible breach in etiquette—but only Erin had seemed embarrassed at the time. She and Nik—and Potok certainly!—knew that these two seals were the result of a lucky hunt, that they were here in the *igloo* because they were too small to be cached. Everyone also knew that he and Sitok had captured them when on sea ice with each other only two sleeps ago—in fact, Nik himself had captured these two and they were here for first use because they *were* so paltry. Potok was certainly aware that they were not from any group hunt in which he had participated. The man was rebuking Sitok for not hunting more often these days with him and with the villagers. Anger flooded through Nik. He turned away to hide his feelings.

Sitok did what he must. "These poor creatures," he told the man, "are far too small to be of interest to any hunter such as Potok." He picked up with each hand one of the gutted and now stiffly frozen seals. "But a guest would oblige this clumsy hunter by taking them—" he placed one into each of Potok's waiting mitts—"perhaps to feed someone's least worthy dogs."

Again, *"Nakorami,* thank you," this not so heartfelt as the thanks following Kiti's tale. In fact, their neighbor smiled disdainfully as he thrust one seal into the eager arms of his wife Maleet. Now he got down on hands and knees to lead his family through the exit tunnel and up into the raging storm, each parent pushing a seal in front.

After they were gone, Kiti wrinkled her nose but said no word. Regardless of circumstance, certain laws of hospitality must be observed.

That night in the sleep time and throughout the next two days and nights, wind whipped frozen grains of ice-laden snow back and forth across the coastal plains. Nor did the storm abate, only increase. In spite of eating the negligible portions allowed by Kiti the one little seal that Potok had not spied became a memory in what seemed to Nik a far-distant past. It was time to go out to forage in the supply hole.

"Someone should wait," Kiti counseled him, "and allow the wind to subside."

"But a grandmother said that same thing before the sleep—and also before the sleep prior to that one."

She was silent. He spoke truth.

"It is better to die quickly from cold than slowly from starvation," Nik said. His belly was a separate, voracious creature demanding food.

Kiti made no more objection. Nik would go. But he agreed to use the guideline she supplied, a long cable of twisted sealskin strips. After tying one end around his waist, Nik looped the other around the big soapstone food bowl; but Kiti pulled it free and knotted it around her own waist. They grinned at each other. The boy crawled outside and tried to feel his way to the storage pit. The angry howl of a full blizzard gale deafened him. Its force did not permit him to stand upright. He crouched low against the wind, clenched his eyes shut, turned his head, chin down, away from the stinging pellets that assaulted his face, from the deafening cacophony that made his ears ring even through his parka. No right or left or up or down existed. No forward, no backward. He could of course pivot slowly, but could not be sure how far he had turned.

At last, he located the ice-blasted boulder which guarded the small igloo over the storage cavity. He slashed through the adjacent drift, then grunted to push the rock away—certainly it should stand strong before ravening dogs and wild creatures. He was careful not to breathe through his mouth, and he kept even his small, nearly bridgeless nose pressed deeply into hood fur so that air could warm before he inhaled it. Even so, with the effort of getting entry into the storage, his lungs felt as if they breathed fire.

Down in the declivity and out of direct wind, he tugged and boosted one big icy split of seal carcass onto a tiny, sagging plate of stiff walrus hide lashed to short bone runners. He would make two trips. He caught his lash through the near crosspiece. All the spirits together should bless his grandmother for this guideline. He knew he would never leave the cache cellar safely without it, even as close as it was to their *igloo*. And he knew also that, should he have to return without a line, his lungs would freeze long before he found the porch opening. Villagers would then discover his stiffened body after the storm . . . under the snow . . . whatever the dogs and other predators had not consumed. . . .

Nik snorted at his imaginings. "A boy wastes time to keep from returning to the tempest," he scolded himself. He tugged on the crossbar of the hand-sled, heaved himself and the cargo up the slick ice ramp and out. Then he followed the line to the snowhouse porch, this time with the wind at his back, and pushed the sled before him as he crawled down through the tunnel.

"It happens," Kiti told him as he prepared to go out for the other split, "that no more food is needed for several sleeps." Grateful, Nik coiled the line and gave it to her for safekeeping.

The storm continued. All the wind since time began had surely howled past in proud review by now, had groaned and wailed beyond the bleak *igloo* by the frozen sea—then circuited the sphere of earth to return with new lament.

Nik and Sitok with Kiti stayed curled in their sleep robes on the ledge as much as possible. Here was the only warmth, for lamp oil and blubber had been consumed two sleeps ago. Also, lying snug to wait for weather change, they gradually got beyond the pain in their bellies. Kiti allowed them to eat lightly and late, once each day, right before the true sleep period which they lengthened gradually. Respiration slowed; necessary movements were made at half speed, a mere turning over on the *iglerk*. Nik perceived himself to be a twig afloat on a late-summer stream nearly without current. Bobbling. . . .

But even with Kiti's careful husbanding of provision, the half seal Nik had brought was finished off at sleep time the very night before a gaunt and hollow-eyed Urgit with his Aunt Saruna tottered through the baffle down into their *igloo* and asked for aid. Saruna was ill, her small face flushed, eyes bright with fever. Both were cold, both hungry. Nik knew that they had come here only as a last resort—especially proud Saruna. He also knew that they would not be turned away. A matter of *peeusinga,* the Way of the People, as Kiti would interpret the situation.

Ananatsiak hurried Saruna to warmth within the sleep robes, sent a reluctant Urgit back outside for snow—warned not to leave the porch entry—to first melt and then bathe his aunt's fevered face. Nik noticed that his grandmother tied a line around her waist. But she did not offer Urgit the other end. Rather, with no explanation needed, she gave the guideline to him, to Nik, to her younger grandson. They must have more food. Nik took the hide sled from a storage bulge in the tunnel.

The wind seemed to him as bitter as before. But the stabbing ice pellets driven along the ground might have been fewer. With his mittens, he grabbed the guideline at his waist for added security. Someone could still become easily confused, and the small extra time to find one's bearings could mean death. As always in extreme cold, he reflected as he made his way to the storage hole, *Inuk* could freeze from the inside out by carelessly breathing through the mouth. Or he could be attacked by a great white sea-bear starving and desperate in the storm. But none of these things would happen to Nik— because he had a special sense when danger was nearby, he had recently decided. And because his imagination during the extended sleep time had been conjuring calamities far worse, surely, than any disaster that might befall him in this storm.

Nik had to hack with his snow knife to get through doorway drift at the storage pit. But after he was through it, he discovered that the actual stone to block the door had been ajar before the gap iced in. He crawled inside and went down, felt around in darkness. Nothing. He pushed back panic. No wild creature could manipulate that stone block up there, even if it had the strength. Certainly no dog nor wolf pack. Still, what human would take the food of another without asking? Even starving—*Inuit* would first *ask.* Like Urgit and Saruna. And *Inuit* who went in for food would replace the boulder on leaving.

But had Nik replaced the boulder when he was here previously? Of course he planned at that time to return immediately for more food. But he did not remember letting go of the hand-sled to turn and block the opening. Could he have been so irresponsible? And had the dogs then nosed in and eaten the remaining seal split? He recalled the unusual silence of *kringmerk* throughout this storm. Only a few sleeps back, in fact, the family had discussed how quiet they were. He and Sitok both thought them probably dead, frozen, starved.

But Kiti insisted that the animals would take action before that would happen. Their warm fur in the snow caves would protect them from the cold. "If desperately hungry," she said, "they would gnaw their lines and scratch through ice right into this *igloo.* "

"Someone wonders," Nik thought aloud at the time, "how it is that a grandmother knows so much about what a dog would do."

As usual, Kiti ignored his implied question and continued her assertions about *kringmerk,* the sled dogs. "They have found food somewhere," she assured her worried grandsons, "and with full bellies, they have burrowed deep and comfortable in drifts to outwait the storm."

Full bellies indeed! With a sick feeling, Nik accepted what had surely happened. His fault, too, and this could be the end for everyone. He left the sled inside the cellar, followed the guideline back. He was in no rush to return with bad news. Nothing at all remained with which to feed their guests or themselves.

Silence greeted his confession. No accusations came, only acceptance. *Pirtok.* What's done cannot be undone. Throughout that sleep and two more, the five of them huddled beneath *iglerk* robes in the cold, dark snowhouse. At first, stimulated by having guests present, someone would speak, another might answer . . . or not. Ideas were left unfinished. No one noticed. Stomachs that had previously churned with hunger ceased to complain. Breathing slowed once more. The five stayed warm on the fur-piled ledge, closed their eyes . . . cleared their minds . . . drowsed . . . dreamed of sleds filled with seal, of walruses flopping through the porch tunnel to give themselves outright, envisioned fish and summer berries, eggs picked from the inland tundra . . . *food* to offer bodies so famished that they no longer made demands. . . .

From deep sleep, Nik awoke and came alert to silence . . . echoing, unaccustomed quiet. He thought at first his ears were plugged. He slipped off the ledge, then *heard* his fur-shod feet pad to the baffle. He *heard* the flutter as he moved beyond the drape, *heard* the stillness above him. Ignoring intense cold, he stood up on the porch, turned to press back the stone closure. Moonlight overhead. Starlight. Glistening snow cover. No wind.

Away from the musk of bodies crowded too long in too small space, away from the close air inside, Nik took one deep saturating breath that seemed to expand not only his lungs but also his fingers and toes, the muscles in his arms.

"Ee-YAI-ee!" he shouted wildly into the clear night. The storm was over at last.

CHAPTER 7.
THROUGH
KALUNAIT EYES

Poona and Kotil were villagers from the north. They were fishing the lead in *kayaks* when they spotted *agviq,* the great bowhead whale. Since the mammal moved slowly south and west, they paddled rapidly to the next village—to Nik's village. Startling news, for the creature was not only out of season but also out of place. The big whales normally passed only in springtime and then kept to deep water well east of those near-shore ice floes, the *siku.* A paddler with his *kayak* never saw them. Sedna for some reason was outdoing herself this early winter, Nik thought. *Perhaps the Sea Queen perceives the brothers' need for extra food before they make their trip.*

The village was agog from the moment it learned of the whale. Nik wanted to join the *kayaks.* Sitok of course said *No,* that it was far too dangerous for someone without experience. Kiti agreed.

"Someone learns to paddle a *kayak* by **paddling** a *kayak,*" Nik grumbled.

Sitok laughed, wrinkled his nose. He put his hand on the boy's shoulder. "Someone first removes one's tunic in summer," he said gently, "and learns by putting his craft into a gentle inland stream."

Nik remembered the summer Sitok mastered handling the *kayak.* His brother spent much time under water, often upside down. He would extricate himself from the craft with difficulty in shallow streams, stand up snorting and spluttering, then try again. Because the family *kayak* had disappeared in Urgit's great wave, Sitok had to borrow a craft to go today. He with Kiti had started building to replace the *kayak* lost inland. Carefully tanned, the sturdy hide covering still needed to be stretched across the bone frame already prepared.

People hurried toward the open lead guiding dogsleds loaded with weapons. The whole village helped to get everything needed onto sea ice. Each sled was brought down, every *kayak.* Even toddlers were proud to carry flensing tools for removing skin and blubber.

Nik walked with both hands and his left shoulder supporting a side of the *umiak,* the big rounded boat belonging to Arajik but used by the whole village. Sometimes called the "woman's boat," and on days like this a "whale boat," the relatively sturdy craft on which Nik would ride today was considered deepwater safe even though, like kayaks, it was without a keel. Made with bone ribs and a few precious sticks of stabilizing driftwood and—like *kayaks*—covered with thick walrus hide, it was bulky and awkward to transport on land, but not heavy. Bobbing in the water, it responded rapidly to paddles.

As they assembled, the sun peeping above the south horizon to light the scene, villagers heard an unfamiliar sound in the distance. Sustained, the noise increased rapidly, a roar coming from the sky. Everyone paused. Nik with his companions lowered the big boat onto water, then looked up. In the southwest, they saw a dot enlarging.

"*Tingmisut!* Airplane!" The word passed in hushed tones from one person to another. Everyone knew *about* planes. No one present had ever seen one, not even Kiti. Such a noisy bird approaching from the heavens—the stuff of legends. The machine passed over, circled, passed again and then landed on smooth sea ice nearby. People dropped what they held, ceased whatever they were doing, to converge upon the featherless sky-thing. A door opened upward just as a racing Nik reached the plane. A ladder came down. A pale face appeared at the opening—a *kalunait* face with shaggy eyebrows and a beard. Hair red as dried seal blood. The "surprise" Sitok had mentioned, the dog-person whom Potok had spoken about—the *scientist* who *studies!*—must be here. A whale, an airplane and now this dog-visitor—all in one day? . . . Here was a happening to remember and recount for a lifetime. . . .

While the man came down the ladder backwards, Nik's eyes caught more motion at the hatch. Another of them? Smaller, but in ways a duplicate of the first. Again red hair, pale eyes like sunlit sea ice. This one had small spots sprinkled across nose and cheeks, some sort of tattooing, Nik decided, rosy in color without design. A youngster nearly Nik's own age—the son of the *scientist* had come to *study* also?

Because Arajik had made the original arrangement, that man's eldest son Sitok was now responsible. He pushed past others to greet the visitor, Potok not far behind. Nik wondered whether he and his brother could still take part in the whale hunt today. The boy moved in closer to watch the smaller *kalunait* spring down the steps face forward. A stranger from warm lands to the south. The dog-child looked at Nik and smiled. The Inupiat boy moved forward to give a formal greeting; but as he spoke, he could see from the eyes that the stranger understood nothing. Nik turned to the big man when *he* spoke.

"This man is Cliff Belson from a school in Missouri, a man who studies people," the stranger boomed in clear *Inupiaq*. "It happens that he is an anthropologist."

That word *studies* again, Nik thought. *Pehl-son.*

84

Then the man turned to the youngster. "And the small person here is Bonnie Belson, the half-grown child who accompanies the parent." Nik understood every word the man spoke. He had good *tune.*

"Pehl-son," Sitok repeated carefully, then looked over at the younger kalunait. "Pah-nee." Nik said both names several times to himself. He was excited. No young people anywhere near his own age lived in the village. Among the children, only Potok's two youngest were old enough to be permanently out of their mother's hood. But they were still small children and were *girls.*

Pehl-son and his *Pah-nee* wanted to go hunt whale with the village. Now. So it was decided that the man and his child would ride most safely in the big *umiak.* Sitok put Nik in charge of them. Kiti suggested that the newcomers might be more comfortable waiting in the village. Belson declined for both of them. Another dog-person in the plane handed down a few bags and boxes. Villagers stacked these on an emptied sled as the plane took off across ice with an astonishing roar. Again, Kiti offered to accompany the guests and their belongings up to the snowhouse. But Nik heard Pehl-son say three times that he—**they**, himself and Pah-nee, too—*wanted* to go on the whale hunt, "if it is permitted to accompany the hunters."

Of course it was permitted! All things are permitted guests, and these two flame-haired descendants of mighty Sedna and her cruel consort—these dog people—could not have been more welcome.

The rounded, rudderless *umiak* with a waterproof skin of tightly sewn hide hopped and skidded atop the mild waves. In the middle, Belson and Bonnie sat among robes Kiti insisted on putting into the boat for them. Nik and two broad-shouldered harpooners, Tukla and Wutik, knelt around the gunwale. All three dipped oars. A dozen *kayaks* swarmed back and forth like lemmings on tundra moss. Included among these were paddlers Poona and Kotil, who had originally brought the good news about the whale. Everyone looked north anxiously, hoping to spot the creature. Nik prayed to his favorite spirits that the creature had not already passed. How much time was lost when Pehl-son and Pah-nee arrived? Not much, he decided. He had heard that whales at ease swim slowly.

Belson looked over at Bonnie. "Pretty sure this Inupiat lad thinks you're a boy."

Bonnie shrugged. "So tell him, Pop!"

Belson hesitated. "If I do, you're likely to be stuck in an *igloo* for the time we're here."

Bonnie frowned. "For sure?"

"Females generally don't hunt unless they have to in order to eat—orphans, widows? The wife or friend on a long trip. And a female guest really isn't *permitted* to hunt—believe me!"

"Then *don't* tell him," Bonnie said. She glanced at Nik, but he like the others was intent on searching water to the north.

"Pop, do you think all the villagers were on the ice when we got here?"

He nodded. "Everyone strong enough to make the walk, anyway."

"I didn't see anyone near my age except this boy— well, those two *little* girls."

"Possible. Small communities up here—just what local land and sea can support—so not very many people in one place."

"Guess it's best not to say whether I'm a boy *or* girl, ok?"

Nik understood none of the words he heard the dog-people speak to each other. He would like to have turned to watch their faces and body movements while they talked, see whether he could get the gist of the dialogue in that way. But he dared not, for that would be intrusive and therefore discourteous. Instead, he moved over to look at Tukla's supplies.

The man's harpoon, with grooved and tapered shaft, was made in part from the jawbone of a walrus. Skillfully carved upon it was a variety of sea creatures—Sedna's *puyee*—two seals, a walrus, fish, and there the delicate narwhal with its jutting tusk. A polished toggle point of walrus ivory on its own separate shaft was fitted cunningly to slip from a groove when the point struck. The toggle was connected to a long lash of split and twisted walrus skin tied to a bald sealskin on the other end. The sealskin was inflated and plugged, ready to fly from the *umiak* with the toggle when it left the shaft, then bounce along the surface of the sea, afloat, to mark the location of a whale harpooned.

Lined up by Tukla on the hide floor of the boat, along with the harpoon, was a killing spear of whalebone, its sharp stone point lashed securely with sinew from caribou. Also, a broad snow knife of charred and sharpened bone. On board for towing was a coil of sealskin line and grapples of various shapes and sizes made from caribou antlers. Nik saw that Wutik, the other harpooner, had similar weapons and tools at his own feet.

"*Agviq!* The big-headed whale . . . spouting . . . here he comes!" Calls from *kayakers* echoed on the water. A veil of fog blowing in softened the cries. Within moments, each *kayak* became a phantom stick twisting on a ghostly lagoon. Mist cloaked even *siku,* the giant ice island on the far side of the open water lead.

"Each person must help to balance the boat, now, and must steady himself by holding onto something," Nik told Belson. The man translated to Bonnie. They each took themselves and a robe, hunching to keep their weight low as they duck-walked across the bone skeleton to different sections of gunwale so that weight was distributed. Nik was glad to see that Pah-nee came to crouch close to where he sat. All paddles stopped as the alarm cries ceased. Everyone listened, trying to see through churning mist. Nik heard only the small lap of waves against the boat. *Churm, churr-rr, churm* . . . patience, now . . . patience, he told himself. When he knew with certainty that he would explode into as many pieces as stars in a moonlit sky unless something happened—soon, oh please . . . a great ***Whoo-oo-oosh-hh!*** sounded on the far side of the boat and vapor thicker than the fog shot up above the heads of those afloat in the *umiak.*

"It happens that a whale is close by," Nik said to Pehlson, his eyes shifting to Pah-nee as the parent translated. Pah-nee's nose was wrinkled up at the smell. Nik took the dog-child's arm and hooked it hard over the gunwale just as the boat shuddered, then skidded erratically across the calm water. The mighty creature had brushed them as it moved. A *kayak* would have been destroyed, Nik realized with a shiver.

Then suddenly, wondrously—alarmingly!—the whale came shooting headfirst straight up from the sea as it breached. Unforgettable even in fog . . . a tall, temporary coastal cliff formed suddenly . . . and sank slowly down as the dark mass subsided.

"Dad!" Bonnie sighed in rapture. "Oh-hh-hh, Dad . . ."

Belson looked at his daughter, nodded. In *Inupiaq* he told Nik, "Neither *kalunait* has ever before seen such a sight." He touched his head. "Nor *dreamed* of anything so splendid."

Nik smiled, caught Pah-nee's eye. Something beyond language passed between them, a bond based on shared *feelings*. Nik knew that his glory in this moment—for he as well had never seen a breaching whale—was far greater because he could share it.

Then the spell was broken as both youngsters grabbed once more for the gunwale when the backwash caught them. Twice more, the whale came up. And when it rested near the surface, *kayaks* pulled back to let the sturdy whaleboat come in rapidly. In the circling mist, Nik saw Tukla brace himself, harpoon poised and ready as they neared the vast creature. And then with a grunt, Tukla sent the shaft into the killing spot near the eye. The deed was done!

The whale dived. The sealskin float popped off the deck and skimmed half-submerged near the surface of the water. Tukla leaped clear as lashing sizzled off its coil to follow the descending creature. Wutik stepped across to help by heaving the float line over the side and far from the lashing. Now there would be no opportunity for the float to become enmeshed in the lashing as it became hot from the friction of its unwinding, no chance of its being burned and burst and destroyed. All watched the last of the long rope run out. Then slowly, the *umiak* began to move.

Nik sighed. And once again, they must wait. The sky had cleared, but the brief, early-winter sun was gone, the afterglow nearly faded. Some *kayaks* and the big round *umiak* collected at coastal ice on the west. Other craft hugged *siku* on the east. A harpooned whale must have plenty of space. Because of mist and darkness, people on one side could not see across to those on the other. And no one saw the whale, although Tukla and Wutik claimed to see the float. Time stopped. Nik napped, his hood resting on the gunwale . . . then awakened. The whale had certainly changed air by now—but no one saw or even heard it happen. He dozed again.

The end of the hunt was as impossible as the *fact* of finding a whale in early winter. Nik awoke to *"Ai-ee-ee!"* and looked around. There was the float—barely visible, three full *kayak* lengths south down the lead, glowing dark in moonlight. And further, at the end of the lashing, lines being thrown and snugged around its body, lay the whale motionless, a great shadow. *Kayaks* still approached the creature cautiously. But *agviq,* the whale with the huge head, had surrendered his spirits.

Nik had a lump of sorrow in his throat. Without doubt, the whale had given itself willingly, lovingly. Songs would be sung and tales told, stories enacted . . . of this day when nourishment for all the winter came to his village—whale for the belly and even more important, if such were possible, visitors for the soul.

The creature was hauled up onto deeply grounded ice. Before flensing began, the peeling away of skin and blubber, Potok stepped forward. Everyone grew silent. He removed a mitten and placed his bare hand high upon the right flipper, near the eye.

"It happens, a whale has given itself," he said in his deep, carrying voice, "and all are grateful to him and to Sedna, Queen of *Puyee* that swim the sea."

Villagers sucked in breath to show approval and respect, chanted *"Ee-ee,"* Yes, to each other, raised their eyebrows in agreement. And then, with no sign seen or heard, at least nothing Nik could pick up, the time for thanks gave way to time for action. The butchering began.

Much meat went to all. Poona and Kotil were honored for alerting the village. They promised to return for the drum feast now planned to celebrate such good fortune. They left happily with borrowed teams and sleds piled with whale meat for their families and their village. Their *kayaks* rode smooth and high, lashed atop the packs.

Late that afternoon, Nik and Sitok filled a large new cache on inland prairie with whale meat Kiti declared "excess" over present need to be retained in the snowhouse and for storing in the nearby cellar. Potok importantly helped Sitok build a special new snowhouse for Belson and Bonnie, a blister on the *igloo* of their host. A vaulting, grand affair—for Clifford Belson was a tall man—it contained its own porch tunnel as well as a robe-draped doorway straightaway into Nik's house. The *kalunait* visitors were to eat with his family. Although still delicate, Saruna recovered enough to help Kiti operate the two households—seven people, now, to feed. It was well that Sedna had been generous.

Nik enjoyed the role of guide for Pah-nee and sometimes—when his older brother was out with villagers or on the trail alone—even taking Pehl-son with Pah-nee out to hunt. The *kalunait* were gracious about their "finding" so little, capturing even less. But for Nik, increasingly, everything was tentative, not quite real. What his family did each day was *pleasant,* he had to admit to himself, but was not what they *should* be doing. Eh, *pirtok!* One cannot undo what is already happening. Every night before sleep, Nik went over in his mind the steps still necessary before he and Sitok could go inland. Soon they would have enough food, sufficient to leave for Kiti and their four guests as well as adequate to carry on their own sled. Were they deeply enough into the winter season to make traveling to the southwest ice-covered—and therefore rapid with dogsled—and trouble free? Surely soon it would be frozen hard enough inland to satisfy even cautious Sitok.

CHAPTER 8.
FRIENDS

That Pah-nee! Beginning after the whale hunt, Nik and Bonnie were together constantly, chattering non-stop, with pantomime to echo every thought, for neither understood the other's words. Nik found this dog boy an amusing companion because he was quick to see what was needed, then to *do* it. He and his father had arrived in proper clothing, fur *silapak* with heavy bearskin trousers over *illupak,* underwear of light pelt with fur side in.

But this winter was already proving itself especially cold, and the wind rarely ceased blowing a gale from one direction or another. Although he never complained, the dog child got very cold—for Nik had several times seen telltale white patches of frostbite on cheeks and nose. The *inuk* boy would hurry, then, to tighten the drawstring on Pah-nee's hood, to rush his guest into the shelter of robes or *igloo*.

Nik noticed that Pah-nee seemed fascinated by what was routine for the *Inuit* boy. As an example, Pah-nee almost never missed an opportunity to watch the mudding and icing of sled runners before and during a trip. Nik noted that he showed no fear of *kringmerk,* the half-wild sled dogs—nor of anything else, for that matter—and the fierce, standoffish canines accepted this dog-person almost immediately. Pah-nee spent extra time getting to know Nuko, seeming to recognize instinctively her many special qualities. The lead dog loved getting unaccustomed attention and rapidly warmed to the newcomer.

The dog-child and Nik understood barely one word the other said. But both were alert and observant, increasingly attuned to each other. Both used arm and hand motions, facial expressions, to get across what was important. Nik's hunting improved because he himself now had someone to teach. On rare days, Sitok took both of them out with him—for fish, for seal, or even upon the inland prairie to find smaller creatures like hare and ptarmigan.

Often, though, Sitok must go with village hunters. Here was a social obligation he fulfilled reluctantly, but the village and especially Potok were resentful when he did not join them. After all, they would share with Sitok and his family anything captured by a group of village hunters together on the trail, would they not? In fact, *insisted* on sharing despite his protests. Sitok surely knew that he could do better alone—and he would take the trail by himself—or with his brother—following every few sleeps. Nik had lately and finally become more an asset than a liability.

What Sitok said he wanted to do was to store everything captured beyond daily need, and this was difficult to do when villagers rationed out the take according to need—always, as it turned out, with Potok making final decisions on *need*. That man insisted that the "share" for Arajik's family was to be for that family alone, the three people remaining. Urgit and Saruna did not count for sharing because Potok had recently proclaimed that neither was a member of the village, anymore, because neither contributed. And as Cliff Belson and Bonnie were official "guests" of Arajik and not part of his family, certainly not part of the village, they were not included in distribution, either. According to Potok, the village was not obligated to feed them although Arajik was—Arajik in this case represented by Kiti, Sitok and Nik. Of course Potok was not a village leader officially, for an Inupiat village consisted of a collection of families, each independent of another and recognizing no higher authority than that within a single household. But Potok was older, spoke loudly and with confidence—demanded—and did in the minds of villagers retain a certain status conferred largely by his former close association with Arajik. Nik and Sitok's father was indeed a man now missing, but he had been looked up to, previously, for his travel experience and for his wisdom gleaned from years of interaction with other places and people.

The older brother Sitok became increasingly agitated —unwilling to participate in the continual intrigues Potok initiated, yet heeding Kiti's counsel and foregoing any challenge of the man. Sitok must not break from the village before and until he and Nik finished their search for Arajik and Mawena. With seven people eating on the allotment for three, less and less food would be available as the boys delayed the trip inland. So still more secret caches of food were needed to feed themselves and the dogs and to provision *Ananatsiak* Kiti and all guests while the brothers were away. When Sitok was with the villagers—and Nik noticed that no one ever asked Sitok's brother to go hunting with them—the boy took a sled and team and Pah-nee, sometimes Pehl-son as well, to go onto the trail independently.

In morning darkness, Nik was getting ready to pack his sled runners—*mud* them with a smooth layer of melted permafrost—when Pah-nee came out of the Pehl-son snowhouse dressed for the trail. Sitok was off to find seal with villagers today, and Nik had a plan. *Thwack!—shuu-uush-sh . . .* he slapped melted permafrost onto a whalebone runner, smoothed it with his knife as it froze, then put on a new section, evened the join so rapidly that it came together as a seamless coat. He was not yet as good with the mud pack as he had become with icing.

Pah-nee put out a hand to stop his arm when he was ready to prepare the other runner. The dog-person brought from his parka a hide bag of something that steamed in the icy air.

"Oatmeal!" he announced. Then he removed a mitten, took a handful of the stuff and splattered it onto the runner. After, he licked his fingers and Nik wrinkled his nose. *No, don't do that.* But the visitor wanted him to use this "oatmeal" mud, and he tried it. Excitement grew as he worked the new material. It was just rough enough to hold the icing of water yet to come, but unlike permafrost contained no pebbles or stems or twigs. Freezing rapidly, it was easy to trim.

The two went inside for morning food while snow thawed over the lamp so that Nik could ice the runners. Belson and Kiti were there, and of course the omnipresent Urgit and his aunt.

"Circles!" Bonnie told Nik as she held up her eating utensil, then looked to her father for translation.

The man frowned and shrugged. "What about them?"

"So many *circles,* here! The snowhouses. And the *umiak* we rode in is rounded, too—who ever heard of a round boat? Look at the knife they use to cut the whale meat—"

"An *ulu,*" he said. "And it's cutting the much-prized *muktuk,* whale skin with blubber attached."

Everyone looked at him when they heard *muktuk* and *ulu,* raising eyebrows and smacking lips loudly. Kiti's favorite edible much enjoyed by all, she managed to get from a whale the most possible *muktuk.*

"*Mumuktopaluk!*" Nik told Pehl-son. Delicious!

"So now ask about circles, Dad!"

"I don't have the words, Sweetheart," he told her.

She paused. "I'll figure something!" She turned to Nik. "Circles!"

"Sir-koz," he repeated, with no notion of what was meant.

Then he watched as Pah-nee bounced thumbs and index fingers against each other to make a ring. "Circles!" he said again, then chuckled. Sooner or later, the idea would get across. . . .

Outside once more, Nik stooped to ice the runners, then stopped.

Pah-nee came up behind him, bent to look down in the cloudy moonlight. "Oh, no!" the dog-boy moaned. "What happened?"

The bone runner on which Nik had put the smooth stuff Pah-nee called *oatmeal* was now bare. And as their eyes accustomed themselves once more to the dim moonlight, visible all around them were sled dogs contentedly licking their chops. Pah-nee walked over to scold Nuko, the lead dog and his favorite, even while he rubbed her ears. Laughing, Nik went inside to re-heat permafrost.

Sitok would be surprised! Nik and Pah-nee were near the rocks where he and his brother had gone for seals on their first hunt together. This was the place Sitok said the paddlers planned to take their *kayaks* today. If they were fortunate in capturing, they would be delighted to have a sled to help transport meat back to the village. Always delicate but normally buoyant and responsive, *kayaks* heavily loaded become sluggish, hard to maneuver safely around sea ice. Too, the ravenous white sea-bear *nanuk* could sense the food and would sometimes attack a *kayak* right from the water. It would tip the craft enough to off-load the tasty cargo, sometimes injure the paddler, all too often send him into the sea and down to Sedna forever.

Nik had brought the usual: robes, some food for themselves and the dogs, a small bladder of seal oil to provide light and warmth if they should be delayed overnight. In his hunting bag permanently were his fire stone and easily flamed dry moss in a small pouch, waterproof, plenty of sinew and hooks for fishing, then more and finer sinew as thread to use with circular bone needles. Any rip or tear in clothing or boots must be mended immediately when someone was on the trail. Nik of course had his hunting tools and weapons along with a snow knife. On the sled was plenty of space for meat, if they connected with the hunters—and if they did not, transportation for whatever they themselves might be lucky enough to capture.

The sun would rise soon but briefly—if it was going to show at all today. The wind moaned ominously out of the northwest. By the time they neared the seal rocks, Nik realized that gusting blasts stopped even the dogs for moments at a time. The temperature was dropping fast, and snow dust billowed up from the ground like smoke. It was hard to see anything. *They must find or build shelter.* Nik wondered what was happening to paddlers in their *kayaks* as waves built high even in the narrow and sheltered leads.

He turned the team toward rocky outcrops he remembered from the time he had crawled past while stalking those seals with Sitok. But fortune was smiling despite the sudden storm. Nik found almost immediately a cavity going back in under adjacent ice-encrusted boulders. Protected on three sides, the space would require only a front wall of snow to make it cozy. It was not high enough to stand in, but they could crawl during the short time before they lay down. Also, the small size meant that body heat would warm it more easily.

Pah-nee picked up right away on what he was doing. The dog-boy carried in cargo from the sled while

Nik cut blocks of snow to wall the front. This new friend was intelligent, strong and willing, Nik decided. Without being shown, Pah-nee found armloads of snow to chink the seams of his construction. Before building, Nik had pushed loose snow and a good-sized rock inside what was to be the shelter. The clean snow would melt in a bladder, after he got a fire going, to become drinking water. The rock would block the opening when they were inside. After he fed the dogs all that he had brought for them, he used his snow knife to cut through the icy scab of nearby drifts, then watched his team dig in to avoid the storm. All but Nuko. She clearly wanted to go inside the shelter with him.

"The storm will not last," Nik assured her. "The lead dog must make her own *igloo!*" But Nuko was still watching as he crawled inside the low cave and then pushed the rock back firmly to close the entry.

While building the wall, Nik had searched among scattered stones from under the snow until he found one which, although lopsided, had a hollow which could hold a little seal oil for burning: light and a bit of warmth. Now he set Pah-nee to filling a clean drinking bladder from the hunting bag with loose snow while he dug out the bladder of oil and fumbled in the dark with flint and tinder to get fire. He knew that Kiti would have had a spark long before he was successful. He reflected on what great value lay in his people's practice of having a female on the trail—not only the rapid making of a good fire but also the mending of trail-torn garments or punctured *kamik*. A woman in the shelter, while he was building the wall and tending to the dogs, would mean that a lamp would be burning and food ready when he came in.

Despite what people said while chatting over a meal, Nik had previously thought that taking a woman along for a hunting trip was a great deal of unnecessary trouble. Here would be one more mouth to feed in unpredictable hunting ground, and for no good purpose other than human companionship and sexual indulgence.

Now, he changed his mind. He could even imagine himself asking a female to accompany *him* on his very next journey. Eh, the village women would laugh, those old enough to be of actual assistance—he knew they would. First, Nik was perceived as a child, not a hunter. Second, he never had gone out on the trail overnight alone. Until now—well, Pah-nee was here, but the dog-child would be considered yet another responsibility. He smiled, then began to chuckle. *Ananatsiak* Kiti might have accompanied them on this very trip, even though she ordinarily did not take the trail, anymore, except to reach summer camp and return. He had heard her turn down villager requests. But at least she would not have made fun of him for asking. Never mind, he and the dog-boy had not expected to be gone over a sleep.

And see? Nik knelt close to his tinder and *pshht!* the gentlest breath upon a wisp of smoke. *The mighty Inupiat hunter has finally managed to bring up a spark to light the lamp oil!*

The two youngsters ate, feeling cozy and content, listening to wind whistle beyond and somewhat through their wall. Each privately used the waste bladder which Nik had placed in deep shadow far back in the small cavern. Bonnie rolled up in a robe and was soon breathing evenly. Nik, though, twisted in his bedroll, turning, listening to voices that rode the gale.

He regretted that Pehl-son would very likely worry about his inexperienced son out on the trail during a storm. Nor was there anyone the big red-haired *kalunait* could send to search; for all of the male adults including Sitok would be holed up out of the wind on land or sea ice somewhere far from the village, as he and Pah-nee were, or would have buried their *kayaks* and constructed *igloo* to shelter themselves.

Kiti would reassure Pehl-son, Nik knew, regardless of her own misgivings. This time, she had no Sitok to send out and collect the younger brother. Good.

Still restless, Nik lulled himself by counting Pah-nee's rhythmic breaths as he slept so soundly rolled up in two robes. Count the breaths, time and more time marching like endless rows of ice forms large and small floating down a stream at late spring break-up. *Why did he not sleep?* Count them, count the breaths. *Why did he have a sense of foreboding? Why was he uneasy?* Count, count. At last, he realized that the low-domed cave was filled with too much smoke and too little air. If his grandmother were here to tend this makeshift lamp, smoke and fumes would not plague them. He sighed, unrolled himself, fumbled in his hunting bag, crawled over to the block wall. There, he plunged his broad snow knife between the thick blocks to make a slender nostril, heard stale air and smoke *whoo-oo-oosh* out.

He also heard Nuko whine at the crack. *Ai-ee,* a cold night. He supposed her warm coat and breath might after all be welcome inside. He rolled the rock back enough for her to squeeze through, then replaced it. He noted that the dog went over to curl tightly against the back of sleeping Pah-nee.

Nik lay down once more, brought his robes up, staring toward a roof that he could touch but not see. Now what?! He was startled to realize that jealousy over Nuko nibbled a corner of his consciousness. Eh, foolish boy, what a *soospuk!* Was it not natural that any dog would be drawn toward a *dog-boy*? And Nuko was more sensitive than most, a creature of sapient intuition. Was she not great-great-granddaughter to the celebrated *Nuna* who, according to *Ananatsiak,* was pre-eminent among *kringmerk* ever born or yet to be? And now here was Nik, delighted to have a companion of his own age, finally and for the first time ever—then allowing himself bad feeling over this small matter with Nuko.

Eh, before Pehl-son and Pah-nee arrived, he had made up his mind to speak with Kiti and Sitok about finding some other village in which to live. That decision was made after the strange conclusion in favor of Unipak. So wrong. So unfair. So *political!* And then Potok's influencing people to stay away from the *igloo*-building? In fact, the mood of the whole village made him uncomfortable, then and still, especially as Potok increasingly gained unearned respect and unwarranted power. Too, Nik disliked having ugly Urgit with his ailing aunt eating right there on the floor robe with Nik's own family and sleeping with them on the *iglerk.* Yes, Nik reflected now—his family should consider a permanent move; for their village seemed to be changing, and he did not feel good about the differences.

Still, he had never broached the subject, and for one all-important reason. . . . If Arajik and Mawena somehow survived the tundra and reached the coast on their own, they would come to this village. He could not take the chance of missing them. Eh, all the more reason to search inland! Yes, the brothers would surely leave soon! Not right now, not while Pehl-son and Pah-nee were here. They must defend Arajik's honor. Pehl-son had been told only that Arajik was "away." He had not questioned this because Arajik was known to be a great traveler—else Pehl-son would not have met him. Besides, no firm arrangement had been made regarding even the season of the dog-person's possible arrival. So the two brothers would capture and cache provision, then be ready to go immediately after *tingmisut* departed. Sitok and *Ananatsiak* would agree with Nik on this matter. Relieved with that decision, Nik burrowed deep into his robes and slept.

When he awoke later in darkness and cold—for the lamp had gone out entirely—Pah-nee still lay motionless although Nuko came over when Nik sat up. The big dog flopped down beside him, muzzle pressing against Nik's trouser leg as the boy buried the unlit end of twisted sinew into freshly poured seal oil, then got a fire going. In the dim light, Nik crawled over to once more plunge his snow knife through the chink he had opened in the night and which had since closed in with blowing snow. He listened.

The gale outside might not be quite so fierce, he decided; or did he only *hope* that this was so? He brought up the bag containing what little food remained. If the storm did not permit their going home today, he would have to get out somehow and capture food—at least for the dogs. Pah-nee was stirring and then awake when they both heard sounds of determined digging and scratching at the ice wall.

Nuko was inside, and Nik wondered why the other dogs would be out of their warm drifts while the storm still raged. He crawled forward, rolled aside the boulder, then leapt back as a dark-furred creature rushed in hissing and snarling, shadowy lips drawn up and away from fearsome fangs. Then the draft that accompanied the beast blew out the shallow lamp.

Wolverine! Nik made a dive to the back of the cave for his spear just as Bonnie hurled the loose robes up to cover them all. The beast attacked the pelts, slashing and growling furiously at hides which now tented both youngsters and Nuko as well.

Nik got his spear in one hand, felt around until he got his snow knife in the other. His hunting bag remained at the back of the cavity. He hoped the animal would not get so close that he had to use the shorter weapon.

What was it doing? After the first fearsome attack, the boy heard nothing but the pounding of his own heart and the shallow, rapid intake of his breath and Pah-nee's. Or was that Nuko's? No, Nuko was growling low. When Nik got the fire going, she had still been asleep, tail over nose and nestled partly under a robe. Now she was fully roused, as were he and Pah-nee. He tried to center his awareness on hearing only. There! He heard claws scrabble on the ice floor. Moving away? He heard wind *whoo-oo-ooshing* around the unreplaced stone at the cave opening. Then he heard the food bag rip, the sound of gulping even above the storm as the animal devoured their meager food supply. Nik worked himself out from under the robe. He heard a muffle of frustrated growls as the dog tried to free herself from the tent Pah-nee had thrown over them. Nik put down his weapons, reached beneath the robe and took the dog-boy's hands. He wrapped Pah-nee's fingers into Nuko's ruff. Nuko must stay out of the fight to come. The wolverine would kill her easily, in this small space, would rip her apart if she got free and rushed in. So Pah-nee must hold her, and he seemed to understand; for Nik felt him wrap both arms around the dog's neck and one front leg besides, bury his face in the neck fur, so close to Nuko that she could not bite against the restraint even if she wanted to.

And now—while the beast was eating—was the time to use a spear. Nik wished the snow cave were high enough that he could stand up straight to get his body weight behind the thrust. He slid out fully from the robes, silent, trying to force his eyes to see in darkness, for the lamp had of course gone out again. But the wolverine must surely have the same problem. Again he listened. The creature chewed noisily enough—but where was the body in relation to the mouth? In a high crouch, Nik barely inched forward to insure that his *kamik* were soundless on the ice floor. He raised his spear.

And it grated on the rock surface overhead!

The wolverine was on him immediately, snapping, clawing, a heavy, writhing bundle of hissing fury, shrieking, spitting half-chewed food, expelling a musk that brought tears to the eye. Nik swung the snow knife around and plunged it blindly into the creature as it continued to claw his furs, moving up on his body, ripping at his tunic, snapping, biting. It must not reach his face!

He heard a grunt, sensed a lapse in the attack. He drew his knife away and stabbed again, at the same time bringing his right arm with the spear around to protect his eyes. The tightly-clutched spear knocked the heavy animal away momentarily, and Nik slid his bare hand down for a short grip on the handle and rammed it to the floor, backing the thrust with all his power. If he could hit the wolverine hard enough—anywhere!—he could pin it to the ice and the punishment it dealt might be controlled.

Then he heard a long choking gasp and smelled a fresh ration of stink as the animal's bowels and glands relaxed. He felt a shudder through his spear, heard a few weak hisses, then silence. Nik stood motionless for a long time, partly to be certain the creature's life spirits were gone . . . mostly to collect his own spirits, to control his breathing and to still his quaking limbs. *Count, count the breaths*—this time his own. He kept his hand on the impaling spear to sense restored vigor, any movement at all by the creature, but mostly he concentrated on what his ears could tell him. No sound came from Pah-nee, either. Even Nuko's protests had ceased. And still Nik waited. *Count, count . . . count.*

And then he knew it was over. He gently lifted the robes from the dog-boy and Nuko.

"Ai-ee-ee!" But his cry of conquest was subdued. He was still too terrified to feel any great triumph.

No special rite was wanted here, for no wolverine ever gave itself willingly, at least none Nik had ever heard about, certainly not this one. These were the servants of violent Paija, the most vicious spirit of all. *Kapvik* the wolverine was afforded as much distance as possible even by the mighty sea-bear as well as by frail *Inuit,* the true people of this open land.

Still trembling, Nik rolled the stone all the way back from the opening, for fresh air was needed in this place. He then struggled to light the lamp wick once again, sheltering it with a lump of robes. At last able to laugh, he pulled Pahnee's fingers away from where they still clamped a once-more-struggling Nuko. With a little light at last, Nik went to inspect the reeking animal and was followed closely by the dog-child. Silent still, the *kalunait* had not uttered a sound throughout the struggle. Nik smiled. Perhaps great beasts unknown to his own people were commonplace in this *Miss-oo-luh* where Pehl-son said they had their permanent *igloo.*

Nuko came to inspect the creature as well. She was not mute, however, her growl a deep threat. Stiff-legged, she circled the wolverine—even knowing as she must that it was dead. A large and savage creature, Nik thought as he got the skinning knife from his pack. For its weight, *kapviq* was surely most dangerous among all animals. The white bear was far heavier, fearless of people, intelligent and persistent— so was therefore more deadly than the wolverine at any given moment . . . but *nanuk* could sometimes be reasoned with. A bear killed in order to eat and to feed its young. A wolverine seemed to slaughter and destroy with fetor merely for pleasure well beyond need. And so far as Nik had ever heard, not even another wolverine ever tried to reason with these strange beasts.

Eh, how Kiti would delight over the pelt—one of but two furs in the whole land on which frost would not accumulate. Such exquisite and enduring material that it was removed when one hood wore out so that it could be fastened as trim to the very next *nuilak,* the rough around the face opening. If properly cared for, it remained gleaming and imperishable. Wolverine fur made it possible to breathe easily outdoors during a blizzard . . . so even this killer creature possessed unique value.

Bonnie now showed alarm for the first time. The dog-boy fussed over the cuts on Nik's arms and legs, tried with rabbit skins to stem blood which streamed from a dozen wounds bleeding through his torn parka and trousers. Misplaced concern, Nik thought—his friend should worry about Nik's torn clothing instead. A body would heal soon enough. But cold entering these rents in his fur would kill him when he went outside. He rummaged in his hunting bag for needle and sinew, then handed these to his companion.

"Infection!" Pah-nee repeated so many times that Nik could say the word perfectly. He thought it meant holes in his skin. He shrugged off the dog-boy's attention to his punctured flesh. Instead, he removed his ripped furs and handed them over, covering himself with robes to stay warm. He finally got across the idea that these needed repair immediately, and he pantomimed the process.

When Pah-nee took a look at one of the slim bone needles, he raised it triumphantly. "More *circles!*" he proclaimed.

"Sir-koz," Nik said agreeably, in recognition of the now-familiar word although he still had no real inkling of its meaning.

Bonnie worked awkwardly but persistently on the holes in Nik's clothing while Nik skinned the evil-smelling wolverine. Both he and Bonnie were gagging throughout. Nuko lay in the door opening, her nose outside, breathing audibly, head lifting from time to time, eyes rolling back to view her master reproachfully. Nik chuckled, wished that *he* had someone to blame for the offensive stink. Clutching a robe around him, he finally pushed past Pah-nee and the dog to go bury the carcass in a drift outside. Brr-rr! Definitely, he could not go out to find food until his clothing was repaired.

The storm continued through that day and for another sleep. On the second morning, in dying winds, Nik put on his hood and the roughly mended tunic over his light fur underwear. Pah-nee was still working on the tattered trousers, so he doubled the heaviest robe and tucked it around him, securing it with a sealskin lash. He dared not be gone long. He took his fishing gear and snow knife down to the ice. Eleven fish gave themselves, and he thanked Sedna, for his need was great. The dogs could not take them home without nourishment, and *kringmerk* would not touch wolverine flesh. He fed the team when he returned, brought two of the big, stiffly frozen fish inside—one for Nuko and one for Pah-nee and himself to share.

Inside after being for several hours in open air, Nik found the lingering stench of wolverine to be nearly overwhelming. But Pah-nee was still mending the final tears. Nik took the trousers outside in the wind and brief twilight of mid-day to test that they were air-tight. The stitches seemed taut enough but were uneven, certainly not beautiful. Kiti would shriek with laughter, rip out every one of them and start over. But Kiti was not here and Pah-nee was. Besides, he knew that even *Ananatsiak* would admit, when they got back, that the dog-boy had done a far better job than Nik himself would have managed. At least no cold would enter. *Ananatsiak* could apply her craftsmanship and artistry to his furs on return to the village. Then once again, all would be water-tight and beautiful.

They took the sled out onto ice because Nik wanted to look around the lead near the seal rocks. Still, he would have missed the snow-drifted mound if Pah-nee had not pointed it out. Frozen down solidly was a hillock of five big seals doubtless stacked by hunters. The village men had been here, then, and had been favored before the storm arrived—just *how* fortunate they were, Nik could not guess. Either they had been caught by the storm and left their entire catch while they raced their *kayaks* down the lead for shelter—or these were the seals that could not be carried back on *kayaks.* Nik loaded the carcasses onto his sled after mudding and icing the runners.

Ready to go at last, Pah-nee tugged on his sleeve and pointed toward the lead. Three white bears—a mother and two cubs, one nearly grown—were strolling toward them. The wind silent after the storm, Nik heard the *"Whuff-**whuff**"* of their unhurried approach. The dogs began a chorus of low moans, edging forward in their traces, wishing to move away. Here was a warning to their master as well as an expression of their ancient fear of an enemy having enormous power in its raking claws and ravaging teeth.

Nik snapped the whip in the air, and the dogs raced off toward land on new snow over smooth sea ice. After a short period of bumping along coastal plains, the boy halted the team at the crest of a rise. There, with Pah-nee's puzzled help, he loosened lashings enough to drag out and roll off one of the seals. *Inuk* the true man must not be greedy.

He waited only a few minutes after re-tightening load straps before he could point out to Pah-nee the still-approaching bears. How could Nik explain to his new friend that these great shambling creatures would likely follow their trail of seal scent to the moon, if necessary, until they got their meal? He sighed.

CHAPTER 9.
DRUM FEAST

A few knolls before they reached the village late in the day, Nik and Bonnie met a sled with Wutik and Tukla. Smiling, the men transferred the seals over to be borne by their own fresh team. "It happens that village hunters were going back for these seals following the feast."

Feast? Ah! The whale—so with Wutik and Tukla as honored guests. *Muktuk,* his favorite. Seals, too, Nik supposed.

Cliff Belson met them all as they came in among the snowhouses. Inside, strain showed around his eyes as he hugged his daughter.

"I tried not to worry," he told her, "but I didn't know where to look."

"The storm, Pop. We came home as soon as we could."

He nodded, then turned to Nik, took in the ragged condition of his clothing. "A father thanks a hunter for bringing his child back safely."

Yes, he *had* done that, hadn't he? Pehl-son called him a *hunter?* Nik glowed. A hunter!

They had missed the first part of the drum feast, the *Kalunait* told them. Wutik and Tukla had wrestled earlier, leaving immediately after they finished to go search for Nik and Bonnie.

Belson pointed out to Bonnie the snow ring where two other village men presently strained to get one another off balance however slightly and thereby conclude the wrestling match.

"Another circle!" Pah-nee announced with satisfaction.

"Sir-ko," Nik echoed, wondering what on earth the strange syllables meant.

He had forgotten the feast planned even on the very day they caught the whale—that day when Pehl-son and Pah-nee arrived. Perhaps if he had remembered the celebration, he might have pushed the weary dogs to move faster, but he doubted it. And they could not have taken the trail safely before the gales abated mid-morning. Too bad, Pah-nee missed the blanket toss. Nik was too heavy, anymore, for that fine aerial game, but the dog-boy was lightweight and wiry, would enjoy being bounced high into the sky. He *did* get to see the huge round "blanket"—many robes tightly stitched together—where it lay abandoned on the snow.

"Circle!" exclaimed the dog-person, pointing to it in great glee.

Nik only raised his eyebrows. He supposed that he should ask Pehl-son about those two syllables Pah-nee kept repeating—*sir-ko*—but he wanted to figure out the meaning for himself.

They had missed the singing and the laughing contest, too, the special mask drumming, the mimics. Had the throat-singers performed, Nik wondered, or would they save their talent (and breath) for the wife-changing entertainment to come? Pah-nee and he had missed the feast, as well, and that fact bothered ravenous Nik the most. Kiti, though, motioned them both out of the big snowhouse, a large but temporary ice structure built especially for this occasion. They followed her to their own *igloo*, where she stuffed them with *muktuk,* the whale skin with blubber, Nik's favorite and Kiti's as well.

Atik came in for Kiti as they finished the meal. "The people are ready."

She sucked in breath, Yes. "But it happens that the story-teller is *not!*" She shooed everyone back to the festivities, and Nik tried to explain to Pah-nee that his grandmother was about to tell a tale.

Kiti carried the small drum from her own household, one Arajik had built especially for the talented woman he considered to be his mother. An unclouded moon of beautifully tanned hide half an arm in diameter stretched taut in the perfectly rounded frame of precious driftwood. The woman tapped a prelude lightly along the rim with the stubby bone beater, then settled into a clear rhythm. Unipak held the big dueling drum and stood quietly in flickering shadows behind her, as did empty-handed Tukla, both men ready to assist.

Kiti put her white bear pelt down on the ice floor, then with dignity sank down in one fluid motion. Solemnly, she looked at each member of the audience in turn. Next, she tossed a special robe of colorful feathers over her lap, arranging it while Unipak and Tukla strung finely braided sinew high overhead, a sturdy line nearly invisible. Then Unipak thumped a restrained ***Boom-boom-BOOM*** as percussive background while Tukla hung three stiff leather masks on the line, each visage taller and wider than Nik.

First, the head of a snowshoe hare, that furry Big Foot of the north. Second, ptarmigan, the chubby, ground-nesting Arctic grouse which changes feather color with the season. Third, caribou, a venerable tribal chief—for unlike Inupiat, caribou have formal leaders. When the set was hung and all spectators quiet, Kiti began.

"Long ago, before the moon was placed securely in the sky, a small Inupiat boy spent much of his time in tears."

Kiti's little drum went lightly *Tat-a-TAT!* to emphasize the words as she continued her tale.

"The reason? All the other children, even those still naked in their mother's hood, poked fun at him. In age, he was fourteen winters—and making no progress at all toward becoming a hunter."

She speaks of Nik, the boy thought. *Oh, Grandmother, please do not!*

"His loving father carved him a bow, fashioned him ten arrows, each balanced with a cleverly trimmed eider duck feather so that it flew true. But Koogee-Kahgee, for that was his name—"

—"*Phht!*" the audience tittered, for none had ever heard of such an appellation, and the sound was ludicrous to the ear.

Kiti sternly eyed the people around her, then continued by describing the fate of the ten arrows and five harpoons fashioned and then gifted to the boy: "The last harpoon was used to feel ever more deeply and broadly into a seal's breathing hole—until *nathek,* that sweet-tempered mother, lost all patience and with her mouth took the harpoon right down through the ice and buried its tip in the floor of the sea. Koogee-Kahgee cried when his last weapon disappeared."

Please no, Ananatsiak, *do not humiliate a grandson before the village.* Then Nik remembered that she knew nothing of his first attempt with Sitok at seal-hunting on ice. His embarrassment over the event was still too great for him to share with her; and Sitok would never mortify a fellow hunter, even his troublesome brother, by relating details of that hunt. His brother would not speak about Nik's folly to *Ananatsiak* nor to anyone.

Rat-a-TAT-a, TAT-a-TAT-a continued lightly from Kiti's drum, then during pauses, a startling *BOOM-bah-bah-BOOM* from Unipak behind her.

The listeners, though, could not stay silent. . . . Whoever heard of having the mellow seal tug a hunter's weapon right out of his hand? What a *soospuk!* This Koogee-Kahgee—*Hoo-oo, such a name!*—must have been clumsy indeed.

Pretending to be annoyed by her noisy audience, Kiti resumed only after raising her chin to sweep the circle of listeners with a stern stare.

". . . But this old woman will not use feast time to recount calamities! Oh, the fishing sinew . . . one needs to know that the moon above was brilliant blue as dancing lights in the north sky before Koogee-Kahgee snarled his line on it, tipped it slantwise and drained out all its color!"

Kiti's voice softened as she continued.

"But Koogee-Kahgee's parents, older brothers and many relatives were loving ones, and patient—as someone may by now have guessed."

The spectators giggled. All who know the Inupiat—certainly Belson if not Bonnie—know also that in all the world are no more devoted parents than the *Inuit.* Adults will step back and laugh at themselves, exchange with each other tales of how their impish young ones rule their existence day and night, summer and winter—turn them into slaves, fathers as well as mothers—make their lives a misery, so these parents say with great pride. But then these same adults go right back to indulging their children—*"Our little one wishes to continue suckling his mother, even though he is now of seven winters? Why then, he must do so for as long as he likes."*

Kiti tapped her drum as she continued her story in a half tuneful chant accompanied by the strong rim beat. She ignored the giggling audience. She carefully rearranged on her lap the blanket of soft birdskins sewn together. She patted it here and there until all spectator sound had ceased. Then she brought the handsome robe up with her as she stood, her face one more—and very small—among the hanging masks.

"Some laugh," she said accusingly, "but that young boy did *not!* Desperate, Koogee-Kahgee left his loving family to go out upon the frozen tundra to seek new kin among creatures for whom hunting and the skill of wielding weapons were not vital."

Now using the great masks, the wrinkled woman told of the boy's attempts to join other groups on the tundra.

Ananatsiak got behind the rabbit mask and let her big lap quilt of feathers fall in such a way that the folds became huge feet. She raised her hands to control both sides of the whiskery face, and the furs of her *silapak* were already bounding up and down. Her giant left foot lifted to go ***Thump-a-THUMP*** as spectators drew in breath to show appreciation for her skill. Behind her, Unipak ***Boom***ed deeply to build suspense

The furs swirled, a big feather-foot thumped, and some stiff, ropy whiskers on the mask twitched as the woman recounted the first unsuccessful effort of the hapless and sobbing boy.

No, Nik finally decided, *a grandmother does not speak of her younger grandson—for all know Nik is not one to cry.*

Next Kiti went behind the ptarmigan mask, and her movements became short and jerky in the manner of birds. Here, too, Koogee-Kahgee's request was heard courteously, Kiti told her listeners, and then the ptarmigan explained the dangers of being a big bird in a hungry land. However, the birds decided that this boy would be too noticeable, would attract even more predators to prey on them, and in the end refused to let him join them.

When Kiti came forward from the bird mask, she folded up the blanket as she came. "One has spoken long enough," she announced mildly. "This old woman will finish the tale at the next drum feast."

"*Owka,* no—***Hoo-oo!***" her audience wailed, as she had known they would. "Please do continue, *Ananatsiak.*" This was the general clamor.

With an air of reluctance, she returned to the dangling masks, gave an exaggerated sigh, and stepped behind the caribou.

"Here with Long-legs, in fact, the bumbling boy met success. That is, he *did* get accepted and actually took the caribou form . . .But Koogee-Kahgee became homesick, as it turned out, and would have to change back to *Inuit* and go home."

"'But one's antlers!' wailed the boy, 'and one's hooves and tail and ears and furry legs!'"

"The caribou chief chuckled. 'This old man tells a child to return to his family,' he commanded not too severely, 'and promises all will be well.'"

Kiti sighed with feigned weariness. She came out from behind the caribou mask to be only herself, an Inupiat storyteller who had in this instance stretched more hides to cure than she wanted to chew.

"Now to finish the telling before Koogee-Kahgee becomes an old man: the boy trotted home—and those four hooves served him well on the trip! Approaching, he saw his two older brothers . . . hunting . . .together raising their spears—

"—'Owka! Don't hurt this creature!' he shouted, 'for your prey is not as it seems!'"

"'That's certain,' the eldest agreed, 'for never before has this hunter heard *tuktu* speak.'"

But uniting with the family was not the end of the tale. Kiti said that Koogee-Kahgee insisted, on his return, that the household move to the seacoast and there learn to hunt walrus. Also seal and whale. *But not caribou.*

"What happened?" asked someone in the audience. For Inupiat today hunted caribou with great enthusiasm and considerable success. They depended on the creatures not only for meat and hide but for sewing sinew and *kayak* as well as *umiak* skin, sled ribs, snow knives and other nearly countless necessities of both household and trail.

Ananatsiak Kiti explained then that this Koogee-Kahgee lived a very long time ago. And that the advantage of hunting caribou, as time passed, seemed to outweigh the matter of obedience to some ancient child whose spirit was doubtless involved right now in making this present decision.

"Because his family loved him so strongly, and because they were so glad he was not lost after all, they did as he bid them.

"And Koogee-Kahgee did learn gradually to become a good hunter who used weapons skillfully and brought back plenty of food for his family. And although he went out during inland summers to pluck eggs from ground nests and to capture ptarmigan and giant hare, he himself always held firm about not hunting caribou. However, he never would reveal the reason, and his family always wondered.

"All who knew, in fact, were Koogee-Kahgee, his two brothers—who were never *absolutely* certain—and of course the caribou themselves. And these were all who needed to know."

Kiti folded up her quilt and bear hide. The snowshoe hare ceased to hop, the ptarmigan to lurch, the caribou to stride sturdily. Tukla came forward to untie, nest and carry off the bulky masks as Unipak's *Boom-**boom**-a-BOOM*s rose ever more loudly to make a finale.

Then, amid great shouting and stomping, Kiti with head held high disappeared among the spectators and their shadows. Her tale was told, and she did not wish to talk more.

Nik and Bonnie both found themselves fading. Pehl-son walked back to the snowhouse with them.

"If we'd come to visit Jupiter," Bonnie told her father later, "life *could not* be more different—oh, what I've seen here! What I've done, Pop . . . what I've *eaten!*" Her father had warned her before coming that the *Inuit* diet up here was meat, especially fat, and was served raw. He had not expected her to eat it as he did, but at the same time had worried about her ability to withstand the cold unless she ingested the fat. Nevertheless, he had brought some food to sustain her. Somehow, she had managed to consume with neither enthusiasm nor complaint whatever Kiti served.

Remarkable. This daughter whose mother had died when Bonnie was but a toddler. This twelve-year-old whom he had raised as best he could while others advised him to remarry and assure his child a "proper" home. Here she was— mature and versatile, accepting and adjusting to unfamiliar ways. Not for the first time, he was extremely proud of her.

Now Bonnie told her father about the storm, the wolverine attack, the *ransom* Nik paid to polar bears. Cliff Belson considered his daughter's account, compared it with Nik's own tale supplied earlier in the evening. A mild event to the *Inuit* boy, an unforgettable adventure to the girl from Missouri. He smiled, nodded in the dim glow of their lamp, brought his mind back to the present.

"The climate's hostile," he explained. "People have to live differently, just to survive. And Bonnie-girl, day by day you've done *well!* You can be pleased with yourself."

"I'm loving it, Pop—oh, maybe not so much the raw meat."

He chuckled. "How could someone cook it? No wood to burn, no coal or available gas, certainly no electricity. But my dear, you've been a trouper about food."

"You warned me before we came. That was the deal—you'd take me with you, but I wasn't to complain about the food."

Belson laughed. "It's one thing to agree beforehand, quite another to do as promised in the fact. We could have gone into our own stores, more—not too exciting, but at least familiar."

"That would have hurt everyone's feelings. You know that!"

"It would, but also would have taken some pressure off their hunting."

"Maybe. But I'm used to the food now. Oh! And I haven't had a bath since we got here, Pop. Neither has anyone else!"

"You mind **so** much?" They both laughed. "We're both a bit ripe. Tell you what—let's take a team out to the lead and have ourselves a quick dip."

"Be serious!"

"Summers, people wade in lakes and rivers—mostly snowmelt, and still cold, I promise you."

"Everyone back home's always talking about bacteria, infection—"

"—Too cold here for much of that!"

"Nik got really deep bites, all scratched up by that wolverine—and he only worried about his torn-up clothing!"

"Rightly so. Cold through a ripped seam kills someone fast!"

"But . . . no iodine, peroxide—nothing!"

"No need, Bonnie. What self-respecting germ—oh, unless . . ." his voice trailed off.

"—Unless *what?*"

"Unless someone like you or me brings in a disease. That's why I insisted on all the health checks before we came up—plus those shots you loved so much."

"Not to keep us from *getting* something?"

He shook his head. "To keep us from *giving*. *Inuit* live far away from any other people. Their bodies don't carry the same kinds of protection we do."

"Yeah, antibodies. Everyone here seems really healthy, though."

He nodded. "Maybe the most vigorous on earth. But measles? Chicken pox? A common cold, even. And 'Flu'— let alone tuberculosis—is lethal here. Wipes out the entire community, even a whole territory—*and it has!*"

Bonnie shivered. She could not imagine Nik or even Kiti becoming ill and dying from something simple like measles or chicken pox. "Healthy. . . . and all they eat is *flesh*—meat, fish—lots of *fat!*"

"*Fat* keeps them alive in the cold. Blubber gives body warmth as well as lamp oil."

"Vitamins, Pop? Minerals? No vegetables or fruit."

"Berries in the summer, depending on how far south they go inland—sourberries, cranberries, low-bush fruit that grows up here on the tundra."

"Without sugar? Brrrr! You brought some home once, remember?"

"And in the stomach of the caribou might be—usually is, I'm told—a bit of partially digested green matter. Lichen. Highly prized, and I've tasted it. Palatable enough if you forget the source—and you're right. Fruit and vegetables are not part of the diet."

"I don't get it."

Cliff Belson grinned. "Science doesn't know everything, Honey. Doctors and nutritionists don't get it, either! They go wild trying to understand why *Inuit* are *alive*, let alone bright, vital and robust."

"Maybe just the intense cold?"

The man shrugged. "Climate's more a *problem* here, I'd think, than a *solution.*"

"Also been wondering, Pop. People here are beautiful—and smallish in height, mostly. Plus short arms and legs, have you noticed?"

"Physical adaptation, Sweetheart. Current theory, anyway. Toes and fingertips closer to the heart, easier to warm. Padded cheeks . . . small ears, nose practically bridgeless—same reason, all the harder to freeze. Neat, compact people."

Bonnie was quiet for so long that her father thought she had fallen asleep. Then, "Pop?"

"Present, accounted for."

"I'd like to stay here for a while."

"Umm-mm."

"I mean it—well, it would be a challenge, like a game!"

"Grim game, Dear. Death to any loser."

"Pop!"

"Chess, then? Opponents are harsh climate and lack of resource. Then all living creatures, especially people, become mere pawns."

"So rooks and knights and bishops are the blizzards and high winds—"

"—And the king and queen—"

"—Are the *cold!*" Bonnie concluded triumphantly.

Her father nodded. "Cold sometimes so intense that it freezes your lungs to breathe air through your mouth!"

When Bonnie remained silent, Belson reached off the *iglerk* to snuff the lamp.

120

"I read in a book at school that everyone who lives in the High Arctic has a stone-age culture."

"Well, yes . . . stone plus animal parts. That's what's here—and it's *all* that's here."

Bonnie spoke thoughtfully. "Maybe driftwood?"

"Undependably—they can't count on it. *We*'d be stone-age, too, if we had to live here. And if—big IF!—we were ingenious enough to survive at all."

"That book I read? Made them sound—not just primitive, Pop, but—you know—simple-minded? Unintelligent?"

"And we both know better, don't we? You can't use something like fuel if you don't have it, regardless of how smart you are."

"Nik's really sharp, Pop. Sitok, too, in a different way—and look at Kiti!"

"No one not bright endures here for long. Nor does someone physically handicapped."

"I've wondered about that. No one here's lame or blind or even seems to be hard of hearing."

"That's essentially true for all Inupiat."

"So this is a 'perfect' race? No one's ever handicapped?"

"Oh yes, just as in our world."

"Then where *are* these people? I haven't seen anyone who's not totally healthy—vigorous!"

"Bonnie, I don't think you want me to answer that question."

"But—oh! You mean such people are set out to freeze—aw, Pop! Are you sure?"

Belson nodded, but Bonnie couldn't see him in the dark. His silence, though, confirmed the suspicion.

"You have to remember, though. . . . These people believe that the valuable part of someone is the spirit—and that these spirits live forever, continuing generation after generation."

"So in a way, reincarnation?"

"Of the spirit."

Bonnie was silent for many minutes. Then, "They believe that someone's spirit goes on and on forever, but inhabiting different bodies?"

"Human spirits to a newborn human body. Whale spirits to whales, and so forth."

"I like that idea. Is it true?"

"That's not how I was brought up. It's not a part of our belief, yours and mine."

"So it's *not* true, right?"

"I can't say that, Bonnie."

"Maybe it's true just for them," Bonnie suggested.

"And maybe it's true for us all."

Silence. Then from Bonnie: "If you'd seen Nik and that wolverine? Pitch black, nothing to guide him except sound. But he figured out what to do, then *did* it!"

"It is my understanding," Belson said slowly, "that a kid Nik calls **Pah-nee** gave a fair accounting, as well."

"Pop, who told you that? I didn't do *any*thing. Well, yeah. I hid under the robes. Hung onto Nuko. I was *so* scared!"

"Nik gave me his version this afternoon when I asked about his torn clothes."

"I don't sew too well."

"He got home without freezing. You should be proud of yourself—kept your wits about you, used your head."

"Thanks," Bonnie said quietly. "And I *still* want to stay up here for a while."

Belson rolled up more tightly in the sleeping robes. He had explained to Bonnie how much he worried when she was on a trip like this last one. Still, he tried to trust Nik and the others to keep her safe. "You sleepy, sweetheart?"

Bonnie turned toward his voice in the dark snowhouse. "Not so very—but plenty of food plus soft robes and warmth?—I feel terrific!"

"Sometime, we'll talk about those circles of yours."

"—And I'm finding more all the time."

He grunted. "All these years, studying Inupiat, *I* never noticed—then you're up here twenty minutes and develop this theory."

"Pop, no *theory,* just—*observation.*"

"Thing is, sweetheart," and his voice sounded thick with sleep, "you may have hit on an important theme."

CHAPTER 10.
WALRUS

"It happens that the brother not yet a man will accompany the dog-persons in the big boat." Sitok's voice was firm, but Nik looked over to his grandmother to assess her viewpoint. The blackberry eyes were resolute. No help there.

"Someone learns to handle a *kayak* by *handling* one," Nik grumbled.

"True. But skill with *kayak* is developed in the shallow waters inland during summer."

The boy wanted to argue. "And Nik could not do that, last summer." His parents had taken the family's *kayak* on their ill-fated fishing trip. Sitok of course had borrowed *kayaks* last summer to maintain and sharpen his own boating skills.

No one would have loaned a *kayak* to an amateur like Nik. He knew that. Only a boy's family would endanger such a precious craft to a beginner. The careful fitting of caribou ribs to form the skeleton. Those hides with special processing to form a waterproof, tough skin for the slim boat. It must be rugged enough to bump on ice without rupturing; but only triple seaming insured that the craft was at once light weight and water tight—a sturdy bird skimming the water but obedient to the paddle.

Today, though, Sitok was offered several *kayaks* for the walrus hunt. It was Potok who insisted that Nik's brother do him the great honor of borrowing the older man's second craft. All knew that Sitok would do well and thus honor Potok.

"We will have no peace otherwise," Sitok explained to an irritated Kiti and Nik.

"Nor no peace in any case," Kiti had muttered.

Sitok was something to see, this morning. His borrowed *kayak* was perched on the sled atop half a dozen big fur robes—and little else beside his hunting bag. He was using the team Nik usually took. The older brother explained that he, Sitok, would be exceedingly tired after the hunt and Nik must drive them back to the village over smooth sea ice.

Nik suspected his elder brother of wanting to see how his pupil was doing. He hoped that this today was a check of his dog team skills before they started their journey. The inland tundra was bound to be well frozen half a moon from now, with winter well established. They planned to leave then or even earlier, if Pehl-son and Pah-nee departed. Perhaps, knowing how disappointed Nik was in not being among the paddlers, Sitok planned to give him special responsibility. Driving the team when a sled is piled high with meat requires smooth control of dogs and rapid decision-making, even on the smoother sea ice and especially with ever-changing and often unfamiliar trail. Nik could not have managed at the beginning of winter. Now? *Ee-ee,* Yes. He was confident. But . . . he wanted to paddle a kayak!

Kiti spoke. "Be patient. The younger boy's time will come. On this day, though, he will explain to our guests what is happening on the hunt."

Nik did not respond. He looked over at Pehl-son and Pah-nee who were chatting together in their strange language as they accompanied everyone walking across the shelf of sea ice attached to land. Nik felt nothing but affection for the two, especially for Pah-nee, the dog-boy with whom he had spent so much time during the eight sleeps since *tingmisut* had brought him here from the sky.

The presence of *kalunait* had no real bearing on Nik's role in the walrus hunt to come, for Nik's being consigned to the big round boat, the *umiak,* would have occurred in any case. Sitok, with Kiti firmly supporting him, would never let Nik paddle in the sea, even if he had *fifty* winters behind him—before he had learned to manage a *kayak* in the shallow fresh water of summertime.

Nik helped the others lower the *umiak* into the lead. This broad trail of calm water sliced through to separate mainland ice from one huge *siku* of floating but unattached ice so large that its edges could not be seen even in bright moonlight. The lead also contained bobbling pans of smaller ice, but some sizable. And it was on these that their quarry basked. Never mind. At least Nik had an important role in this walrus hunt. The function of the *umiak* was to tow walrus kills to shore, and Nik was in charge of having the boat there when needed and keeping it otherwise out of the way.

The craft were now in the water, all the *kayaks* plus the *umiak* with its *kalunait* and Nik along with two paddlers from the village, young men who had no access to *kayaks.* No harpooners were aboard, this time. Wutik and Tukla preferred putting their harpoons on *kayaks* for this kind of hunt. They wanted to be at water level, where more action was likely to occur. Human voices hushed, paddles dipped slowly to be silent in the oily sea.

"Hear *avik* speak," Nik told Pehl-son, and the man rapidly translated for Bonnie. Together, they listened to the oddly rhythmic bark, cough-like, a half-strangled sound that no sled dog ever made.

"The herd bull is in *conversation* with other herds, other clan groups, to report that all is well."

The boy watched in moonlight as paddlers arranged their equipment. In a low voice, he explained what was happening to Pehl-son, giving the man time to tell Bonnie quietly as well. Before and behind each *kayaker* were coarse bowls of formed pelt sacks containing neatly coiled line made from oiled and braided strips of split walrus hide. These strips were knotted smoothly together by tough sinew woven in at the joins. The harpoon tip was attached to the longer line in the front bowl.

"A partly-inflated sealskin float is attached to the rope in the stern," Nik said.

Pehl-son pointed this float out to Bonnie.

"It is true," Nik continued, "that *avik* the walrus weighs far less than a whale. But *avik* can be more dangerous to the hunter."

Nik waited for Pehl-son to translate. Then the man turned back to him. "Pahnee wants to know how a walrus can be more hazardous when the whale is so much larger."

Nik explained. *"Avik* is nervous, always suspicious, and can be aggressive."

Pehl-son translated. "Then . . . ?"

"Avik has a tendency to panic. The huge males especially are contentious when disturbed."

"But why are your floats only filled halfway?"

Nik sighed. Did the dog-people know *nothing?* "One walrus pulling a seal carcass only half-inflated results in less drag than the several fully inflated floats normally used for the heavy whale."

"And the advantage of less drag?"

"The lesser tug is still enough to wear *avik* down—but without causing it such consternation that it panics and attacks."

Nik pointed out the single spear that lay ready on every *kayak* deck. "It is hoped that the weapon will not be needed."

"Yet it is there, at the ready?"

"Ee-ee, yes/ Only for close up, desperate encounters."

Then, "There!" Nik grasped Pah-nee's shoulder, pointed to an ice pan nearby. Dark shapes of walrus were huddled on it, black silhouettes and blots in the uncertain luster of starlight and a cloud-shadowed moon. Then, moving his arm slowly so as to give no alarm, he pointed out another herd on a blob of ice farther out in the lead.

Belson and Bonnie spoke softly to each other, the man occasionally asking Nik something, then turning back to his child.

Nik felt restlessness rise in him gradually, a twitchiness born not of fear but of the old familiar impatience. He wished to be out of the *umiak,* wanted to waltz wildly on the sea. But no, and time passed slowly as the dog-persons chatted softly to each other, the *shu-ush-ush* of ripples the only other sound nearby, sharp ice cracks in the distance. Count, count the wash against the boat. Learn patience. . . . *Count.*

Winter-morning moonlight was tempered by a swirl of respiration from the heavy drift of brown heads and shoulderless bodies packed tight on floes upwind nearby. In silver light, as Nik followed the paddlers to go in closer, the creatures could be seen to do their own dance. Back and forth, then back again, they rocked together in slow cadence. Did they, Nik wondered, communicate with some mighty walrus spirit in the sky? Some malignant shadow soul which had directed them to travel to this place so close to land so late in the season? A soul in league with *Inuk* which treacherously drew them here from their usual and safely distant, unattached sea ice, the far-floating *siku?*

Nik pressed Pah-nee's mitts hard against the gunwale. He must hang on, for action was sure to begin soon. The walruses would note the presence of converging hunters at any moment. Sure enough, the swaying stopped even as he watched. Silence. Suspicion. Something different. Amiss.

A bellow came across the water, an inquiring roar

from deep in some cavernous throat. Pause. And then again, this time challenging, a different note, irritated. The hunters dotting the lead stayed motionless, paddles out of the water and still as stones. The mighty mammals on the ice were near-sighted; and with *kayaks* and *umiak* downwind, no scent could reach them. Yet they knew that something around them was altered, so danger must be present. Where did it lurk?

Another bellow came across the water and echoed off shore cliffs. Paddlers now dipped their oars carefully, silently into the sea to close in on whatever piece of shadowed floating ice they had selected. A shuffling started in the midst of the herd closest to Nik. But no alarm, not yet. One gigantic body emerged from the group, thrusting with powerful flippers to be free of the others, to get out to the edge and investigate. This would be the lead bull, master of his cows. He dived at a steep angle.

The *kayaks* swept forward, silence no longer important. Sitok skimmed by, impatiently motioned the *umiak* back. The big boat would be needed later if the hunt was successful, for then Nik's craft must tow the one or several carcasses to firm ice near shore where sleds and teams waited. Like the *kayaks,* Nik's boat of bone and hide, waterproof with special seams, was all too easily ripped by a flipper. Unlike *kayaks,* the *umiak* was a little sluggish, not so easy to maneuver. It presented a larger target Sitok would not want to risk.

Nevertheless, the great bull walrus came threshing up beside the *umiak* suddenly, angry eyes rolling, whites glinting. Nik knew those eyes would show red if there were more light. He held his breath, was grateful that Pehl-son and Pah-nee as well as the paddlers stayed silent and motionless also. If *avik* perceived the craft to be a threat, he would attack. But the creature did not comprehend his own power, and no sound or movement in the larger craft attracted him. Now his head rotated to inspect the surrounding sea.

129

Surely, *avik* searched for a target to explain this change in his environment—a change he sensed and disapproved but was unable to pinpoint.

The two *kayaks* of harpooners Tukla and Wutik darted in, took a position where their weapons could be used without endangering each other or Nik's *umiak*. And it was in these light low craft that the walrus could actually *see* creatures he now decided had disturbed his ease. He lunged for one *kayak,* then the other when the first darted back. Silently, Nik motioned his own oarsmen to help him get the *umiak* away toward more dependable ice on the coastal side of the lead.

Now Wutik with the first *kayak* moved in, harpoon poised in one arm, the other dragging his paddle at the last moment to skid the craft sideways. The weapon flashed, imbedded, broke down into three loosely-connected parts as it was designed to do. The walrus dived. Wutik reached back and tossed the partly-inflated seal hide to water, then reversed the motion of his craft once again to give the beast space. He had struck first, and successfully. So this particular herd bull was technically his kill.

Nik told Pehl-son, "Wutik will get that first warm bite—"

"—You mean the liver." Pehl-son nodded.

"But otherwise, the meat will be distributed according to need—"

"—And who decides?" Pehl-son wondered aloud.

"Probably Potok, since Arajik is not here."

Tukla in the second *kayak* had been under attack when Wutik intervened. Tukla also turned away now, but neither he nor Wutik went far. In the moments without action while Nik could study the water after the *umiak* was snugged against ice, he saw peripherally that other paddlers were engaging walrus on other ice pans dotting the lead.

But suddenly, big Unipak slid out into open water from some invisible lead nearby. He paddled with strong, noisy strokes. Ignoring Nik and the *umiak* completely, his glance swept first Wutik and then Tukla but gave the two waiting harpooners no regard. He then considered more carefully the proximity of other craft, all well away. Now Unipak swung in close to the half-submerged float, his spear raised high while he examined the sea surface around him.

Precipitately, the big bull erupted from the water— terrified, enraged, snorting with pain, air-hungry. His head faced Unipak's *kayak,* and it was for this craft that he plunged. The big man back-paddled, tried to turn, but *avik* came too fast. Unipak exchanged the spear for his harpoon, held it horizontally to use as a buffer to protect himself as he twisted within the craft to follow his target. But half a *kayak's* length away, before the weapon could be dispatched, the walrus dived.

The animal came up under the boat almost immediately. Unipak in his *kayak* took to air like a pale gyrfalcon. Then the craft broke into pieces, a shattered Unipak going one way, the smashed *kayak* spraying parts in all directions. And while the walrus charged at first one and then another among the larger pieces that fell near him, Nik saw limp, disjointed Unipak strike and then sink beneath the churning black water. The boy stared in shock at the spot where the sea had swallowed the man. Pah-nee crept over, and he felt the dog-boy's shoulder press against his arm for courage. Neither Pehl-son nor his child uttered any sound.

No more time was available for Nik to consider the *kalunait* guests, for Tukla moved in rapidly and thrust his own harpoon. It raced to the mark and broke down. He hurled his float to the water, paddled back.

Small Atik joined the fray, his killing spear held high to support the harpooners as needed. Two floats now jigged across the surface, and the beast came up between them, this time charging Atik, the newcomer. That hunter thrust his spear solidly into the creature, held on and used the animal's momentum to force him and his *kayak* safely back until the walrus changed course suddenly and Atik could release his grip on the spear and escape attack.

The walrus dived again, now with three *kayaks* moving away rapidly in different directions. All must wait once more. Nik looked anxiously at the ice against which they rested in the *umiak*. Should he have Pah-nee and Pehl-son leave the boat? For if *avik* broached beneath the *umiak*, all of them would tumble out. But see, the *umiak* already twisted and bobbled on wave action in the lead, not only that of the battle nearby but also from other hunting groups. Nik decided rapidly that trying to leap onto ice from a churning craft was more dangerous than taking one's chance with a frantic creature of the sea.

He looked about. Other paddlers were picking up floats having lines with walruses attached. This would be a successful hunt, Nik reflected, for all who survived.

Unipak . . . *pirtok,* there was a happening with no repair possible from the outset. No one had caused the accident. No one besides Unipak could have prevented it. If indeed that *was* his motivation—something Nik doubted—Unipak had come in to help bring in the giant walrus bull. But it was Sedna herself who had orchestrated what was, after all, a familiar *Inuit* tragedy. No words would be said for Unipak now; probably not ever. The present—here on the ice at the scene of triumph—was a time for *doing,* for rejoicing in one's own vitality, not for dwelling on Unipak's fate—Unipak, whose vital and of course eternal spirit might by now have already entered a new infant born at this time in some village somewhere. Now was the time for a village to celebrate good fortune in the hunt.

At last, Nik saw Wutik's huge walrus come slowly to the surface nearby, its valiant spirits flown. Blood showed black on the dark water. Sitok arrived soon, hauling another walrus behind his kayak. He motioned the *umiak* over to take the big bull with which Wutik and Tukla as well as Atik had struggled. And by means of which Unipak had been destroyed. That extra-heavy carcass required more than *kayaks* to tow it.

No additional dark forms dotted the ice pans. All creatures not captured had fled. Human cries of triumph filled the air as an echoing victory chant began. *Oo-oo-oo-LAH! Oo-oo-oo-LAH!* And reverberating softly came harmony from other village paddlers, these voices more distant, the singers invisible: *Oo-lo-ah! Oo-lo-ah!*

When the village catch was finally brought up onto firm ice at the shore side of the lead, it was once again Potok who did the ceremony of thanks to the nine great mammals who had given themselves, and to Sedna who had allowed them to make the sacrifice. He cut rapidly into the abdomen of each beast and withdrew the liver, still warm and now steaming. This delicacy he gave to the hunter who had made that kill. After one ritual mouthful, this man sent the tasty treat around the group for every other to cut off a share. One piece of this organ from each creature magically remained. And these, Atik collected at Potok's gesture. Atik took them over and dropped them into the lead as special thanks to generous Sedna and her *puyee,* her great creatures of the deep.

Belson would return to the village on the big boat. But Bonnie insisted on going with the heavily laden sled, said now to be returning by land.

"You'll be sprinting along beside the team most of the

way," her father warned. "The sled's too loaded to ride, and remember that any land trail has hidden rocks and bumps."

But the sight of Unipak's accident seemed to have drained her interest in the sea, at least temporarily. Two sleds brought out from the village raced off together over land. Nik waited for Sitok's signal to go, but his brother stood studying the sky.

The sun by now was at its apex, the top arc barely visible but nevertheless halfway across its brief but glowing trip along the south horizon. Just above the glow was a peculiar dark-ice green fading to purple-blue where it met land. An early-winter day of great beauty. A time of good luck in the hunt.

CHAPTER 11.
DISASTER

Nik and Bonnie took turns sliding down a hummock while they waited for Sitok's signal. The ridge of ice and drifted snow let them descend laughing into a soft mound that they had collected for the purpose. Surely no one could doubt, Nik thought, but that winter was the wonder season of the year. And to think: that glorious season was just now beginning!

At last, Sitok returned. He studied the sky. "This sled will go back by sea ice, after all," he said simply. Nik went over to get the team moving. A mid-day glow brightened the southern horizon. He pulled out and adjusted his snow spectacles, his *idjak,* while he ran beside the sled. Then he put on speed to get ahead of Pah-nee.

Nik felt *good,* weightless as goose down blowing on a wind along the ice trail. The dog-boy was racing beside Nuko at front and center of the fanned-out team, not the safest place to be if he should fall. Nik should point out the hazard. How?

Also, Pah-nee should be using spectacles for protection from snow blindness even in this pale light. Nik beside her, now, Pah-nee finally understood his pantomime and produced the small bone goggles, the *idjak* that Sitok had fashioned to fit his freckled face. Kiti had found in her Big Feed large *idjak* to fit Pehl-son.

Eh, that Big Feed of Kiti's, that woman's box of wonders—what *wasn't* in it?! Nik remembered as a small boy daydreaming of the miracles that might be hidden in the

135

woman's cache of his *Ananatsiak* Kiti—that mysterious and forbidden Big Feed nested right into the wall wherever they lived. As he ran along the ice now, he smiled at his childish imaginings—wings for humans to wear, a hole through the bottom of the container to connect with the hot center of the earth, a baby brother or sister all ready to pop into Mawena's hood at will. Not merely possible but *likely,* he had thought then.

Thus Nik's mind was flowing when the white bear came out suddenly from behind a hummock and barred the way. The dogs stopped. Sitok yanked the bone anchor on the handles to keep the sled from over-running them.

Nanuk could not have communicated more clearly if he had spoken *Inupiaq: **Give me your walrus meat.*** His four furry feet were planted on the ice—not moving forward, not giving way. The great body swayed slowly back and forth, ready to act. The flattish head on the sinuous neck was extended, it too weaving slightly. His mouth was half open, a deep pink visible behind long, pale and very sharp teeth glinting in moonlight.

At another time in other circumstance, Nik might have marveled at the sight of the powerful male, could have admired its beauty combined with size and raw strength. But not here. Not now. His focus was on saving the meat on which his people depended and especially on making sure that his brother and he—Pah-nee, too, of course—lived to enjoy it. As with all of his people now and the long line before, his intent was human survival, every sense attuned to that single goal.

Hampered by harness, the dogs hunkered low on their haunches to stop, their ears flat against their heads as they keened their "bear song" that Nik with Bonnie had together heard once before and recently. All but Nuko—the lead dog closest to the creature. She held her ground, crouching despite

136

the harness, muscles flexed, her ears disappearing into rising fur on head and shoulders. Lines and all, she was ready to spring. Her lips were raised to expose many sharp teeth pitiful when compared to the fangs exposed in the bear's answering grin.

And Nuko did not moan. She snarled long and low.

Sitok had managed to stop the sled before it overran the dogs. Now, he raced ahead of the team, bringing out as he came the precious metal knife he kept in his clothing. Brought back from one of Arajik's fur-trading expeditions with dog-people in the south and given to Sitok last summer before the disastrous fishing trip, the knife was made of something their father called "metal." Very strong but brittle in the cold, it had to be carried inside the tunic for body warmth in winter or—so said Arajik—it would snap like burnt cartilage when used. Sitok always kept it sharp and oiled in its hide holder within his *silipak*. Now, it gleamed in moonlight.

Nik raced back to fumble at the sled. He pulled out a bone snow knife, grabbed Sitok's killing spear and his own, then dashed forward, offering the weapons to his brother, whose eyes and full focus were on the sea-bear. Advancing very slowly, knife in hand, Sitok's gaze never left the creature. He waggled his left hand at Nik. *Stay back, keep weapons available.* Then he jabbed a mittened thumb toward Nuko. *Unharness the dog.*

Nik bent to the task, thinking as he did so that Nuko had been a good leader. She had no chance against the bear, but she might hold its attention long enough to let Sitok strike. The boy's throat tightened, and for a moment he clasped the dog, held her back.

Free, Nuko touched ice only twice before she surged to the furry throat of the startled bear, canines slashing. Her back legs found momentary purchase on the right front leg to let her leap away—but not before the bear's left front paw with its dreadful claws dealt her body a swipe, a mighty blow that increased her arc of flight by the distance of at least two *kayaks.* There she crumpled, blood darkening the ice.

Bonnie let out a shriek and shot forward past the crouching team, past Nik and Sitok and even past the bear, to bend over motionless Nuko, then commence dragging the dog's considerable weight back to the sled.

Nanuk paid this interruption no more regard than he would give some shrill summer insect—glancing only for a moment in the direction of the small dog-boy. But that moment with the prior interlude by Nuko afforded Sitok what he needed. He darted in, sank the knife deeply into a spot above and behind the left front leg, then bounded away.

"Whuff-ff!" The creature looked over to inspect blood darkening its fur. Then with a snarl of fury, he reared onto his back legs, a monster more than twice Sitok's height. At that instant, Sitok grabbed the spear from Nik and dashed in to sink the point deeply into the killing spot just below the chest and angled up.

"Whuff-ff-ff!" The bear swept his right paw across. Those permanently extended talons caught Sitok solidly on the left shoulder and arm.

Blood bloomed on *Nanuk* from the original knife cut and now pulsed richly from the mortal wound aimed at his heart. He took a couple of dabs with his tongue, looked around him, peered at Sitok his attacker who lay motionless on ice nearby. *Nanuk* did not seem to be interested in walrus meat at this moment, but would clearly consider revenge. The big yellowish-white bulk came back down onto all four legs and turned toward the injured *Inuk* who had caused him pain.

Nik dashed in from the left, brandishing his own spear and chanting spontaneous prayers to every spirit whose name he could remember, even evil *Paija*. With all his force, he thrust again at the exposed original side wound left by the metal knife.

This time, the bear toppled. Poised to leap away, Nik stood long minutes above the creature until he was certain its life spirits were gone. At last, bewildered by such rapid events, the boy looked around him.

Pah-nee was with Sitok. She was stemming the heavy flow of blood with hareskins from Nik's hunting bag, the contents of which were now scattered across the ice. Nik saw the dog-child secure the supple skins to shoulder and chest with fishing sinew, now try unsuccessfully to roll the injured young man onto a blanket. Nik went to help.

"He's still breathing, but he's hurt really bad!" Pah-nee told Nik in her foreign words, but the younger brother already knew that the elder boy struggled to hold his spirits together within him.

Nik raised his eyebrows, *"Ee-ee."* Yes. The miracle was that Sitok still breathed. Few *Inuit* survive even the most casual caress from a sea bear. He eased his brother onto the big fur, then wrapped him warmly with other robes Pah-nee dragged over. Sitok's parka was shredded where the claws had struck. Next, Nik got the dogs quiet, then reharnessed a new lead to take Nuko's place. Still keening, the creatures moved the heavy sled forward to where the injured man lay. Nik unstrapped the load. Sitok was the priority now. The *kayak* which had been on top must be left on end here to mark the place with its dark outline—this location on the ice where lay a dead bear with the pile of walrus meat for which it died. A dead bear and a dying dog. He dared not feel sympathy for the two creatures. Getting his brother home to Kiti filled his mind.

Unconscious Sitok secure and warm on the sled, Nik with Bonnie retrieved all weapons, reassembled the hunting bag and loaded it in case of emergency. Nik wiped the metal knife clean on snow, replaced it onto the sled in its holder within his brother's clothing. Finally and gently, Nik lifted the bundled Nuko and placed her on the ice as well. The dog was conscious now. She growled feebly at the bear carcass, licked Nik's mittens, stretched her nose toward a puzzled Pah-nee.

"No!" Pah-nee said when Nik's intent became clear. *"Owka, owka, owka!* No, no, no! A predator will get her. . . . She'll freeze or die from wounds, maybe starve if something else takes the walrus."

But of course Nik understood only the emphatic *no*, the *"owka"* in clear *Inupiaq,* and he disagreed.

Sniffing loudly—was the dog-boy catching cold?—Pah-nee walked over and dragged Nuko gently back to the sled, looked over to Nik for help in getting her up and tied secure. Water ran from the *kalunait's* eyes and froze on his cheeks. What was this?

Nik did not want to be burdened by a dog. And certainly not by the mere *carcass* of a dog, for how could Nuko live? They needed to travel as rapidly as the team could go, as fast as Sitok's wounds permitted, get the injured man to *Ananatsiak* before it was too late. Nuko was a fine dog, had been. But she would never survive the bear's blow. . . . Why should the team carry her weight only to have her finally give up her spirits on the trail or back at the village?

Nik leveled on Pah-nee one of those resolute stares that Sitok still used sometimes to control his younger brother. Then Nik heaved Nuko up once more and returned her to the ice. Without another glance, he started the team.

They went carefully around or over each treacherous pressure ridge, places where a floe riding the tide had struck grounded ice with such force that both edges rested against each other high in the air. They passed three of these and bypassed a dozen hummocks before Nik thought to look back. Pah-nee was not behind. Still jogging beside the team, the boy searched ice on both sides and ahead. He let his pace slow, allowed the sled to come up to him. The dog-boy was not tucked in around Sitok's robes, either.

Nik stopped the dogs altogether, called, *"Oo-oo-oo!"* It would not do to call out someone's actual name loudly and make things easier for vicious trail spirits which seemed already to be active on this day. He called again and once more, heard his yodel echo on shore cliffs like a grieving wolf, but received no answering reply.

With a sigh, he turned the team and backtracked. Where could Pah-nee be? Why would he not have stayed up with the sled as he generally did, or else climbed onto it?

After what seemed a long time but was probably no more than it takes to eat a trail meal, Nik spied in starlight something solitary and dark on ice far ahead. He kept going back, recognized the dog-person. Pah-nee was carrying Nuko, and very slow going it was. The *kalunait* was wheezing with fatigue when he reached the sled. The dog whimpered with movement that irritated her wounds.

Nik sighed. Could it be that Pah-nee had not understood his gaze? Or had the dog-person deliberately disobeyed? Nik was probably the elder of the two, certainly the more experienced among those with spirits alert—and therefore *Nik was the boss.* Did dog people not realize that it never works to have two leaders on a trail? Or did Pah-nee not care? A knotty matter, and no time now for untangling.

He took the sled back, glumly loaded Nuko, avoided meeting Pah-nee's eyes, for the dog-boy had disobeyed. *Ooangniktook,* the north wind, was presently flexing his muscles. The moon had long furry clouds chasing across its face. They must try to reach the village before the storm struck. He would discuss with Kiti at home this deliberate defiance by Pah-nee. They would probably take the matter to Pehl-son.

For now, though, Nik would drop it. Actually, he was not sorry to have Nuko with them, no—however futile their effort might be. He cut his eyes to his guest without letting him know that he was looking. The weary dog-boy had chattered some words but now dragged himself up onto the sled. Nik could not stay angry with his friend, especially when he saw Pah-nee tucking robes around Sitok, finally lashing him to the antler hand-grips to make sure the precious human cargo was not lost. Then the dog-boy tended to Nuko.

Pah-nee must surely be relieved to relax for a time while the dogs streaked across ice for home.

The wind at their backs became a rage, and ominous creaking stirred the ice. Nik turned toward land, despite its uneven surface. He would not wish them to find themselves suddenly afloat—on a moving, ungrounded island of ice, on *siku*. By the time they reached the shoreline, Nik was letting the dogs take their own direction, for he could see nothing. The temperature dropped rapidly, and he chilled even as he ran. They would not reach the village tonight. He must find a cave or build an *igloo*. Snow blow increased, shrieking parallel to the trail, and he could not see even the front of the sled. White-out.

He pulled up the dogs. No point searching for a cave. Visibility was so poor, they might actually be standing on buried shelter right now—who could tell? He took the snow knife and wished he could recognize the right kind of snow to make a trail house. Never mind, he would cut where he stood—use any snow that would hold together.

Nik's first snowhouse built by himself was not long enough to lie down in without curling up. Nor was it high enough to stand in. But it did have arching walls that stayed up when he put on the capstone. Pah-nee helped him get Sitok inside, then insisted on adding the dog. Still alive, Nuko's warmth and fur would be like having an extra robe, Nik decided. He had no food for the team, having neglected to save out any walrus even for themselves. But the dogs were anxious to dig into snow and escape the wailing ice wind, and for once made no complaint. Finally, he helped Pah-nee finish chinking the blocks of the *igloo*. His last act was to fill a bladder from his hunting bag with clean snow. This he placed between his outer furs and underfurs when he rolled into the robes. Soon, they would have water for drinking. And tomorrow, for icing the runners. He was pleased when everyone was packed inside with a mound of snow drawn up to secure the opening. Very little wind whistled through the cracks. What more could someone ask? His belly rumbled. Food would be good. He hoped for a short storm.

Sitok came awake much later—thirsty, weak, in pain. Nik could let him have water.

"Someone's elder brother killed a bear," the younger boy announced.

"That cannot be!" Sitok said slowly, "for even after two killing blows, the spirits of *nanuk* were strong."

"*Ee-ee,* Yes, but then he died." Sitok's were the important strikes, Nik knew. So did Sitok.

"Nik is certain that the spirit left him truly?" A wounded sea bear left for dead was known to follow its persecutors and exact terrible vengeance. White bears can hold a grudge.

"The liver of the magnificent creature is packaged for *Ananatsiak* Kiti. It happens that she may use it to heal a brave man's wounds. . . . So sleep!" Nik ordered.

And Sitok slept. With morning came cessation of the storm followed by a brilliant moon. Nik packed and iced runners, harnessed the dogs while Bonnie prepared the sled for two invalids. They arrived in the village before the sun glimmered at mid-day. While Kiti murmured and scolded as she ministered to Sitok's wounds with Aunt Saruna helping, Bonnie got healing herbs and advice-by-demonstration. The young girl worked on Nuko in the small snowhouse shared with her much relieved father.

"What I don't understand," Belson told her as sternly as he could, considering that he was limp with delight to have her safely home, "is the reason why you and that boy always have to do things *differently.*"

"Pop, it's not like that!" she protested. "In fact, returning on sea ice was Sitok's idea." She paused. "I don't *try* always to be going in another direction—nor does Nik. It just sometimes turns out that way."

"*Some*times!" the man exclaimed. And then more mildly, "Until we go, you are to check with me before you leave this village—with anyone, for any reason."

"Pop, I already do. I have."

"Hmm." It was true, and he knew it. Should he have brought her here? He had planned originally to be gone only three weeks—a long time to be away from his precious daughter. With her, he could stay for five. And he had thought coming up here would be a valuable experience for her, a broadening of horizons. And it was. But taking a child into the High Arctic. . . . He just hadn't considered the vast changes for her—or the dangers.

Both patients improved so rapidly that Nik could not believe what he saw when he returned the next day from making the trip back to get the bear and walrus meat as well as Potok's *kayak.* Atik had accompanied him—rather, he *chose* Atik from the whole handful who clamored to go. Urgit was among these—*Urgit!?*

The intense dislike he had felt for that young man was dissipating. He'd had opportunity to observe him after he and his aunt came to them during the storm, then stayed because they had no other place to go. Nik realized that Urgit was *inept* but not evil. *Clumsy* but not treacherous. He had not been taught to hunt. Neither had Nik been taught until now, this winter, by Sitok; but Urgit had no older brother. Besides, Urgit seemed to lack the inner unrest which made Nik so often miserable . . . but which also made Nik anxious to learn.

Yes, Urgit *seemed* to lack. . . . Eh, what did Nik know of that orphan's anxieties? Certainly, Urgit knew nothing at all about *Nik's*. Who could say what pain might plague Urgit's spirits? His mother died while he was still in her hood. His father Pak had not remarried. He with his widowed sister Saruna spoiled and indulged the child even more than most small Inupiat are spoiled and indulged, so Nik had heard. They never noticed when the dependent child grew up to become a still-dependent *man.*

No, Urgit was not wicked, Nik knew at last—only ignorant and weak because until now he had no need to be canny and strong. Until now? Perhaps too late. So why would he then wish to go with Nik on an icy trip to retrieve a dead bear and some walrus meat? Some sort of hunter instinct must be stirring in Urgit. But then, why did *any* of these grown men come around to suggest that Nik should take them along? And they *had*—at least seven had made the request—including Poona and Kotil, mere visitors from another village and themselves distinguished hunters.

Why?

As days passed, Nik became a little dizzy, in fact, with his improved stature among his people. Before, he had been tolerated as a village youngster—considered by others, in fact, to be the *peculiar* one of Arajik's two boys. Now suddenly, he was sought out. Asked to go on the trail for food with other villagers. Consulted on hunting matters?! Yet, he knew himself to be barely competent as a hunter. All right, he was better than he'd been before, true—but still had far, far to go. This was fact! One does not practice false humility when examining a matter within one's own head. Eh, he must speak to Kiti!

To soften her up, since he intended to ask a few direct questions, Nik got Sitok's permission to give her the bear pelt. Then he told her what had happened with Pah-nee on the trail.

"Only explain," he begged her. "Can the dog-boy be unable—"

"—The person you call a dog-boy is *most* able!"

"Then why would he not obey?"

Kiti shrugged off the question. "Some sleeps ago, this person had a thought about this friend of yours. And when someone spoke quietly with Pehl-son, he said that the idea held truth."

Nik waited what seemed a long time before he prompted, "And?"

"And?!" She seemed startled, then smiled. "On the matter of obeying? Here is no long-term problem for Nik. Has a grandson not *studied* these people? Their code is not ours—and this old woman suspects that they have no *trail* code at all . . . are in fact strangers to the hunt." She chuckled. "On the other matter, the thought which Pehl-son says holds truth . . . all will come clear before *tingmisut* flies off with the visitors."

How easy it was to forget that Pah-nee and his father must leave someday soon. Nik shook his head. For the first sleeps of their visit, he had felt impatient and trapped. No trip inland was possible while guests were visiting. Certainly not guests invited by their father. At least not when they were newly arrived. And most emphatically not guests living in their *igloo* and dependent for food on Sitok and yes, even Nik. But then in short time, he had been caught up first in the novelty of their differences and finally in the warm companionship of Pah-nee. Now he wished they would *never* go back to their dog-country, that place Pah-nee called *Miss-oo-luh*. He sighed. Sitok and he would go inland, find their parents, rapidly return. Pah-nee and her father would be waiting. Behl-son and Arajik would be overjoyed to see each other. He snorted. And Nik was having a pleasant dream! Oh that his imagination were *allowed* to arrange reality! He looked over to capture his grandmother's eyes.

"Another matter is even more troubling, *Ananatsiak.* All this attention from village men, these questions a boy gets about hunting—'Shall a hunter go on *this* day or on *that* one?' and 'What trail is better? Land or sea ice?' *Phfft!* What does Nik know?!"

"*Ai-ee!* The glorious hunter!" Kiti laughed heartily.

But this was no matter for mirth. "*Ananatsiak* knows her younger grandson is not yet even a *good* hunter! Certainly not someone to give advice."

Grandmother raised her eyebrows, Yes. She agreed. Now she walked over to sit on the *iglerk* and with narrowed eyes and a cocked head observe him where he sprawled on floor robes.

"Nik is serious in his questioning? He truly *does not know* the reason for this sudden favor among hunters?"

The boy stared over at her. He raised his eyebrows, kept them high to show his affirmation and puzzlement. Yes, he was serious. No, he didn't know.

Kiti chuckled. "True, Nik's skills are shaped but not yet sharpened, although he has shown himself to be valiant and surprisingly sensible. But the reason hunters seek his advice?" Her eyes narrowed and a smile crinkled up. "Truly?! Nik is unaware?"

"Grandmother!" This serious matter was nothing to be teased about.

"Eh. Nik has proven himself to have something which every hunter in this village desires and admires more than skill."

The boy looked about. He owned nothing but his clothing and a few rough tools and weapons, his hunting bag. He had made himself a new spear rather than return to the bluff where he lost his old one to the musk oxen. ***"What,*** Grandmother?"

Her eyes crinkled. "One had believed Nik to be more attuned to the ways of this village," she chuckled.

"Now is no time for riddling," Nik said impatiently.

"Eh, any time at all is right for a good riddle!" she teased.

"So what does someone HAVE!?" the boy demanded, his ears going red and his eyes narrowing.

Kiti raised both her arms to him, bare palms outward, fingers splayed, the signal for surrender. "What the boy has," she said slowly with great expression, "is *incredibly good luck!"*

CHAPTER 12.
NIK THE HUNTER;
SITOK THE ARTIST

The anticipated search inland suffered two setbacks. First, Sitok's wounds. His shoulder had to be re-set and he needed time for his body to mend. Second, inexperienced Nik had eight mouths to feed before he could cache any more food for the trip. Indeed, he would certainly have to *remove* some of the cached food in order to feed the people dependent on this *igloo*. Besides themselves and Pehl-son and Pah-nee, besides Aunt Saruna and Urgit, there was now Nuko to receive generous portions of the richest provision.

Nik thought sometimes that his grandmother would starve the people including herself before she would let that dog go hungry. Kiti declared that this *kringmerk,* this sled dog, had earned a place in the household—right up on the *iglerk,* too, among robes on the sleeping ledge. She said that Nuko was the great-great grandchild of a dog named Nuna that she had known long ago, a *kringmerk* having a pure Inupiat spirit. This dog Nuko, she insisted, had confirmed her ancestry and was now fully welcome in the *igloo.* The strong bond between Kiti and Bonnie had been toughened when the visitor insisted on saving Nuko.

Nik contended that space was too small, what with seven at a meal and five people on the *iglerk* for sleep time— but to no avail. *Ananatsiak* was resolute. Yes, Kiti seemed to be in league with Pah-nee, especially where that dog was concerned. Unable to reason with them on the matter, unsuccessful even at teasing them into submission, Nik grimly reminded them of what happened to Sedna when she allied herself with a sled dog. Ah, Sedna—forced by her fierce *kringmerk* husband to dispatch her litters of dog-children on the water, where they floated south to become all the pale-skinned, heavy-eyebrowed, hairy people who do not live in the Arctic. That Sedna, whose parents failed her, so that she finally sank to the sandy bottom where she rules today as Queen of the Icy Seas.

"Sedna was forced by her father," Kiti reproved him. "Besides, it happens that no one plans to mate with Nuko, no more than with any other member of the present household."

Nik should know by now that it was not possible to win an argument with *Ananatsiak.*

And to end the dispute Kiti added, "Nuko is family—as Arajik will agree when he returns—and she is entitled." When the privileged *kringmerk* was finally past danger, then *yes*—the old woman would accede to Pah-nee's entreaties and allow Nuko to stay on the *iglerk* in the visitors' bubble.

But for now, his grandmother's words rang with finality. No more discussion. Nik tried to understand the strong tie as he watched Kiti finger the disfigured lobe of her ear. Yes, it was the great-grandmother of Nuko's mother who as a pup had fastened her sharp teeth on Kiti's ear while the child toddled on the ground away from her mother's hood. *Ee-ee,* a distinguished bloodline. And yes, he too respected Nuko. He trusted and admired the courageous creature. But she was, after all, a *dog.*

The older woman nursed Sitok and still to some extent Saruna, although Urgit's aunt seemed much stronger. Kiti also continued to instruct Bonnie in care of the sled dog. More, Kiti practiced prudence with the food supply, although no one went hungry. Nik knew she was thinking not only of Nuko but also of the coming trip inland, the need not to take any more than necessary from the caches now because all would be needed later. Grandmother Kiti was sensitive to Nik's limitations as a hunter. She knew well that with Sitok unable to take the trail, all responsibility for food day to day rested on her younger grandson. Nothing was wasted. Kiti also made sure the household looked and smelled good—which meant that she assigned tasks to Nik and now to Urgit and even to Pah-nee . . .

"—Certainly it is appropriate for Nik to continue his former job of emptying the waste bladder following each sleep. No one could wish a guest to be given this most unpleasant among household tasks."

Kiti checked furs daily to see that all were in good condition—"Here are needle and sinew for Pah-nee. A youngster can finish mending that rip."

Or to Urgit, "The hunter's outer furs are matted from the trail. The scraping knife is beside the lamp." Although women did the mending expertly, *Inuit* adult men as well as women were expected to keep their own apparel clean and glossy. When not in use, the *kamik* (boots) and outer furs, the *silapak,* were to be dried if necessary, then vigorously brushed, folded down and stored safely overnight in a waterproof bladder or hide bag. So if Urgit did not begin immediately on this task he should have undertaken when he entered the *igloo* and without her suggesting it, she would fix the young man twice her height and weight with a long, steady gaze and place *silapak* and knife directly into his hands. No further action was necessary, for Urgit held *Ananatsiak* in awe.

Kiti of course tended the lamp, making sure that the extra one in Pehl-son's adjoining snow house also had plenty of the golden seal oil and well-trimmed wicks. Kiti always kept track of who was doing what in which place. During spare time usually spent visiting with Sitok while his torn body healed, she worked on the new bearskin. She would make something wonderful with it, Nik knew. Only see how gently she handled that huge rich pelt of ivory hue! But she refused to tell her plan for its use—not to him or to anyone.

Each day had fewer moments of light as winter deepened. Soon—and certainly by the time the brothers would leave to go inland—nothing but moon, stars, and spirit lights would brighten the way. For once glad to be young and inexperienced, Nik knew he was not compelled by local practice to hunt with villagers—although with his strange new rank, the men invited him daily. Considered a man, Sitok—if uninjured—would have had to go with some frequency or be considered selfish.

Nik was not stingy, but he did have an agenda that villagers did not share. Even with a fair portion of their whale meat still in storage, and a not-so-fair part of the walrus, along with seal that Sitok and he had captured, Nik sensed an urgent need to collect beyond daily needs so that he might even continue to cache. Building to their reserve was not likely if he hunted with the group, where all was shared according to need. Immediate need. And when Potok pronounced "need," as he usually did, these days, he continued to ignore not only Urgit and Saruna in Nik's household, but also the two visitors who always ate with them. Still, if this *good fortune* Kiti spoke of was with Nik truly . . . *ahmi,* who could foresee the future?!

The boy went onto ice near the village for daily provision—for fish and sometimes successfully seal. Most times when asked, Pehl-son would sigh and give permission for Pah-nee to accompany him. And as the dark days passed, Nik and the dog-boy were actually able to take a little food out for storage on the prairie. Pehl-son and Pah-nee did not eat much, Nik reflected. With so little fat stored on their bodies, he wondered how they could survive times of famine in their own village.

Bonnie and Nik had almost reached the seals, three cows and a bull on a few flat rocks above the sea, airing themselves to get rid of the annoying sea lice. Nik was excited because he and Pah-nee were crawling here successfully in full view of the creatures. He could almost taste the warm liver . . . the skin lined with blubber . . . and oh, the warm blood broth sliding down his throat. He rolled onto his side and flapped his arm, hoped that Pah-nee had understood his earlier demonstration, and now continued forward slowly, using his elbows, dragging his legs held tightly together.

But then for no reason Nik could sense, the four beasts flopped off the rocks and took to water.

"*Ai-ee!*" His frustration bubbled up. Now they must go to find a seal hole on the ice. He had learned to wait, out there. He had learned to *attend* what he was doing, not let his imagination roam too far for too long while all movement halted at a seal hole. But he had not yet learned to *enjoy* this practice of patient focus.

"My fault," Pah-nee chattered as they walked out in search of *aglu* with a Nuko nicely recovering but not yet ready for harness. "Remembered to do all that other stuff—hey! I *was* a seal, there for a while. Even thought about fish and clams and sea snails—yum! What else do these guys eat, anyhow?"

Nik caught the questioning inflection. He smiled over at his friend, not having understood one word of the chatter.

"So there we are," Bonnie continued, "Nik, crawling so carefully. I'm dragging my legs, kind of *swimming* along on my elbows. . . . Then? *I forget to scratch!* Some seal, huh?

So I spooked 'em!"

Spooked? Something like *soospuk?* But Pah-nee was no fool! The sounds of the dog-boy's language were so often in the front of the mouth, Nik observed silently. *If his people had to open their mouths that much to talk, they would probably freeze their tongues.*

Nuko sniffed at what looked like a twist in a drift. "Here?" Nik murmured, using his spear to poke about gingerly. "Ee-ee, the seal's *aglu*—it is good."

Pah-nee used the spear Nik had made for him only to get fish, but the dog-child would stand silent with Nik above a seal hole for a long time and without complaint. The Inupiat boy set the floater, placed his utensils on the ice, brought out the *two* rings of bearskin he carried these days, tied Pah-nee's and then his own about the calves over their fur boots.

Under shrouded moon and reluctant stars, without even the glow and glimmer of spirit lights, those bright specters north and overhead, Nik with his friend stood hunched above the seal hole, mittened fists on cheeks, elbows on knees, bottoms in the air. They remained nearly silent and motionless through the long black afternoon and evening and then through the night and the following morning. No, Nik did not like lingering at an *aglu*—and he never would. But even that long wait was easier with a companion.

From time to time, he would reach slowly into his hunting bag and pull up something to chew—silently—after giving a portion to Pah-nee. One or the other might creep away to answer nature's call behind a hummock. The dog-boy insisted on privacy for them both at such times. Nik respected this odd *Kalunait* custom, even if he did not understand it.

Sitok lay on the sleeping ledge waiting for skin, muscles and tendons to heal. He was learning a new kind of patience.

Instead of going out to hunt, he did the only other thing he *knew* to do—lie still and *think* about hunting. He realized as time passed that he had never before possessed such periods of leisure, nor wanted to. Nor had he ever before contemplated hunting—only done it. Without consideration. Ever. Now, idle thoughts circled to catch each other and flow upward like formed smoke.

Sea and ice beneath *kamik*,
Sky churning color up beyond the *nuilak,*
Inupiat beside the dogs in front,
Sled behind, with runners hissing smoothly,
On slick sea ice.
A master's line held snugly in a mitten
To sizzle through the air . . .
All is well.

After he heard the chant aloud, he experimented to find a tune which lent itself to the word bones and to their marrow of meaning. Shy, he lifted a robe and sent the song down into the furs. Beside the lamp at the far end of the sleeping ledge, the *iglerk,* Kiti scraped at the white bearskin. Although her scraper and the fingers which held the tool never slowed, a broad and private grin split her face.

Out on the prairie and inland plains, Sitok had heard the rhythm of his brother's poetry dispatched with bright melody into the air. The older brother had displayed neither approval nor disapproval to Nik—nor for that matter, appeared to show much interest at all. But privately, he had thrilled and swelled with pride in talented Nik, had gloried in those clear notes that the boy sent out to ride the wind.

Sila, the outer and inner worlds—the environment and the soul-spirit. Hunter and poet. Every *Inupiat* man and woman knew that the one side was incomplete without the other. And Sitok, too, knew it to be so. . . .

155

Sedna sings in deafening tones tonight.
One hears her mighty voice
In the thunder of the tide
And the crack and boom of heaving ice.
And in quiet moments,
Someone hears seals chirping on the rocks
And walrus barking at the lead.

Can it happen
That a gift is on its way?

The grandmother only smiled. She knew that a single word from her or from anyone—even of approval and encouragement—would send her grandson's timid efforts scuttling off to some hidden recess of his mind. Big Sitok, the man of physical action since the day he left his mother's hood to join the outer world. But always tangled and perplexed by flux of spirit, by that inner world of chant and performance.

Kiti chuckled softly and reached up to rub her right ear lobe. Eh, this winter was to be a time of great growth for two boys. They were nephews, not grandsons. For their father Arajik was her youngest brother—and even *he,* Arajik, did not know. But whatever the relationship, she loved Arajik and both his boys far more strongly than she could ever love herself.

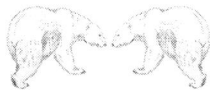

Bonnie jostled his arm, and Nik automatically looked to the jiggling float flag, then picked up his long lance and held it high, waiting. When the flag began to settle back, he plunged the killing spear through the hole—and struck *nathek,* the seal. He hung on through the floundering, Bonnie rapidly enlarging the hole with a snow knife. Then they hauled their dying seal onto ice at their feet.

With his *ulu,* the sharp semi-circular knife having so many uses, Nik cut a small incision to remove the liver. From this he took one big bite before handing it to Pah-nee. After the dog-person closed his eyes to first taste and then return the dripping organ to him, Nik cut off one more generous portion and dropped it into the *aglu.* Then the Inupiat put his mouth to the seal's nose and breathed deeply three times.

"*Nathek* the seal came for air, and here it is," he said. "The two young hunters thank her for giving herself. It happens that a family needs her meat and blubber and oils and sacs when Sitok and his younger brother go to seek Arajik and Mawena."

Pah-nee narrowed her eyes as she heard the words, only "Kiti" and "Sitok" familiar. Then she smiled.

Dr. Cliff Belson looked up from sheaves of paper spread across robes on the sleeping shelf, the *iglerk.* "No, Sweetheart, I didn't worry a bit! Made up my mind that Destiny has written our lives, so fear is useless."

"You're such a philosopher!" Bonnie knew that he was not. Pop was a worrier.

He nodded cheerfully. "That, and I gave Wutik for services rendered a couple of razor blades plus three needles from our sewing kit."

"Oh?" Bonnie beat dry snow from each part of her outer fur, then folded everything carefully, as Kiti had taught her, and pushed it into a caribou skin bag.

"And in return, Wutik keeps track of you two without your knowing it, makes sure you're ok—and keeps me posted."

Bonnie snorted.

"Best trade I ever made! Wutik's carving every bone he can get his hands on with those blades—and I sleep much better when you decide to go out and sit on ice."

"Those needles, Pop? Any woman in the village—except maybe Kiti—would sew and mend for you forever, just to get her fingers on a steel needle."

"Except Kiti?"

"She already has a few. She showed me—keeps 'em in a little membrane bag of blubber. In her Big Feed. Warms them behind her ears before use. Treasures! Of course she still uses bone needles—especially the rounded ones—for the toughest skins. You know, boots and boats—the *kamik* as well as *kayak* and *umiak.*"

"Good! You're picking up words! But where do you suppose Kiti—"

"—Arajik. Nik's dad—the man you say invited us but who's not here now."

Belson shook his head in wonder.

Bonnie planted herself before her father accusingly. "What **about** those needles and razor blades? You always say not to muddle a culture by throwing in something new that they can't make or get for themselves!"

"Guilty. Do as I preach, not as I practice?"

"Hunh! Anyway, Sitok already has a sharp metal knife his dad gave him, if I understand it right. He used it on the bear."

"That fellow Arajik got around, all right. Hope he's *still* getting around! They're going to look for him, you know."

"I know—but when?"

"After we go, and when Sitok and Nuko are well enough."

"All the villagers?"

He shook his head. "Nik and Sitok only, as I understand."

"I've been wondering why Nik tries so hard to cache every bit of extra food. Now I know."

Belson nodded. "Sitok's accident will delay them even more than our visit. Oh yes, are those caches round, honey?"

Bonnie frowned. "Roughly, yes, I guess—they sure aren't squared off! You've seen 'em."

"Only from a distance, the ones here. So let's talk in circles." Belson grinned and put a clean sheet of paper on top of his stack. "Proper heading. 15 November 1935—eh?" He studied the thermometer he had hung from a chink of ice. "And twenty-eight degrees Fahrenheit—that's here inside where it's warmer."

Bonnie said nothing.

"Now a list, sweetheart. Circular items in the culture."

The girl hesitated. "Dad, *not* just the culture! Today, when we broke open a seal's breathing hole?—which is round, by the way. But then Nik showed me this circular ledge—a hollowed out half-doughnut above the water line."

"Ok. Seals build that as a resting place for their babies." He did not write.

"And the horizon's always round, up here, because with no trees or mountains you can see forever—when there's a little light—in all directions. We climb up onto a pressure ridge—the whole world's spread out, three hundred sixty degrees. Round!"

He nodded. "Sure, ok." Still, he didn't write.

"Ok. An *igloo*, then—any snowhouse, even our little blister of an *igloo* attached."

Now he wrote.

"The skylight, that clear-ice capstone from freshwater at the very top—" she pointed—"and the stone food dish we melted it in before we refroze it."

Belson shrugged. "Probably depends on the shape of the stone they found."

"But to work as a capstone, wouldn't it have to be round?"

Belson agreed. "Roughly." But he didn't write. "What else?"

"Wrestling ring! You know, at the drum feast? Drum duel ring, too—and how about the drums themselves?"

Belson scribbled on the page, then looked up. "Our drums are round, too."

"You asked about *round,*" Bonnie told him. "That big blanket of hides sewn together for the blanket toss? Round. The *umiak,* Pop! Who ever heard of a round boat?"

"Round*ed.* Several other cultures, I'm told. But I don't think any of the others resemble an *umiak.*" He wrote. He knew that rounded ocean craft existed elsewhere in the world, but his daughter did not. He also knew that the *umiak* had unique features.

"The hole for ice fishing?"

"Seems only natural, somehow."

"Hunh! At home, we'd probably square it off—"

He laughed. "Probably buy a template at Woolworth's—"

"—Right!" Bonnie giggled. "For whenever we went fishing or sealing through that Missouri River ice at St. Joe." Belson's pencil was ready, nested under his jaw.

"The rounded knife for clipping off food at their lips? Other uses, too."

He nodded and said *"ulu"* while he wrote.

"Bone or driftwood needles, whittled circular—but not our steel ones."

Again he wrote. "Anything else?"

"I'll let you know."

He was counting. "Nine for sure, with a couple three more iffy. Hmm. Culturally, a basic shape in daily use. . . ."

PHYL MANNING

Environmentally, too. More than coincidence? Have to chat with the statisticians when we get back."

"Does it matter?"

Belson laughed, nodded. "Still, Sweetheart, if you've happened onto a cultural theme . . ."

Bonnie shrugged impatiently, was silent for a while. Then, "Pop, I'm going to make a big dinner, right before we leave. Use up that food we brought but haven't needed."

Her father raised his eyebrows and stuck out his lower lip. "Much of what we brought needs to be *cooked*—at least warmed, most of it. And you're sure we have enough?"

"Not for the whole village. But *yes,* for Kiti and Nik, Sitok, Urgit and Saruna." She laughed, then added "and Nuko," nodding with excitement. "I'll plan everything ahead!"

"Just remember, these are **big eaters,** sweetie. Not very easy, someone from our culture fixing them a satisfactory meal . . ."

But Bonnie was examining supplies, pulling out bags and packages. "Pickles, olives, peanuts and peanut butter, cheese, salt, sugar—ah, powdered milk. Now I see why you put everything into bags—oh, a few cans?—fruit cocktail. We'll use up everything we have!"

"We need to carry any metal containers back with us—can't clutter up the ground—but empty's easier than full."

"Flour! We have lots of flour!"

"How about biscuits? Then melt down some seal blubber to make gravy?"

Bonnie wrinkled her nose. "We have a package of jelly."

Belson laughed.

"For meat—bacon or jerky, d'you think?"

"Bacon **and** jerky! Trot out the works. Once we board the plane, everything edible left over is excess baggage."

"We'll leave any remaining food right here!"

He nodded. "Sure, if they like it. The paper and cardboard containers will burn—we'll show them. But the cans really cannot stay up here."

Bonnie was thinking. "We'll have a *feast!*"

Her father laughed. "I dunno, sweetie. What we have's mostly 'ingredients.' Nothing familiar to them; and besides, there's no fuel. That's why they don't cook."

"We *will* cook, though, you and I. Slowly, over the seal oil lamp." Then, "Can you use that heat to fix bacon on your knife, d'you think?"

"Good idea! I better start right now, though—it's going to take forever."

"And please save every single drop of the grease for me!"

"Big project. I'll help, but—you *sure* you want to do this?"

"—Positive!" Then she laughed. "You always say, 'Challenge builds character.'"

"Actually, that's *adversity.* Challenge all the time only builds blood pressure."

"Anyway, I want to make something circular—a big round cake or pie . . . sure could use some eggs, though."

"Talk to Kiti. Heaven knows what's in her Big Feed."

"Pop! No chickens are up here, and you know it!"

His eyes twinkled as he tapped his papers and put them neatly into a folder. "More than chickens lay eggs, city girl."

CHAPTER 13.
RELATIONSHIPS

Sitok reproached Nik one evening just before the sleep, "Someone might have told his elder brother that poetry is not *so* difficult."

Nik sat between the food bowl and the robe-covered *iglerk*, so that he could hand over choice morsels to his brother.

"Would a favored Grandmother kindly loan her drum?" Sitok asked Kiti formally, and she brought it to him.

Sitok twisted in the furs until his left arm was free to use the beater, his right to steady the instrument. Such movement with that left shoulder would have been impossible before it was replaced in its socket. Now he gave a few experimental knocks on the rim, then started a regular triple beat . . . *Thum-pa-pa, Thum-pa-pa.* In a voice which at first quavered uncertainly, he began.

> Once, were two brothers,
> Alike as a walrus and seal.
> One big and strong, unsightly to look at
> But heavy in value on hazardous trail
> And free with his giving.
> The other, the seal, was nervous and cunning,
> Head filled with visions and feet always running!
> Both were of Sila—
> The elder without
> And the younger within.

Nik exploded with joy. He did not care, suddenly, that this was his fourteenth winter. He hugged Sitok, rubbing his nose against his cheek, slapping his back until he realized that the sounds Sitok made were shouts of pain.

He pulled away. "A person must forgive—" he began remorsefully.

"—Nothing to pardon," Sitok gasped, "but Nik *must* stop pounding on someone's shoulder!"

Beaming, Nik shouted, "The elder brother has rehearsed while the younger was freezing his tail feathers on the hunt!"

"Only fair," Sitok retorted, "since that elder with Arajik has been feeding a useless child for many years!"

The two grinned at each other. Then Pehl-son's voice filled the *igloo*. He with Pah-nee crouched at the low arch which joined their quarters.

In formal *Inupiaq:* "It happens that this intrusion must be excused. These *Kalunait,* these lowly dog-persons, did not realize before that Sitok was an artist."

The boy in the bed-robes flushed with pleasure. Then he gave the typical Inupiat response. "One's vile wolf-howls have disturbed some honored guests. This one begs forgiveness."

Pah-nee looked up at her father. "Did you invite them yet?"

"No." Pehl-son looked at Kiti, cleared his throat. "The airplane, *tingmisut,* will come for us after four sleeps—a day we call *Sunday."*

"Hoo-oo!" exclaimed Kiti and both brothers in distress.

Nik stepped toward their guests. "It may be that *tingmisut* will not arrive!"

The man looked at the boy and read his pain with surprise. He knew that Bonnie and Nik had spent much time together. But he also knew what their visit had meant for their host family in the consumption of extra food, the taking of extra care and time and patience with ignorant newcomers. And the visit might also have kept the two brothers from an earlier inland search for Arajik and Mawena. Had the boys been on the tundra, Sitok might not have been injured.

Belson nodded at Nik slowly. *"Ee-ee,* Yes . . . a storm could occur . . . or the spirit of *tingmisut* could fail."

Bonnie was as unsettled as Nik. The five weeks had flown by. "Pop, *I* don't want to go—and neither do *you!* Can't you cancel the plane or postpone it or something?"

"How?" He grinned at her woefully. "Actually do sometimes wish I'd arranged a later pickup. But who knew what kind of reception we'd get?"

"You!" She was close to tears. "You've always said your *Inupiat* are friendly and hospitable, caring—" she broke off with a sob.

Nik did not know what was bothering the dog-boy, but he knew what was bothering *him*—their departure. He, too, wanted to let tears fall instead of keeping them fiercely in check.

"Yes, they are all those things, a loving people in *general* . . . . But in *particular?* Who knew? What's turning out to be a speedy five weeks could have been a very long time to sit hungry and neglected in a snowdrift."

Bonnie had herself under control. "Pop, the invitation?"

Cliff Belson turned back to Kiti. "It happens we brought food for emergency," he said, hoping their hostess would not take offense, "but you have been so generous, we have not touched our supply."

"Only a little oatmeal," Bonnie corrected, flushing at the recollection.

He ignored her.

"You ate our poor fare," Kiti said gravely, "and it happens that we had plenty because Sedna has been generous this winter—perhaps to favor the children of her children." The two dog-people. The woman could have no idea of how dissimilar their food had been to that which was familiar to her visitors from the south.

"We do not have enough to feed the village," Belson continued, "but we wish to provide a meal for your family, Urgit and Aunt Saruna of course included."

Kiti smiled, nodded, "And Nuko."

Belson acknowledged her addition with a grin. "In the evening following three sleeps from now," the man concluded.

The Inupiat looked at each other. For the boys, this was a future time beyond comprehension. Nik was excited by the prospect, Sitok distressed, Kiti doubtful. She knew how little Pehl-son and Pah-nee ate. No *Inuit*, she believed, could stay alive long on even three times what these dog-persons consumed both together!

Besides, where did they *keep* this food they spoke of? In their parka pockets? Among the thin white leaves of hide that Pehl-son used for making marks? She knew they had no great cask of food packed in their snowhouse, some odd little packets only, and some heavy circular things of a hard material. And she knew that anything less than great plenty would leave her family with stomachs rumbling.

"We shall be pleased to eat the food of *Kalunait* in the same spirit that they eat the food of *Inupiat*," she said graciously. There. That left them room to eat very little, should the flavors not appeal. And most likely, they would eat very little in any case—because so far as Kiti could tell, there would be very little to eat.

Two large seals and one small one were lashed to the sled, for Sedna had once again been generous. Alone, Nik did not want to go back to the village, not yet. He staked the dogs and walked back toward the open lead. The northern sky crackled and glowed and shimmered with a slow wash of color, a brilliant fall with an encompassing current that streamed sometimes upward, sometimes down, often sideways. And such display with silvered moonlight elsewhere made this day and this place and this time alone something which he did not want to end.

He heard the lonely *skree-ee!* of a wandering bird above, listened to the *cree-ee-eak* and **boom!** of ice as it rearranged itself somewhere nearby. He climbed a pressure ridge, heedless of danger, pulled from the hunting bag strapped on his shoulder both circles of bear fur, then arranged one for his buttocks, the other for his feet.

Then he sat at the top of the ridge, facing northeast to survey his world. From a pocket inside his parka, his *illupak*, he pulled a slab of *muktuk,* chewed it slowly to fully savor the crackling richness. He touched the sharp ice crystals of the ridge, smelled the fresh dry cold, felt every part of him attune to the surroundings. North sky hues and tints cast color on the ice and bathed his eyes until—full to bursting with the beauty—he looked over to fasten his gaze on the lead. Here was Sedna's mysterious waterway, black with moonlit sparks atop each ripple. Pack ice beyond, seeming permanent and stable but—as all knew—a traveling giant with a secret destination.

Movement at the corner of his eye brought his head around slowly. Heaving from the lead further north was a white sea bear with one good-sized yearling beside her back legs. The two animals came his way, but Nik was downwind.

He signaled the moaning dogs to silence, then himself remained motionless. His spear was over on the sled. He had only a knife with him—and besides, he had no reason to kill. For once, he was not hungry, and his and Sitok's caches overflowed. Capture from this trip would feed everyone easily until the *kalunait* left and the brothers began their journey.

As the sow lumbered past, between Nik's icy crest and the lead from which she had emerged, he saw that she was bulging with new pregnancy. Most likely, she had already built an ice cave nearby on some *siku*, some ice island, where her tiny cub would be born. She would nurse her baby day and night until her own hunger became too much. Then the yearling would keep the small one warm and safe while she, lean and ravenous, went out to find food for all.

Graceful and long, the bear with her child was nearly out of sight to the south along the lead. Pastel glimmers from the northern sky reflected on the hind quarters of the swaying beast. She had ignored Nik and his team totally, even though she must have sensed their presence. No move toward the sled, although she could not help, as she got downwind, but smell what that sled contained. If she turned, Nik would have to go protect his staked dogs and the food. But he knew, somehow, that she would not—no more than he would consider killing her as she walked forth. She too was not hungry. Her thoughts were on her ice cave, on her family to come.

And Nik's thoughts—eh! He waited for the bears to vanish on the far ice before beginning to drum absently upon an icy block beside him. After a time, and echoing the practice of his people for at least five thousand years, he opened his mouth to free with chant and melody what his heart could no longer contain.

The circle of this wide winter world
Is bright with moon today.

The soul is reaching up
As spirits play
Their noisy color game
Within the northern sky.
Ai-ee!

One's spirit sings unbidden
As creatures pass upon their errands:
Food and shelter.
Walrus, seal, whale—sea bear!
Wolverine . . . And inland . . .
Caribou and hare,
Fish and muskox, too.
Someone wonders what these others ponder.
Ai-ee!

How can such beauty be
Without exploding all around
And draining the horizon?
Ai-ee!

The heart is full,
The throat is tight with ache.
For now the friend will go away
While one's own home is here.
Hoo-oo-oo . . .
Ai-ee!

Soon Pah-nee would go . . . the *real* source of his thoughtful mood. His first friend ever. Nik had forced himself to ignore the building sadness until now, when the strength of their relationship came out in song. He had known all along that the dog-person would leave. As light must always follow dark and summer follow winter. The mood broken by the reality, he folded up his furs and slid down from the ridge. He walked over to unstake and hitch his team, and they were off, runners packed and smoothly iced, hissing on thinly crusted snow above the frozen sea.

The meal Bonnie and Belson served was one to remember and tell of later as a lamp tale. Most filling was a fluffy cloudstuff Bonnie kept cooking as they ate. She used a broad knife similar to Sitok's over a big, smoky seal oil fire on the lamp. Something she called "biscuits" her guests called *pees-keets*. And they used their *ulus* to spread on these their choice of jam or peanut butter: *cham* or *peent-pootr*. Two kinds of meat were served. Rich and warm, the bacon was a little reminiscent of fresh walrus meat heavily marbled from close to the blubber. The other, the jerky, was thin and stringy in appearance, looked to the Inupiat like desiccated caribou hide, dry as stone. But all knew Pah-nee and Pehl-son would not serve leather for food, and they picked up a piece and found it to make magic in the mouth. Almost as salty as the sea, it enlarged with every chew!

Other wonders. What looked like pale seedless berries without skin did not taste like berries and were called "peanuts," *peents.* " Yet, what looked like animal gut floating in its own juices but then *did* taste like berries—the best ones late in summer before the freeze following a moon of much sunshine. *Varoot kakatayer,* that food was named, "fruit cocktail." Olives were perceived as small dark eyeballs, *ah-rees,* and sweet green thumb-shapes with bird-flesh covering were pickles *(peek-os).*

At last, Pah-nee brought two circles of something pale yellow that steamed. *Hot blubber!* Nik thought with great excitement.

"My lord!" Belson exclaimed. "You made a miracle—actual custard pies!"

Bonnie laughed. "And Pop, please translate *exactly* what I say." She presented the dessert. "Please tell them that one discovered these old muskox droppings on the prairie, that only a *soospuk* such as Pah-nee would waste effort to carry them home. That these guests will be great fools to spend their energy in chewing and swallowing."

Belson proudly translated, and everyone burst out laughing, for Pah-nee had indeed caught the pattern for gift offerings in the High Arctic. Each guest held out a hand to receive the generous portion served. Nik took a big bite and thought that this certainly was not blubber. He had his bare palm out for more before he swallowed the last bite. Unlike most fare among familiar tastes but present with some frequency in Bonnie's offering was an unaccustomed *sweetness,* something all found themselves enjoying.

Bonnie had extra food prepared in case of emergency, but finally no one could eat another bite. Then Kiti spoke up, still chewing on custard, her face unreadable. "One wishes to say *nakorami,* thank you, for this fine meal prepared by Pehl-son's Pah-nee, his daughter of many talents."

"—Daughter?" Nik examined the *igloo* automatically, as if the father had been secretly harboring some other child, this one female, whose name happened also to be Pah-nee.

"*Ee-ee,*" Pehl-son assured him. "We—your grandmother Kiti and this *kalunait* decided everyone could finally know."

Nik stared at the youngster with whom he had shared for nearly one full moon most hours awake as well as many hours asleep. Then he looked to Kiti for some sign of this being a joke, finally to Pehl-son himself.

"*OWKA!*" No! he shouted finally. *NO!* Complete denial. He stood up, looked at each of the others, at all but

Pah-nee herself. They all watched him curiously, but no one said anything. "Pah-nee has been the companion and friend and helper of Nik—*no girl could be that!*"

Still no one spoke except that Bonnie pulled repeatedly at her father's arm, demanding translation. Nik felt heat rise to redden the very tops of his ears.

Belson stood up also, his head reaching almost to the capstone. "Wait a moment, Son. No harm's been done."

"This *inuk* is the *son* of Arajik and no other!" Nik stormed rudely. He could not think, only *feel*—and what he felt was deep embarrassment. They had made of him a *soospuk,* a nitwit and a fool. He turned with no more words and went into his own adjoining snowhouse, where he threw himself into outdoor furs and was gone by the time Kiti came through to check. Outside, he ran and leaped, kicked and stamped, then pounded drifts with his fists until at last he found himself standing alone on the tundra, breathing hard, exhausted. He trudged back to the village, stood outside Pehl-son's small *igloo* and looked at the friendly lampglow flickering through ice. Friendly for those inside. . . . They would not be missing witless Nik!

At last thoroughly chilled but still in anguish, he crept through the main tunnel into the larger snowhouse, silently removed his outer furs, his *silapak,* knocked off the ice, brushed and then folded them, put them into the hide bag where they belonged. Then he dug deep into sleep robes on the *iglerk*. He would like to creep into one of the folds and disappear forever. Would be pleased to have the *iglerk* sink down and down through ice and permafrost to dissipate entirely in the hot center of the earth. Would welcome *nanuk* the sea bear hunkering through the tunnel past the baffle to seize him and dispatch him bloodily and drag him to her lair. Would, would, would. . . .

"If Nik could fit into Kiti's parka hood, into her *amoutik*, then she would *put* him there!" Having first thrown back his sleeping robes to let morning cold capture his attention, Kiti now hovered over him in the otherwise deserted *igloo*. Her hands were on her hips, and she stared fiercely into his startled eyes.

"It happens that someone in this family acts like a babe just learning to walk!"

"Agh!" In one motion, he pulled up the robe and turned over with extra folds bunched under his stomach.

But now everything above him, every furry blanket resting on the *iglerk*, was suddenly flung away to land in a heap on the ice floor. He sat up, rubbed his eyes and yawned. Although he had been awake and brooding for a while, he pretended to have just now awakened. She might pity him, he thought, might give him a chance to collect his wandering spirits.

Then he snorted softly. He thought such a ruse would work on *Ananatsiak?* She always *knew.* He pulled himself up and off the sleep ledge with a sigh, unbagged his furs. She had even known about Pah-nee! Eh, had deliberately deceived him, said not one word!

But his rising was not good enough. The woman came over and faced him, arms akimbo. "It happens that a boy child will speak with his grandmother on this matter!"

"Peace!" Nik protested. "Let someone dress first?"

"And is a tongue required to do the fastenings on clothes?" she asked the arching roof.

Sarcasm! She is extremely angry. But oh, how he loved her—perhaps most of all when she was like this. He bit back a smile, felt his great resistance softening, his anger and confusion receding. She barely reached his shoulder. But she could scold, intimidate and shame—generally wear down anyone of any size into doing what she demanded. As Potok and Arajik and even big Unipak when he lived had grounds for knowing. Let alone her two grandsons, whom she bullied regularly, whenever she thought they needed it.

And did Nik need her harassment now? "There is tea?" he said aloud. Unlike most other families, Kiti preserved her large hoard of bush leaves collected in summer and served it in winter months for a beverage as well as a component for healing brews.

"*Ee-ee,* Yes." She handed him a small stone bowl deeply hollowed. In it was a steaming herbal drink. A *sir-ko,* this container, as Pah-nee would —*Hoo-oo!* A fresh wave of misery washed over him.

"Two questions, one must ask," Kiti continued. "Their answers should calm some wild spirits within a childish grandson." She waited and glared at him until he was looking at her steadily. *"Had Nik known Pah-nee to be a girl, would he have talked to her freely and taken her on the trail?"*

"Grandmother! Of course not."

"Eh!" The woman raised her eyebrows and sucked in breath. "So then she would learn all about the Inupiat people by sitting in a snowhouse chewing hides for over a moon."

Nik supposed so, yes. But that wasn't the point. *Ananatsiak* Kiti had tricked him. So had Pehl-son. So certainly had Pah-nee. He had been made to look a fool. Villagers would ridicule him when they learned. Nik had thought Pah-nee his friend.

"She confessed to Kiti, but not to Nik," he muttered now.

"*Confessed?* That someone female is thought to be a male requires *confession?* But Nik, no. She did not tell Kiti. Until last evening, she did not know that Kiti was aware. What harm was done?"

"Pehl-son told Kiti?"

"Owka, No—but an old woman has *eyes!* The child's walk, the budding of breasts noticed when she was inside without her *silapak.* The relationship with her father, especially that. A protective spirit."

Nik's head spun with this unexpected information. Mysterious clues about which he knew nothing.

"So then Kiti asked Pehl-son," his grandmother continued, "—oh, many sleeps ago. And he said *'Yes.'* He also explained his reason for letting everyone believe Pahnee to be his son."

"But girls aren't *supposed* to like the trail!"

"Not with a babe in the hood—nor not with one in the belly! But Pah-nee has neither."

Still. Nik felt stubborn and violated. He stood up, started for the porch to go outside.

"Owka! Someone has the second question. Nik did not respond when he was asked before."

Humbled by her revelations, the boy turned back obediently.

"What harm was done?"

Nik tightened his jaw. Did she truly not understand? He looked deeply into his grandmother's dark eyes.

"It happens that someone need not answer that question for Kiti—only for himself," she added.

Nik dropped his eyes. Yes, he would consider the answer. *Later.* He turned once more to leave, but again she spoke.

"It also happens that *tingmisut* comes today to take away the *Kalunait.* It is vital that Nik be present to bid farewell."

His grandmother was skilled at making statements that were really commands.

Quietly, *"Ee-ee,* he will be there."

Nik coiled his fishing sinew when he heard the metal bird, and he was standing silently between Sitok and Kiti when she gave to Pah-nee the beautiful white bear *amoutik,* the woman's parka with a special hood in back.

"It happens that a young *Kalunait* with red hair helped to save a grandson's life," the woman explained.

Bonnie hugged her for a long time, then clasped Sitok's right shoulder, not the injured one, and finally turned to Nik. He stared down at snow beneath the airplane, finally raised sullen eyes to meet hers. She reached inside her furs and brought out a roll of the same white leaves her father used when he made marks with that special stick, that *pencil.* Nik took what she handed him automatically, wishing immediately afterward that he had let it drop onto the snow. Now she looked at him with pain in her eyes, tears rising, turned and hurried up the ladder into the aircraft. Outlined in the doorway, she called back hastily and waved to all. Everyone but Nik waved back.

CHAPTER 14.
INLAND SEARCH

By the fifth dark afternoon of sledding southwest, Sitok and Nik had passed two landmarks Urgit described for them just before they left . . . the remains of an ancient cache with huge boulders atop a steep rise—and then two sleeps later, some gnarled plants twisted on the bank of a frozen creek. Nik insisted on examining these. Each plant stood on one firm foot anchored in snowy tundra. Sitok assured his younger brother that these were stunted examples of the very *trees* their father had described.

Trees? Arajik had reported these to be far taller than any *Inuk*. Their father said that standing at the base and trying to see the top caused neck pain. For this strange vegetation, though, Nik must look *down* to examine the tops. *Trees. . . .*

How does one find parents in an unfamiliar land? By the tenth sleep trailing south and west, they still had seen no sign of people—no sled tracks, no print of *kamik* or snowshoe, not even another cache. Not that so much would be visible, traveling as they did in fog and the full dark of each sunless winter day. As they got well south, and if the skies were not too cloudy, a short period of pale glow would come mid-day just as it had at home in early winter, here to indicate a time when the sun was lighting the *Kalunait* world below the horizon. Never more glow or moonlight, never more flickering spirit lights, than it took to see the rim of the nearest hill in the rolling land. Otherwise, black as the underwing of a wet raven. Nik did not trust the map Urgit marked out for them in snow before they left. Still, it was their only information from someone who had actually made the trip.

From someone who had Arajik as guide for going in, Nik muttered every time he reviewed the instructions, *and then Urgit himself being lost most of the time coming out.*

"We must not go so far south as to be on land beyond *Inuit.*" Sitok, as it turned out, was often anxious in these unfamiliar surroundings. He had always been attentive to the food supply—and for this, Nik was grateful. But he expressed misgiving over everything, these days. He reminded Nik many times between sleeps that the *Irkrelrete,* the Indians to the south, were known to be unfriendly. So Arajik had told them.

"Cruel as wolverines," Sitok said now, "they may hide behind their many trees, and kill both Inupiat boys before the *Irkrelrete* presence is known."

"Behind these trees?" Nik laughed, looking at the low shrubs and snow-covered sprouts surrounding them. "Who can fear such tiny warriors?" he wanted to know, "and why would they wish to kill someone?"

Sitok hesitated. "Perhaps to eat?" The echo in his voice told Nik that his brother had never considered reasons. But only the wolverine was thought to kill even without reason.

"Arajik *never* said such a thing!"

"But he did say they're dangerous," Sitok asserted.

True. Arajik had said so, yes—but had his assertion been made only to design a story all the more compelling? Like the strange tale Kiti sometimes told about an ice serpent who became a great *angakok,* a highly respected shaman of the tundra.

Nik hated having Sitok fearful—even though he believed that his brother's continual trepidation resulted from having inactivity forced upon him. Sitok had been a long time mending—was *still* mending, in fact. And instead of feeling blest by spirits as one of the few *Inuks* to survive bear attack, he had felt helpless and restless, uncomfortably dependent during all that time for recovery. Nik knew Sitok was apprehensive about this trip. Sitok more than anyone else knew how little the older brother could assist the younger if emergency occurred along the trail.

"Besides," Sitok continued, "what else is here for *Irkrelrete* to eat? What sign of game have the two travelers seen since they left the sea?"

"Nothing lately," Nik admitted. "But the sound of wolves is often heard in the distance—and where wolves are, food must be."

"*Ee-ee,* Yes—food consisting of the two brothers who hear them!" Sitok replied. "Along with the dogs that transport those brothers . . . tasty morsels all."

Nik laughed. "Arajik has said many times that wolves do not seek *Inuit.*"

"Then the large, pale creatures consume lemmings?!" Sitok asked with disgust. The boys had learned along this trail that a great many of these furry little rodents were required to make even one meal—and their tiny bones were troublesome, besides. After a few experiments, they agreed to wait until starvation threatened before they would chase down any more of the numerous but elusive and unsatisfying creatures.

"Perhaps wolves do dine on the furry scurriers—but why don't caribou eat them, as well?"

"Caribou do not eat meat."

Nik knew that. He hadn't thought of tiny lemmings as *meat.* "*Tuktu* the caribou leave the plains to go south for winter—perhaps this is the south to which they go!"

"Then caribou sign would be visible," Sitok argued. "Fur on these desiccated plants, perhaps? Manure—" His voice broke off. "Unless fresh, the droppings would be under snow," he conceded.

"If *Irkrelrete* of the southern tundra were to gaze upon the surface of the frozen sea, he would think coastal Inupiat feast on clouds and sky—for nothing is apparent to an unaccustomed eye. So it is for two ignorant brothers in this place."

Sitok did not respond, and Nik hoped this last, vast wisdom he had uttered would shut him up. The younger boy did not know where they were—although he and his brother, and very likely every dog besides, would always know exactly how to get back to their village.

But how were they to locate the parents? Would they not sled right past them? Urgit estimated the walking inland to have been nine sleeps beyond last summer's camp, and that camp was a spot they'd already passed. But remember, Nik told himself, although he did not say so to Sitok, Urgit was lost for many sleeps. In fact, how could he even *guess?*

Ananatsiak had faith, and Nik must remember that. "Urgit is not stupid," Kiti had scolded them right before they left. "He has given directions. Follow them! Use good sense besides, and—" she glanced at Nik—"enjoy good luck."

On the morning of the day following ten sleeps, Nik decided that they should start calling for their parents along the trail. Were Arajik and Mawena even alive? he wondered. Back at the village, he had been certain that they were. Here, he was not so sure. Was this trip complete folly? Then Nik shuddered as another thought came to him. Might Urgit be more clever than Nik or anyone suspected? Might he even be vicious?

Would he deliberately send them on a journey to Nowhere for the purpose of Nothing?

But why? Eh. If Sitok and Nik disappeared, then Urgit would gain stature in the village as a hero who came back from a killing place. Only that theory did not fit what Nik now knew of the talentless—yes—but basically mellow young man.

Still . . . it was Nik who had insisted continually that Urgit repeat his account of the summer. Nik who had pressured him and ridiculed him especially during the time before he and Aunt Saruna moved into their *igloo*. And again, it was Nik who tended to question and disbelieve everything Urgit reported. Would that criticism be enough reason for him to send them to destruction? Nik did not know.

Hoo-oo . . . What he *did* know was that Sitok could have used four or five more sleeps at home to gain additional strength before undertaking this rigorous journey over rough and unfamiliar land. So again, why had Nik pushed so hard for them to leave almost immediately after Pehl-son and Pah-nee flew away? Only two sleeps after, in fact, and then only because Nik declared that he would go by himself if his brother "did not wish" to accompany him. Sitok could finish his recuperation, Nik assured a disapproving Kiti, by lying on the sled along the trail.

No doubt, *Ananatsiak* had been right. Nik was a fool whenever he allowed the little boy inside him to rule. *A great hunter controls the spirits within.* His feelings. His emotion. . . . What must Pah-nee think of him? How he would like the chance to do again that evening of her meal. How he wished that he had handled himself more gracefully. Kiti had been a hunter when she was young, so the whispered tales suggested and so her skill and knowledge established. And his grandmother was the best woman—no! the best *person*— he had met so far in this life.

Pah-nee? Had Nik not been such a nitwit, he might hope that they would someday meet again. Might Pehl-son return next winter—when Arajik surely would be present!—and might he once again bring Pah-nee with him? Eh! Or perhaps he, Nik, could someday go south and find that female dog-person in the land of *Kalunait* to the south, in this place called *Miss-oo-luh*. He shivered. He must take a look at that packet she gave him when they left. He had brought it with him unopened, still carefully wrapped waterproof in layers of ptarmigan skin and lying safe and tantalizing in the bottom of his hunting bag. But he had not yet trusted himself to examine it.

Pah-nee. When Nik grows old enough and is a good hunter, might he find someone like her to marry? No, only one Pah-nee could exist in the world. And, he reminded himself, she did *not* exist—not in his world, not anymore. . . .

On the trip so far, Sitok would trot behind the sled for as long as he could—usually a short time—then sit aboard, hating to have to huddle into robes for warmth. He was perhaps too eager to get back the strength lost by his days on the *iglerk*. Twice between sleeps, and this late afternoon was one of those, he ran so long that he became limp and breathless, hollow eyed. Nik knew his brother had the right idea, but what if he took a hard fall? What if he reinjured himself? What would they do out here alone? If only impatient Nik had waited a few more days in the village.

The land lately was so rough and rocky that Nik had to offload the sled and re-ice runners at least three times between sleeps. Footing even for the dogs was treacherous, and Sitok's running like everything else was of course done mostly in full darkness. But to ask Sitok not to do something on which his mind was set was like requesting the spirit lights to cease their motion. After hot discussion, they finally reached a compromise. Sitok promised to run behind Nik and in Nik's tracks along the trial.

This afternoon, the younger boy slowed the pace to reduce danger not only to the icing on sled runners but also to his brother, who at this very moment followed Nik closely as the younger boy loped along beside the dogs. Shadowed against the horizon, limned silver under a sky filled with moonlight were *trees*, small groves of them more frequent. Not the sort of tree to cause neck pain in viewing the top—but taller than either of the brothers. Nik chuckled as he bounced along. Much taller than the first tree they had recognized as such—that desiccated-looking knot of tangled sinew the size of his palm on a stalk shorter than his forearm.

A stone rolled unexpectedly beneath Nik's foot and sent him headlong and whooping with laughter into a bare bush. But right past him and missing the plant entirely sailed Sitok. And that, Nik remembered with sudden sobering shock, could be a problem. He got the dogs stopped even as he untangled himself from the snarled bare underbrush that helped break his fall. He ran over to his brother.

Sitok was silent, face down in snow, head against an icy boulder. Nik got his arms around his brother's waist and turned him so that he could breathe. Low groans—at least he was close to consciousness if he could groan. Probably, he had lost his wind. Nik left him on his side, ran back to the sled for a robe on which to slide him. Sitok's eyes were partially open when Nik returned, though he did not speak. He would be all right, then? The corners of Nik's mouth rose in relief. Then he laughed aloud. Their two roles were reversed once more: Sitok needy and Nik the caretaker.

Just before he started dragging Sitok back to the sled, Nik stooped to be sure that his brother's eyes were open before he sighed dramatically and looked up at *Tornraksoak*, the moon spirit in the sky.

"Must the younger brother be forever rescuing the elder?" he asked loudly and grinned.

Sitok moaned.

Nik squatted to observe him more closely and saw then that no sense was in his brother's open eyes. He glanced over at the iced boulder where Sitok had come to rest.

"Brother?" he whispered.

Nothing.

Nik untied his brother's tunic enough to see that the bear wounds had reopened and fresh blood was oozing through onto his *illupak*. Closing the tunic, Nik put his hand up gently into the furry hood. *Hoo-oo!* Over Sitok's right ear and behind it was a great lump the size of an egg from the red-throat loon. He clawed up pieces of ice from under the snow cover beside the trail. These he fixed to Sitok's loon egg, tying it on his head with a soft birdskin from his tunic pocket. Body warmth would thaw the ice, and water in his brother's hood would be dangerous on the trail. But Nik knew that ice would reduce the swelling. Their journey was ended for today, perhaps for several days to come.

The boy walked around Sitok to tuck all of the margins from the big robe across him for warmth, planning to drag him back to the sled. But when he tugged on the robe and it began to slide, Sitok's eyes opened wide and he roared with pain. Nik stopped pulling and trotted back to bring the sled up—why had he not done so in the first place? Standing beside his brother, he removed two more robes from under straps. These he could use as a soft ramp. He missed Pah-nee's sturdy help. His experience with accident and emergency was mostly limited to times when the dog-boy—*owka!* that would be dog-*girl*—was with him.

"*No, Pehl-son—no, Grandmother . . . no harm was done,*" he murmured tardily as he finally got Sitok up onto the sled.

"Agh!" his brother groaned with pain, still mostly unaware. Moisture formed on Sitok's forehead, dribbled out from under his hood, rolled off his face.

"A man in pain must take deep breaths," Nik told him because he could think of nothing else to say and thought he should say something.

His brother closed his eyes.

Nik grasped the handles of the sled to pull it behind him back onto level trail where it had rested before. Then he inspected Sitok's chest. Two of the deepest slashes from the bear's claws were open, and blood came from them—oozing, not flowing. Still, Sitok's furs and the snow must have cushioned his fall. Well, except for the big rock. Nik pulled back the hood to examine his brother's head once more. The lump was still rising within the nest of Sitok's hair, now surely the size of an egg from the big yellow-billed loon. This blow would explain his brother's scattered spirits. Nik replaced the hood carefully, but opened the parka front to observe the damage as soon as he could use robes to protect his brother from the cold. Little fresh blood soaked Sitok's *illupak,* and those wounds were likely to heal themselves.

What alarmed him was that the left arm seemed once again to be separated from Sitok's shoulder, there beneath the skin where bones and tendons lay. It looked as it had after the bear struck him, half a moon ago—all shelved away from his main body. Nik knew that this injury would cause his brother agony whenever he was conscious. And Nik knew also that the arm and shoulder must be rejoined. What he did not know was *how.*

When Sitok was unconscious in the village, Kiti with Pehl-son and Potok had together done the job, three knowledgeable adults. Now, Sitok would gain his senses, feel the anguish, have to get the damage mended—and only Nik was here—to do something he did not know how to do and

185

did not at the moment dare to try for fear of causing further injury. What now? Nothing. And when the time came . . . what then?

As Nik sat on the sled beside Sitok's limp form, chewing seal meat and trying to think up alternatives, his brother came gradually awake to acute torment which he would not admit. Perspiration continued to sprout from under his hood as he lay there, eyes slit, jaw clenched and mitts fisted. The moisture made rivulets across his face, dripping down to wet his *silapak* alarmingly—dangerously! When the sweat froze, how was Nik to keep him warm? He reviewed the problem aloud, comforted by the sound of a voice—even his own. Sitok contributed stifled moans. He darted glances at his shoulder when he thought Nik was not looking.

No, the boy decided for the sixth time since the accident, he probably should not attempt to readjust the arm—although he had watched the adults do it in the *igloo,* all three grunting with effort while Sitok lay on the edge of the *iglerk* where his bare arm could hang down. Tonight, then, Nik would not try. Perhaps not tomorrow. Should this accident cancel their search? Certainly yes, for now. And *ahmi,* who can predict future circumstance? He looked down at his brother. A frown of tension marked Sitok's face, but his eyes were closed again, and his hands were flattened out within his mittens. His jaw was relaxed. Nik peeled the frozen sweat from his brother's face and jaw, and only a little moisture came to replace it.

"Sitok?" Nik asked softly, his mouth near the hood opening so that only his brother and no capricious trail spirits would hear the name.

No response. Sitok was unconscious once again, his spirits gamboling frivolously away from the body they were supposed to protect. Could he be awakened? *Should* he be? Well, but he needed to eat, didn't he? The younger brother studied the features in the hood over which he hovered, then drew the robes up softly to cover the still form and keep it warm. *Surely it was better to be hungry and senseless without pain than to be fed while suffering.*

Meantime, food for the dogs and for himself was in order. Then sleep. Fortunately, and only because of Kiti's insistence, they carried eight heavy robes with them.

"How will boys provide for their parents if they take but two robes each? Besides—that mountain of food on the sled needs wrapping to avoid attracting meat-eaters." She did not specify what these might be—and Nik now as then suspected she did not know what hungry creatures might appear during winter on the lower tundra. But no shortage of warmth was likely after Kiti finished with pulling coverings off the *iglerk* and out of her Big Feed.

Dogs fed where they were staked, Nik himself gnawing on a seal flipper, he decided that the next problem to be solved was shelter. Because their travel was in winter time, the boys had brought no skins with which to make a tent. But although ever more abundant as they traveled southwest, and depth seeming to increase with each sleeptime and often even in the day, the snow here was too loose and powdery for a snowhouse. During the last three sleeps, in fact, the brothers had simply rolled up within and over their great hill of robes—and slept snugly enough. Now, though, that practice must change. Sitok could not bear on his shoulder the weight of heavy pelts. Yet, he must have warmth in order not to freeze.

Nik pulled a few more robes onto the ground, then eased Sitok off the sled, which he placed on its side at an angle above him, the caribou antler handles bracing it as these settled onto a drift. Robes for the base, more robes draped and tucked for walls, roof and overhang, Nik set up Sitok's tiny lean-to. His brother's own body heat enclosed would keep him warm. Nik himself would curl up outside in the two remaining robes, for he must not jostle Sitok and cause more pain. Nik knew that he would sleep well. His eyes burned with fatigue, his brain overflowed, and his body was unsteady. Yet, much remained to be done. Using the sled and all the robes was going to leave their food unprotected—but from what? If Nik double-checked that every dog was staked, solidly harnessed as now—and why would he not?—what carnivore would brave dog and human scent to plunder their provision? It would have to be wolverine or else some wandering animal he did not know. They were surely too far from water to be bothered by a sea bear. . . . And other than distant wolf howls, they had yet to recognize signs of any predator.

Yet, such must exist. As if to emphasize his thought, a wavering wolf-note reached his ears, then echoed with diminishing sound from invisible cliffs and boulders on the rough terrain to the west. No longer from very far away, Nik decided now, when compared with the howls sometimes heard on previous nights and even earlier this evening.

From the top of a hill late today, before the accident, Nik had seen twice during moments of bright moonlight some high rock outcroppings well ahead at the time but southwest in the direction they were traveling. He had not been pleased, for such landforms would force a slow trail. Now, though, he remembered them with pleasure. At worst, the rough terrain would contain windbreaks against which a sturdy lean-to of robes could be built. And at best? Caves. He could only guess at how close they might be right now to this boulder-filled place he had seen. Surely not far, for vision was much limited in mid-winter, even when spirit lights danced in the sky.

Nik would take his spear and Nuko right now, and try to find suitable shelter. If he located nothing before sleeptime, they would be all right with Sitok staying in the lean-to and Nik rolled up just outside. Probably with Nuko, he decided. He felt uneasy about the proximity of the wolf calls. He would prefer to talk to his brother about the matter. He bent once more to investigate, placing his head inside the lean-to while he clasped the tenting robes tightly around his parka to conserve the heat building in the shelter. Sitok remained in a troubled sleep, perhaps even unconscious, but his breathing seemed to be a little more regular, and the fur nest where he lay was now very warm. Nik touched his brother's forehead to see whether perspiration continued to drip. Sitok's head was dry.

They needed to find a place to stop for several days. For one, the dogs had earned some rest. Mostly, though—and of course this reason must not be spoken aloud—Sitok must have time and ease to recover from this latest mishap and to gain the strength he should have had before Nik insisted that they leave the village. Most important—if the young man was to regain consciousness without being plagued by intense pain—his arm must be rejoined to his shoulder.

Here was the unwelcome fact which kept bobbing to the surface of Nik's mind like a skin float attached to a walrus. Nik tried once again to remember how Kiti and Pehl-son— yes, and Potok as well, the three of them!—had managed. He could recall the scene well enough, Sitok's arm drooping loosely off the *iglerk.* But Nik had not been able to see the actual process. Had not paid attention.

Never mind, not now. Nik grasped his spear and was heading for Nuko when all the dogs set up a howl, a sustained moaning in chorus. Nik hurried back to the enclosure, lifted a flap of fur.

"Sitok?" he whispered sharply.

No response.

"Brother!" he hissed, then waited in vain to hear so much as a stirring.

With their father, Sitok had several times gone to hunt far enough south and inland that large wolf packs were present. Arajik always said that those few pale creatures they saw up around their own coast and ice islands were wandering males that hunted in huge territories. Nik remembered how his father would describe the tundra wolf dens as cozy and deep in the ground. In these, the one pack female permitted to be a mother raised her litter with the help of all the other members, male and female, young and old. Always inland from the sea and well hidden besides, Arajik insisted, perhaps to avoid the clever and usually ravenous *nanuk,* the big white bear.

Now he needed to know from Sitok the meaning of the approaching, close-in howls, the threat of *amarok* the wolf. And what message lay in the response of the dogs? Sitok's spirits were still scattered, though, and he slept deeply. Nik did not dare to jostle him awake—if indeed that could be done—for fear of causing further pain or even injury.

Eh, then he must listen to the sounds and decide for himself. He brought his head out of the lean-to, carefully turning the robes under to hold warmth inside.

No thought came to mind as he listened to the wild creatures who seemed relentlessly to advance. But from *kringmerk,* this was no frantic bear song—that wail he would recognize, having heard it before. Alarm was here, nonetheless. Mild dismay, he decided finally.

"Only listen," he murmured to Nuko, "and hear no anger, no true terror."

Nuko, though, was for once not attending his words. Her muzzle pointed low to the northwest, and she was restless. Suddenly, she stretched her neck and uttered a long, plaintive howl.

"Hush!" Nik admonished her softly. "If a dog wishes to sing, she must join the others, not sit here and startle Sitok up from his robes."

Nik listened more, tried to imagine himself a member of the team. If he were *kringmerk* the dog, what would he be saying when he uttered such sounds? At last, he gave up, looked down at Nuko.

"They sing. Something is somewhere. A young hunter cannot interpret the music." So much for fear of wolves.

Nik walked forward to the team, checked that every bone stake was solid through snow and ice, then into permafrost. Next he fed every dog but Nuko. Back at the sled, he gave her a fat chunk of whale meat and the promise of more to come.

"A boy and a dog must find an *igloo* in the hills," he told her.

Leaving Sitok's weapons beside his good right arm just outside the lean-to and picking up his own spear, Nik with Nuko made a trail to the west up a series of short rises under a moon partially swaddled in clouds.

They did not go far. If the boy had been able magically to conjure up exactly what he needed from Tornarssuk, from the powerful spirit of the land—a refuge not too large to heat but big enough to protect themselves and to store provision— then this shelter would have appeared. On a gentle incline that would be easy to reach by sled, he found a shallow cave the right size to house them. The entry was low enough and small enough that he could block it with rocks and snow to insure warmth and security. High enough to stand in. And within shouting distance of the place where he had left Sitok and the dogs. Not that he planned to shout.

Excited over the find, filled with new energy, Nik took loose snow inside, piled and packed it by feel to form a narrow *iglerk*, a sleeping ledge, along a side wall. Just right for Sitok.   On the way up here, he had tried repeatedly to visualize what he had seen previously as others fixed his brother's shoulder. He finally remembered that the left arm had hung down off the sleeping ledge when it was gently raised and—so Kiti told him—manipulated back into its socket. How? If only he had seen the movements involved! After the sleep, then, he must try to adjust the injury. If Nik could fix the arm to the shoulder so that pain was less, then his brother might gather his spirits and awaken more brightly.

Nik was making his way carefully back down the rocky decline when he heard his dog team start up their howl afresh. Their bellies were full—why did they complain? Wait . . . ah! The sound this time contained new urgency. Once again, he tried to empty his mind and hear the notes, interpret their meaning. Nuko first whined in sympathy with her teammates, then uttered a low growl deep in her throat as Nik and she neared the lean-to and the team.

Nik heard the wolf pack, then, and realized that his dogs, staked as they were, would be powerless to protect Sitok and themselves. For some illogical reason, wolves hate their sled-dog cousins, or so Arajik always said. Nik ran toward Sitok and the encampment, falling in his haste, picking himself up and stumbling on, glad that Nuko raced ahead.

Nearly there, he heard what sounded like total confusion, and he raised his spear, mildly surprised to find it still in his hand. The moon floated out of a cloud to light up the area. All appeared as he had left it except that every dog was standing, pulling to the north against its restraints, facing away from the sled, away from Sitok and the pile of food, looking back up the trail they had made earlier.

Good, then, *kringmerk* would serve as a buffer to protect the camp from what lay beyond. Nik sprinted to the shelter where Sitok lay, opened the draped fur. His brother was breathing hard, irregularly, obviously still in pain. But he was awake. His head was lifted away from the robe, his hood pushed back.

"What's happening?" Nik asked.

"Wolves. With this ear pressed to scraped earth, someone heard the pounding of approaching paws before *kringmerk* came to their feet. Someone also heard his brother's running footsteps. Let the dogs loose!"

"But—eh, do they stand a chance against wolves in a pack?"

"Untied . . . even working together, unlikely. But still better than staked apart . . . where they would become a meal. *Tuwawi!*" Hurry up! A moan of agony came through the tight, shuddering lips.

Nik dropped the robe flap and rushed forward, Nuko bounding back to meet him, the dog torn between loyalties to team and to master. As Nik freed the animals, commanding each to lie down and stay, his mind raced. Sometimes, in summer when caribou were somewhere near their camp, he heard wolves at night. Always far away. But now the sounds were close.

As he tucked into a robe the last team harness, he looked up, waited for the moon to come out from behind the rag of cloud which hid it. Yes, dark shapes ahead. He did not wait to see if they were advancing. If not, he knew, it would have been his sudden appearance that stopped them. A temporary check. They were many, and he was one.

Wolves were much respected by Inupiat as being clever hunters like themselves in a land where provision was not abundant. Only wolves, Arajik said, like Inupiat cooperated with others of their kind in seeking out and capturing food. His father spoke often of the large and numerous wolf packs to the south—packs that hated sled dogs and would kill them if they could. None among his people Nik could remember had ever reported seeing a wolf up close, even though tracks and scat of the shadowy pale creatures were present year around. Members of packs farther south looked more like big sled dogs themselves, Arajik said, and could be dark in color, spotted, even patchy roan like a fox at season's change. Confusing. But all wolves have close ties to their families and to each other, according to his father. *Like* sled dogs, they are always hungry—but more dignified, more proud.

Eh! Nik pounced on that thought. *Arajik said that wolves have **pride**!*

A daring idea flashed into his head. Sitok would not like it. Every dog was loose and alert, now, crouched low on their master's command, feet unmoving. But they wailed as before. Nik went back to pick up his whip, then stood by Sitok at the pile of provision off-loaded from the sled.

"Drop!" he commanded the keening team, and the dogs flattened where they stood and became silent. *Kringmerk* knew and obeyed this order; for on the hunt, their stillness could mean the difference between success and failure, food and hunger—sometimes, between life and death both for themselves and for the human who drove, fed and protected them.

"Nuko!" the boy called softly, and that great pale animal with her tail arched over her back appeared suddenly at his leg, a canine ghost. "Help me!" Nik whispered.

He slid one end of a line through the notch on her harness collar, fastened it securely, then whipped the rest of the rope three times around the largest seal on the food pile, a carcass nearly as heavy as dog and boy combined. He took the other end of the rope himself and told Nuko, "Pull!"

They both heaved until the mass almost large as two *Inuit* finally slid slowly across the snow. Past the dogs, one by one, they inched their strange cargo until, breathless, they were ahead of the team by two lengths of a long sled.

"Down!" he murmured into Nuko's ear. Quivering with strain from the haul as well as from excitement, the dog heard and obeyed.

Nik dropped, too. He and Nuko were no more than a couple more sled-lengths in front of the wolf pack, midway between them and the hushed team. The wolves also had gone silent. Curious? But their eyes sparked in moonlight.

Wolves are proud. . . . Not like most sled dogs . . . wolves are dignified and proud. Nik realized then that he had left his spear behind. Never mind. No mere spear in the hands of one expert hunter—which Nik still was *not*—could hold off hungry wolves. At least both of his hands were free.

He unfastened the rope from Nuko's harness collar. Then still moving slowly and keeping his body and especially his head very low, he unwound the rope from the carcass, coiling the tie swiftly to take back with him.

"Nuko, Come! Drop!" His own belly dragging the snow, Nik slid along back toward Sitok's tent and the team. The plan might work, but only if they both—he and Nuko alike—kept themselves lower than the wolves. Submission. *Wolves are proud.* But Nuko did not follow him, and the boy hesitated. The dog was confused, after all. No one ever gave orders to drop *and* come at the same time. But if she was to live through the next moments, she *must* drop—*must* obey that command by keeping low and silent—and she *must* at the same time return to the team with him. If some dog anywhere could figure out what surely seemed to be conflicting commands, Nuko could.

Nik looked back two arms' length to catch and hold the dog's gaze once more. "Drop . . . come!" he repeated softly, then continued inching down the trail on his belly.

Nuko emitted a very low, frustrated whine.

"Drop!" he hissed without turning, and her sound ceased. "Come!" Nik crawled a full sled's length back before he turned to check once more. And she followed! Despite the sober circumstance, he had to choke back a chuckle. To see that huge canine with her muzzle *schmoo-oo-ooshing* along the snow, front legs spraddled wide before her, backside slightly in the air as her hind legs propelled her. . . . Eh, Nik realized that he himself probably looked as bizarre as she. He waited for her to get close behind him, then proceeded.

He collected dogs along the way as he crept back to Sitok and the sled. With Nuko to demonstrate for them what was expected, a few even took her cue. Most did not, but their distance from the wolf pack was widening as they moved behind Nik toward the lean-to, so that the posture of their exit became less critical with each moment. When all reached the sled, Nik made every dog drop motionless and silent once again while he ducked his head into the robe tent. Sitok would want to know what was happening—but Sitok was not awake. Nik touched the face, felt perspiration that lay there like spring thaw on sea ice. Pain, not fever. Nik had left so hurriedly, the last time, that he had not re-tucked the furs. The robe nest where his brother lay was barely warm. He withdrew his head and adjusted the blankets.

In the quiet at the sled, Nik listened to the wolves devouring their meal uptrail. No growls or angry snarls came from the feast. Sled dogs in such a situation would be tearing at each other, regardless of how much food was offered. Unstaked and given a whole *whale,* his team would likely dispute every bite.

Now was the time to leave this place. The boy put his head into the lean-to once more, this time speaking with his full voice. "It happens, a cave is nearby," he announced to Sitok. He still dared not touch or try to repair the injured body, so repeated his words ever more loudly until he got an answer.

"Ee-ee, Yes!" Sitok muttered around his suffering and his clenched teeth.

Nik told of the cave quickly. Then, "Can someone bear the jostling of getting there by sled?"

No quick response, but then another *"Ee-ee"* came to his ears in the strained voice. Yes.

"—And can someone also bear the cold?" Nik finished as he lifted away and folded robes to pad the sled. He felt his brother's face again. Perspiration was running, now, but Sitok's furs were not yet iced. The move was risky, for increased pain would increase sweat; but staying here with the pile of food was perilous also. His mind told him this, even though his instinct assured him that Sitok and he were in no physical danger from wolves. Peril attended the sled dogs—most probably, yes. And if he and Sitok had no team and no food, they could not continue their search. Or even survive long enough to get home.

Nik put the sled back onto its runners and piled on robes. The spirits of Sitok scattered again when the younger boy half-rolled, half-dragged him onto the conveyance, then tucked remaining blankets around him, lashed him firmly. The older boy grunted with pain but did not cry out or seem to awaken. Nik checked his handiwork to make sure that he would not lose his passenger along the hilly trail up to the cave. Eh! He had nearly forgotten. He reached under Sitok's hood to assess the bump on his head. Was it smaller now than before? If it was a yellow-bill egg when last he checked—so large? surely not!—it was now the size of an egg from *tullugak,* the great black raven. Here was a good thing, he decided, for Sitok's spirits to be roaming in this time of pain. The agony might not be felt so strongly, at least not remembered. Also, that dangerous perspiration born of anguish when his brother was awake subsided when his spirits scattered.

Suddenly, as if to confound Nik's mute thought, Sitok raised his head, opened his eyes. "The food must come along," he said clearly.

The younger boy did not agree, did not want to argue so did not respond, merely walked away to get the dogs harnessed and back on their lines.

"It happens that moving is useless without food," Sitok persisted in a loud voice.

"Hush!" Nik said as he brought the dogs quietly around, made them once again drop while he walked a few paces back up the trail and gazed through dark shadow to see what he could of the wolf pack.

"Someone must load up the food," Sitok said still too loudly, "or everyone will starve."

Nik walked back, placed his finger firmly beside his brother's mouth. "Someone must be silent," he whispered, "for the wild family is present still."

"Either load the food or *someone* will roll from this sled," Sitok warned in a calmer but fully resolute voice that cut off with a grunt of pain.

Sighing, Nik went back to the carcasses and bladder-enclosed cuts, piling what fit onto that part of the sled not occupied by Sitok.

"Put a seal and some packages up by the caribou horns," Sitok hissed at him through gritted teeth.

"Already done," Nik said.

"Then help someone sit against them."

Nik started to protest, but his brother had loosened the lashes, was now gasping with short breaths of misery and effort as he squirmed on the sled, leaving robes flopping loose behind him. The younger brother sighed once more. He placed what had been Sitok's cover against what was now to become his backrest. Then he lifted him gently at the waist, knowing well what anguish he caused, brought him to a sitting position. Moisture poured off the older boy's face, his eyes slitted shut. His upper lip drew up to reveal his teeth, but he uttered no complaint.

Nik rapidly gathered up the abandoned robes and tossed them over his brother, strapped them down again willy-nilly with Sitok nestled inside like a prize walrus, then packed even more food onto the sled. Three large seals plus several wrapped packets, he secretly left behind. Now he signaled the dogs, and they moved toward the cave slowly, silently, smoothly as possible.

CHAPTER 15.
FINDING TWO LEMMINGS
ON TUNDRA

In the small cavern, Nik got the travel lamp going. He dragged a barely conscious Sitok up onto the slender *iglerk*. He staked all the dogs but Nuko, whom he could not find and did not bother to call. She had served him well on this day, and she would not go far. Sled dogs do not run away. They are staked only to keep them from fighting among themselves and from stealing food from each other and from their masters.

Nik brought the provision and bags and bladders inside, along with the dogs' harnesses. Why is it, he wondered, that much as *kringmerk* love to run before a sled, they will chew up and devour their harnesses at any opportunity? Wearily, he pushed a mound of snow inside the entry. On the hillside, he found and rolled into the opening several large stones, slid past them himself and packed them with snow to be as tight as possible. From inside, he used part of the snow he had stockpiled to chink the many vents.

Sitok was still composed of groggy spirits when Nik finished. Warmth from the small, smoky lamp meant that he would not freeze in his sweat-soaked clothing. Nevertheless, Nik stripped the outer garments off both his brother and himself, beat the snow from them with the sturdy piece of driftwood he carried for that purpose in his hunting bag. He folded his own garments and placed them in a bladder.

Sitok's damp ones, he turned inside out and draped over his brother's long spear placed above the lamp, the two ends resting on seals and meat packets stacked on either side. If he could stay awake long enough, he would turn the clothing. Warmth in the cave had him perspiring in his light *illupak,* and he thrust his snow knife through a chink above the rocks at the doorway, heard the single sigh and wheeze of air flowing through the nostril. From outdoors, Nuko put her muzzle to the opening and whined. Now again, she wanted in. As usual.

Nik hesitated. Pah-nee had felt about Nuko as no Inupiat hunter ever felt about a sled dog, no matter how strong or noble the creature might be. And his grandmother, also, said that Nuko had earned her place within the family. In respect for the feelings of Pah-nee and *Ananatsiak*—certainly not for the satisfaction of Nik or of Nuko!—he let her in and re-sealed the cave opening.

During the night, he remembered to turn Sitok's furs but forgot to pour fresh oil for the lamp, and the wick died. When he awakened later in darkness and mild cold, he realized that Sitok could not leave the shelter until his outer garments dried completely. His brother probably should not go outside at all until the pain had lessened so that he did not perspire. Nik was somehow relieved, for they were in a comfortable place, and he was weary of living on the trail.

Using flint and dry moss from his hunting bag, he got the lamp going once more. He cautiously felt of his brother's inner garments, his *illupak,* to be sure that they were dry. Yes, and so was the person wearing them, under the sleep robes—dry as a sun-baked rock in summer. Nik smiled with satisfaction. Yes, and warm as the liver of a newly-captured seal. The boy brought the lamp over to Sitok so that he could inspect for blood seepage from the wounds. Nothing fresh since late afternoon, and the *tullugak* egg had become more the size of that trim tundra grouse, the rock ptarmigan. Definitely smaller. But the hollow was still there at Sitok's left shoulder, the arm still shelving out. How could Nik return it to the socket? He remembered Kiti's saying that severe pain would not pass so long as an arm was not properly joined.

"Hoo-oo-oo," he breathed aloud in dismay. He had to do something about Sitok's injury, surely before the next sleep.

When Nik had collected the harnesses and was fumbling with rocks to go outside, Sitok awakened. He looked around the small, smoky cave heaped with meat and extra robes.

"Someone did well to find this place," he approved in a voice heavily laced with pain.

"An awkward child stumbled on it blindly in the dark," Nik replied in the expected manner.

"Is all the food here?" No one could tell in the gloom and without knowing the size of the shelter. At least Sitok had not lost his preoccupation with the food supply . . . probably a good sign.

"A small pile remains below. It would not fit on the sled unless a boy left his elder brother behind."

"He should have done so," Sitok replied, "for food is more useful than the brother."

"The team and this person will go now to retrieve it."

Sitok started to laugh but groaned instead. "The wolves will have eaten it."

"They could not **hold** it! They were given a huge seal."

"Then they will have dragged it away."

No use arguing. "It happens," Nik returned cheerfully, "that this *Inuk* will soon know."

"Another *Inuk* already knows! The tired young hunter may as well rest in the warmth of this excellent cave."

"It is necessary to go outside and begin calling for Arajik and Mawena—remember? It was the plan to begin calling at this place—before events intervened. Besides, the dogs are hungry." Actually, air in the cave seemed stifling to Nik. Also to Nuko, for she nosed in front of him to be first past the entrance rocks. And to face his fear honorably, Nik acknowledged to himself that he wanted to postpone for as long as possible the ordeal of working on Sitok's shoulder.

Fresh snow had fallen while they slept, and Nik did not see the food pile until the dogs detoured suddenly to clamor around it. So far as he could tell, the packets were all there. Nothing touched? The hide covers undisturbed? He was incredulous. At least a dozen wolves had been in that pack last night, based on his count of eyes gleaming in moonlight. And even when their sides were bulging after they feasted on the big seal, he would expect them to haul away at least part of the provision left behind. Or perhaps guard it to eat later? He looked around the deserted brush land. But he knew that the dogs would be howling if even one wolf were anywhere near.

After Nik loaded the sled, he walked up to where he and Nuko had left the carcass. He saw by moonlight that deep drag marks depressed the east side of the old trail and were now lightly covered by new snowfall. He smiled. They had eaten what they could, then taken the rest away with them. To one of those underground nurseries for wolf children? He liked the thought of it. Good. It was *their* food, after all—not stolen but freely given. Nik went back and offloaded one more big seal onto the frozen ground. *Nakorami.* Thank you.

"Don't tell Sitok," he cautioned Nuko as they started back up into the hills.

Passing on by the cave, Nik climbed deliberately to the top of the rise above it and called out, "*AIEE-EE-OO-OO-*

AH!" in three directions, waiting for echoes to subside after each long call, then listening closely before he shouted again. He could not of course use his parents' names, for so doing would attract whatever sinister spirits might be in this place. He grunted after waiting many moments following the last call. What had he expected, anyway? Was it too much to ask that his parents were cozy in another cave nearby—on this very hill!—and had been waiting since late summer to hear his rescuing call? Well . . . yes, it was too much.

He chuckled out loud, then went down and cut up seal meat to feed the dogs. They ate while he gathered clean snow in a bladder to melt for drinking water. He opened the door of the cave temporarily to air it out, put a clean, empty bladder near sleeping Sitok's right hand to use for morning functions, if he was so inclined when he awakened. Then Nik used his *ulu* to slice off chunks of meat for his brother and himself.

"It is necessary to return someone's arm to its place on the shoulder," Nik mused aloud after a long period of thoughtful chewing.

Sitok's weak voice startled him. *"Owka,* No. Not yet."

Nik pulled both lips in between his teeth, looked at his brother steadily. "It happens that this thing must be done." The boy wished that he could think of any good reason that it did *not.*

"And Nik knows how?" In lamp glow, the boy watched fluids rise on his brother's forehead at the scalp, runnels that trickled slowly at first, then like rainwater on summer tundra, found other rivulets to join and flow into his ears or drip from his jaw. The pain must be immense.

Nik admitted that he was ignorant of the process. "But someone watched when others did the job following a valiant hunter's fight with *nanuk.* " Not totally true. Nik had watched, certainly; but with three adults hovering over the task, he had seen little. Nor had his attention been complete. Who would dream that he would need so soon whatever he might learn?

"Still, Sitok will wait for a time." The older boy closed his eyes and took a long, ragged breath.

Nik hunkered down to consider his alternatives. He watched that dangerous moisture continue to flow across his brother's face, knew that the drip was collecting and once again dampening the *illupak* as well, wetting the underfurs. Sitok did not dare to let air outside the cave surround him when he was like this, for he would freeze. Desperate to ease the agony, Nik picked up the water bladder, put it to his brother's unsteady lips. "The great pain will surely stop when a shoulder has found its place."

The older boy's eyes remained shut but his brows went up slightly, Yes. "Perhaps. But can one person alone do this job? *Any* one person alone?"

That was kind of Sitok. His brother made the procedure sound as if it required the strength of many rather than more probably the effort from only one person who was knowledgeable. Back in the village, both Kiti and Pehl-son, at least, seemed to know what they were doing, perhaps Potok as well—although he disliked giving Potok credit for much. Yet again, Nik tried to picture in his memory what those three had actually *done* to restore the arm. He could see them clearly, could visualize senseless Sitok on the *iglerk,* his arm drooping toward the floor. Then Grandmother had lifted it up, gently, at a certain angle—that movement he could remember. The two men had then moved in . . . eh, Nik could not see around them. Not now in his recollection and—he realized once more—not even *then.*

He stood up close to Sitok's *iglerk,* reached down to grasp his brother's limp arm. "The proper time is now," he said firmly.

No response. Nik kicked off his *kamik,* then placed his hareskin inner boot against his brother's armpit. He pressed slightly as he lifted the arm straight out and tried to fit the top of it into the hollow spot on the shoulder.

Sitok groaned hoarsely one time, but he did not pull away. A fresh torrent of moisture erupted on his face. Slitted eyes followed every move of his younger brother.

Nik felt something slide and catch at Sitok's shoulder, fit together softly like a hand into its mitten. Was the task complete, then? He caught his brother's eyes with his own. What should he do next? Certainly not let go of the arm he presently held, not just let its weight drop it back to the ground.

He watched his brother's face relax somewhat, saw his eyes close, then reopen fully.

"Lash it," Sitok grated.

Lash what? Nik wondered, even as he looked about him for a coil of split hide.

"Bend the elbow and fasten the useless arm against this worthless body."

Nik remembered then that Sitok had worn a sling around his neck for several sleeps after the shoulder was fixed. Of course! The weight must be reduced to give the arm and shoulder time to become accustomed to each other once again. In moments, Nik slid soft hareskin under the arm, then with broad lashing rigged a sling around Sitok's neck.

His brother smiled in relief. *"Nakorami,"* he murmured. His eyelids drooped, closed.

"Ee-ee, someone must rest." Nik's hand reached into the black hair, felt above Sitok's ear. The egg was now no larger than a songbird's. "Both brothers have a task—the elder's to repair himself, and the younger's to find some parents." He studied his brother anxiously while his voice continued soothingly. He would leave Sitok to mend on this

day and on several more to come, while he himself made short trips to call out and search.

"It happens that Sitok will go along following another sleep." The patient was only half awake, eyes shut, no new perspiration limning his features, but Nik could tell that his spirits were finally beginning to assemble.

"So it may be," Nik calmed him. "But first, someone who seems to learn slowly needs to move in different directions and discover the ways of this land."

Sitok did not answer. His breath came smoothly, deeply and with regularity for the first time since his fall. Nik wiped the peaceful face with a clean birdskin. No moisture replaced the sheen he blotted. Still, his brother had left the village prematurely, so was all the more susceptible to accident and injury. They would keep this cave as their base for several sleeps, Nik decided, whether or not Sitok became fit for the trail. The younger brother was now at last grateful to be burdened with the large quantities of food on which Sitok had insisted. And of course had found use for the many robes Kiti had pressed upon them.

As a matter of fact, what exactly had been Nik's contribution to assure success on this journey? He snorted as he reviewed his role in their abrupt leaving. Why, of course! It had been Nik who prodded them to *go*—ready or not! And of course Sitok was *not* ready, but here they were, an injured hunter and an impatient child. Nik was ashamed.

For eight sleeps, with Sitok ever more restless but still not sufficiently hardy for the trail, Nik wandered in different directions across plains and rough tundra calling for Arajik and Mawena but of course not using their names . . . and always returning to Sitok and the cave at night. The first two days, he went out on foot with his spear, a light pack of food on his back, and Nuko. On the third day, aiming to go farther, he mudded and iced the runners and took the eager team, loading the sled with more food than before and a couple of robes. On the fourth day and thereafter, he did the same, except that he started earlier, fanned out farther, carried more supplies, returned later—always calling, calling whenever he found a high place that let his voice carry far and echo through the deserted woodland and rocky valley walls. He forced himself to wait for an answer after each call.

When *Tornraksoak* the moon spirit hid from him behind heavy clouds, as he did often, Nik lost hope of ever finding his parents. What childish game did he play? Urgit had instructed them, "Go southwest beyond the ancient cache," and they had. The counsel of Urgit . . . like the warmth of a blizzard, the delicacy of a walrus—the wit of a stone.

The white ground cover and drifts got deeper as snowfall continued during nearly every sleep period and sometimes during the dark days as well. More snow here than at home, he realized by now, and at last good for building. In fact, Nik could have cut blocks and made a snowhouse, except that their cave was sufficient, even comfortable. With walrus hide and fur, Nik constructed a sturdier sling well cushioned for Sitok which—his elder brother declared with bright enthusiasm—took strain from his arm and shoulder so that the injured place could mend more rapidly. He moved about with little pain, so he said. But his face remained pale, and Nik sometimes heard him groan in his sleep. Sitok was still weak, clearly in no condition to travel. Nor had he been sufficiently strong before the accident, Nik reminded himself over and again when he felt himself pressed by the old impatience. He asked to see the re-opened bear-claw wounds, but Sitok refused.

As the days passed, Sitok insisted on walking outside to regain lost strength, and Nik knew not to fight him on the matter. But by now far more snow was piled upon the ground than Nik had ever seen before—a southern phenomenon Arajik had failed to mention. Treacherous footing often lay beneath it, along with unfamiliar trail, more often no trail at all. Sitok could easily fall and be helpless to rise. Alone, he could in fact be frozen and spiritless by the time Nik returned at the end of his day's search for their parents. It was necessary that the patient not leave the cave while he was alone, so Nik extracted a promise that Sitok would go outside only when his younger brother was there to assist if a problem occurred.

Late on the ninth day of Nik's search, roaming hills and calling across the low tundra, he came out on a rise overlooking a lake that reflected moonlight on a frozen surface cleared by strong wind. A sense of excitement filled him. For all those days of travel and then search, he had seen no human and no evidence of their having passed. But now? He could not later say how he had sensed *Inuit* presence even before the dogs did. Or how for that matter he sensed it at all. No tracks were visible, certainly. No man smell came to his nostrils. But there in the silvered dark, he knew to call *"Ai-ee-ee!"* And to stand and wait for extra time.

Then came back an answering shout. *"HOO-OO-OO!"*

An owl? But why would an owl answer him? No fools, these great white creatures would far more likely float away on their silent wings.

Containing himself despite the thrill of excitement coursing through him, Nik bellowed again, *"Ai-ee-ee!"* and waited.

Another return call, this one prompt and recognizably human.

Nik must not tremble so. Blood pounding at his ears must subside. He surveyed the lake shoreline spread out far below him. And at last he saw a small pale movement at its edge.

Eh, why had he not thought to bring moss and flint? Then he could signal using fire. But why *would* he? He turned to the team, which was now singing joyfully. Their sharp ears recognized the voice which shouted from the lake.

The dogs ran as though Paija herself pursued them, and Nik stepped up on the back runners and let the team carry him on a path it picked to get down from the bluff to the shoreline and to the person who called.

CHAPTER 16.
A LIAR LIVES AMONG US!

"It happens that someone was fishing," Arajik explained when the two met.

"*Ee-ee,* Yes." Nik stood before him. Their eyes locked and held for one long moment—the man who had nurtured only his elder son. Nik had yearned to be included but then, ignored by his father, developed his artistic side instead. Now each clasped the other closely for a long time, rubbing noses against each other's cheeks and pounding one another's backs, finally breathless, laughing, tears leaking from their eyes, dripping across their *nuilaks* and freezing on their cheeks.

Arajik and Mawena were living in a stick-and-stone shelter built into the side of a hill above the tree-lined lake. They were hungry. They were cold. But they were alive. Mawena lay on a rough caribou hide, covered with the same. She flashed a wan half-smile at Nik, but spoke no words. Arajik wanted to leave for home immediately. He would take little with them on Nik's sled, for there was little to take.

The next days were a blur to all. Mawena's leg had been broken in the flood, according to Arajik, but Nik thought it would surely have healed by now. Still, she did not walk. Nor did she speak. At the cave there followed another warm greeting between Sitok and the father, a cordial smile from this strangely restrained Mawena. Arajik checked Nik's work on Sitok's shoulder, rapidly adjusted the sling so that it bore more weight when the young man stood up.

He studied the injury closely, lightly touched the join with his bare fingers, then regarded the construction of the sling. At last, he turned to look at Nik as if to see him for the first time.

"And does it happen that someone else was here to help with placing this arm to that shoulder?" he asked.

Nik knew that his father's skepticism would become a compliment when the facts were established, but his feelings were hurt. Was it so impossible in Arajik's mind that the younger son could do something right? He turned without a word and left the cave while Sitok explained with great pride that his brother alone had done what was needed.

Outside, the boy's jumble of thoughts glowed and glimmered through his head like spirit lights. The resentment over Arajik's wonder at repair of the injury. Balanced though with belated realization that Nik had not ever exhibited for his father, back in the village, any of his anxiety about becoming a hunter. Arajik knew nothing of his younger son's deep interest and determination where trail skills were concerned. More, Nik had never revealed to his father the extraordinary skill he was developing in chant and dance. Why? Because he thought—eh, still *did* think, for that matter—that nothing short of astonishing perfection would be valued by Arajik. Anything less, the man was likely to ignore or gently ridicule.

But his father was different, now, or so it seemed to Nik. How so? Mawena's great change was evident. She had always been a loving mother but also unpredictable. Ruled by inner storms, he reflected. Certainly, she was under their influence now. Why had he not noticed this in her before? Was she to be mute forever? And lame as well? And could it be that *Nik* was also changed?

For five sleeps, the parents with their sons remained near the cave while Sitok strengthened himself in preparation for the trip back, and while Arajik and Mawena built up their own vitality with plentiful food and dependable warmth. Sitok and Arajik had always been close. Now? Even closer? Nik would find sleep each night with a background of their voices quietly, warmly visiting, laughing in good comradeship based on their history of many hours together on the trail.

On the other hand, Nik and Arajik had always been distant. But here and now, they were at least cordial strangers. The father seemed for the first time to be *aware* of his younger boy. To realize that his son was no longer a baby. And Nik did not for once feel lonely in the man's presence. In fact, he was content because he knew Sitok was representing him well, actually introducing him—Nik!—to their father during the long conversations from which the younger boy seemed excluded. But with each new day, and although the man made no real overtures, Nik recognized fresh interest in Arajik's eyes whenever they met his. Was the *atatak*, the father, beginning to realize that he had *two* sons?

Just as well *not* to visit with Arajik, not quite yet. Nik had too many questions to put in order . . . questions that could not be asked directly but must be fished for like catching char in the depths of a summer lake. One could as usual throw out bait in the form of statements to which the other might respond. Or not. So far, at least, Arajik just wasn't talking about the most important things, not even to Sitok. Nik knew, for until late each night he eavesdropped before sleep claimed him. Also, he checked with Sitok frequently.

"It happens that what would be plenty for two is not sufficient to feed four," Arajik observed one evening as the three visited. And Mawena's curtailment in speech and mobility had in no way reduced her appetite. Both Nik and Sitok were amazed by the gusto with which she greeted food . . . and by the amounts she consumed.

So the trail home was changed on the basis of need and of Arajik's greater knowledge of the terrain. They would, as he suggested and they agreed, cut directly east until they reached the sea, where at this time of year food would be more plentiful than here. And from there, they would cut north and east along the coast to reach their village.

Now fresh seal and the occasional walrus could be added to the supply. And unlimited fish . . . although no one, not even the dogs, ever greeted this fare with great enthusiasm. And after the last meal before sleep time, Arajik revealed gradually how they managed to survive, he and Mawena—and a very poor subsistence it was, by the man's own admission. One had only to see at the lakeside lean-to those skeletal faces, now filling out rapidly.

But their father had not yet described the accident. Arajik referred to Mawena's injury in general terms, but he made no effort to explain her present condition. And Mawena spoke not at all. His mother had gone from her normal *chittering* continually like a phalarope—*kip! kip! kip!*—to these days brooding like the thick-billed murre, silent, hunched and colorless.

On the sled trip home after they left the cave, Arajik included Nik in his conversations. Several sleeps along the trail, their father started filling in some of the empty spots in Nik's picture of what had happened. He told one cold night over a smoky lamp in a trail *igloo* about how unlikely had been their continued existence at all, last summer. No food and, without a hunting bag, no spears or knives with which to supply themselves. Marginal warmth, those late-summer nights; then the days as well as nights gained chill increasingly. Next came howling wind, rain, then snow—yes, ever more of it, here in the south. Misery. Determination to sleep as much as possible and thus with dignity accept the ending of the present life.

A turning point came when a small herd of late-migrating caribou straggled along the lake to make its way south. Desperate, Arajik chased a lone wolf away from its meal of caribou. *"Amarok* the venerable wolf culls lesser creatures from the herd—old or diseased, slower individuals. All know that wolves cannot outrun or take a healthy adult *tuktu,* nor even a juvenile protected by the herd.

"Eh, so this weaponless hunter—this *soospuk*—went charging in with light fur slippers, only his *illupak,* his underwear—all he had—summer wear for berry-gathering. The lunatic *Inuk* raced forward shouting like an assembly of Paija and her familiars, all the time waving two burning brands plucked earlier from the woodland and dried out in summer sunshine."

Although the creature that Arajik stole was old and gaunt with poor fur and tough meat, the two Inupiat now had sinew for snares and fish line. They had bladder and membrane and intestine for storage. They had bone for making weapons and tools. They had hope.

Not until the parents and sons had nearly closed on their coastal village did Arajik give particulars of the accident. Even then, he launched into the tale sideways, as if it were of no importance. That memorable night of clarification began when Arajik brought out his rough bone knife and prepared to feed the dogs. Sitok eyed the dull, chipped edge that his father proposed to use for hacking off seal meat, then pulled out the metal knife Arajik had given him.

"It happens that Urgit lost your knife he brought back . . . uh . . . for safekeeping," Sitok explained as he handed it over.

"Urgit?!" Arajik stopped still. Incredulous. "Here is a matter to ponder," he said finally, as he went to tend the team. He was gone a long time. When he returned, he was preoccupied as he used Sitok's extra *ulu* to cut off seal meat at his lips, one thoughtful bite and then another. The evening meal concluded, Mawena was invisible, tucked deep in a robe while father and sons sat by the lamp on a *tuktu* hide. All were silent, each thinking his own thoughts.

Arajik cleared his throat, looked about him as if to check that no other might be around to overhear his tale. Then he commenced a detailed account of the summer accident.

"Much rain fell in high country above," he began, "but the four who had left the village to go south for fishing were camped comfortably. They were based at an open overhang half a *kayak's* length up the river bank and well above the lake that Nik saw when—eh, when his father found him." Arajik looked at his younger son and chuckled, and the boy felt the corners of his own mouth rise. He could not remember this man ever before joking with him personally.

"The everlasting summer sunshine of that morning came through clouds, overcast. Father with son—so Pak with Urgit—chose to fish. Mawena and this hunter decided to cross the river and seek the bright berries in wet, open woodland on the other side. Trees and bushes—the two sons have seen them now."

"Trees." Both young men echoed that unfamiliar word, then nodded. Yes, they had now seen these strange *trees.* Trees tall enough to cause neck pain if someone stood close to look up.

Arajik cleared his throat and continued. "Across the river, the two would examine any tracks that might show themselves; for fish at every meal of each day grows wearisome."

"*Ee-ee,*" both boys agreed.

"Pak had experimented with smoking the big lake char. He asked that Arajik and Mawena bring back from across the river whatever sticks and brush could be dried for burning. So although the two berry-seekers waded the shallow river, they took the *kayak* also and pulled it high on the far bank—*phfft!*" Arajik lifted his chin impatiently. "Not that such care was useful in the end. The two carried only a few cloths of ptarmigan hide and one large bladder in which to collect whatever they could find.

"They were not far from the river bank when they first felt the ground tremble. Then they heard a roar come from high above—the sound of a mighty spring tide attacking grounded ice . . . except that this place was far from tide and ice. And the two ran!—well so, for water came boiling down the river channel like a moving mountain, first filling and then overflowing the low banks. Here was increasing peril even though the *Inuit* darted from tree to tree, clinging to the rough body of one only long enough to select the next, as water bubbled and *swoo-ooshed* with great current along the ground and up around their feet and legs.

"Suddenly, Mawena shrieked from where she raced the rising river tide. She was perhaps three sled lengths behind her husband. Water with strong current rose to her hips and held her powerless.

"'Clutch a tree!' the husband shouted, even as he himself tried to go back and help. This she did—and fortunate she was to grasp a sturdy one—for Arajik could not *get* back. The outward, downward current of the rising flood curtailed his movement.

"'Climb!' her husband shouted then. 'Float upward!' But the crash and roar of flood was too great. Instead, she rose higher on the tree only as the water level lifted her and forced her clinging arms to grip above where they had been. And sadly, she rose only high enough to keep her head above the flood. What saved her—and what injured her—was a sensible determination to keep herself on the upstream side of the tree trunk that she gripped. Thus braced, she was not torn from her hold and swept away with the current."

"But the father said that so doing *injured* her," Sitok prompted.

"Ee-ee," Arajik said, "for had she not been on that side of a tree too strong to be uprooted, then the tree which *did* uproot and came rushing along with the deluge and which finally broke her leg would never have snagged and remained there. It kept pressing always harder but seemed balanced or tangled. It was unable to continue with the flow."

Nik spoke. "Arajik saw this happen but was not himself in water." The boy was trying to picture the event.

From Mawena's blanket came a soft hiss. They all looked over, but saw no movement and heard no further noise.

"Water bubbled around this man's legs," Arajik continued, "but no longer such strong current so far from the main stream. Every step toward the river, though, caused someone to be that much more likely to be washed away—for water depth increased even though the power in it grew gradually less. Still, a husband was unable to get closer than a *kayak*'s length to his wife, as he returned, without risking all—himself and beautiful Mawena as well—and no help likely."

The man glanced over to the motionless bundle of fur that enclosed his wife. The boys were silent, waiting for their father to continue his tale. The series of events Arajik was describing could never happen near the sea—at least, not on any part of the coastal plains Nik knew. Nor not on any inland tundra Nik had seen before this trip.

"She stayed against that tree," Arajik continued, "for two sleeps. Following the first wild surge came new rising water which did not have the force of the first wave but which gradually widened the river to include the tree where Mawena clung.

"It was during this time, someone decided later, that the camp became flooded and all was lost—" his voice broke, and he looked searchingly at each of his sons—"but it happens that Arajik was in error," he finished quietly. As he knew, Urgit had survived.

Once more, Nik mused about the ways his father seemed to have changed during the time of hardship that followed the flood—or at least since Nik had last seen him. In the silence that ensued following the startling admission of Arajik's being wrong about the fate of the full fishing party, Nik related the account which Urgit favored in his own descriptions of the event. The disaster as he perceived it afterward. His own actions in response to the calamity.

Normally volatile Arajik listened mildly without comment. It was Sitok who kept interjecting angrily to say that Urgit *should* have done this thing, *could* have done that other. Nik was surprised, for it had always been he and never his brother who mistrusted each version of Urgit's tale. And now? Nik had mellowed with time and with experience in the wild . . . along with knowledge of Urgit. Sitok, it was, who was now critical.

Even when Nik concluded telling the tale which the young survivor Urgit had told in the village, Arajik made no comment—neither to Nik's story nor to Sitok's dire accusations. Instead, he turned over in his sleeping robes and soon snored.

Nik's sleep time that night was filled with troubled dreams and half-waking fantasies. Early following the restless night, himself the only one stirring, he trimmed the lamp sinew to bring up the flame, then searched silently as possible at the bottom of his hunting bag. He brought up the packet rolled in ptarmigan hide secured with sinew. This, he opened for the first time—the packet given him by Pahnee before she disappeared inside *tingmisut* and flew away.

218

He listened to the steady breathing of his sleeping family, carefully studied each member for several moments. He wanted privacy and light. Now he adjusted the drawstring to open the hide bag fully, dragged it over to half cover him as he squatted beside the lamp.

He unwrapped the packet with unsteady fingers and examined the contents. Inside were a full man—as many as Nik had fingers and toes—of the split white skins Pah-nee and Pehl-son called *paper*. Two were filled with pictures that he knew Pah-nee had drawn. He recognized her art from times when they together had used bone tools or snow knives to draw in fresh snow. He could identify nothing much on these other than peculiarly dressed *Kalunait* and one strange-looking little animal with almost no neck but a round head with pointed ears and having single hairs jutting out from each side above its mouth to beyond its cheeks. Nik was sure that the figures represented parts of her dog-world to the south. *And was Nik to use the blank slips to draw pictures from **his own world**?* Why else would she include this bit of wood with a point that bled grey when pressed to *paper?*

He found one more item among the delicate hides. A flat, folded bag made also of *paper* had strange markings on one side. Up in one corner was the most remarkable *picture!* It was about the size of his thumbnail, and he did not know what that picture represented—but oh, the colors! He ran his finger across the small square containing blood red, summer fox brown, ocean green, wet-shale black, along with the blues, pinks, purples, yellows and oranges that glowed in his own north sky. Brighter, though, bolder than even the most vivid among spirit lights.

"What does someone have here?" Arajik startled Nik by asking. His father knelt beside him, eyes on the items Nik had spread out on his robe. "Where did Nik find this?"

Nik told him about Pehl-son, about Pah-nee and their visit, realizing with surprise that neither he nor Sitok had mentioned the *kalunait* visitors that their father himself had invited.

Arajik's eyebrows shot up. Then he chuckled. "Every dog-person in the south expresses a desire to visit a village of the frozen isles. He is then invited—but never arrives. In fact, is not seen again."

"Pehl-son speaks *Inupiaq.*"

"*Ee-ee.* And well. Someone remembers. That sets him apart—eh, a high-shouldered man with a voice like the rumble of sea ice at high tide? And hair the color of sunlight on a summer-time weasel?"

Nik raised his eyebrows in agreement.

Arajik sucked in breath, Yes. "A memorable dog-person, clever. He was called an *anthropologist.* Eh. But you say that he brought someone with him?"

"Pah-nee. His . . . child. Nik's age." His father did not have to know immediately that Pah-nee was a female. Nik had not—and had been better off in ignorance.

"This *paper,* then?"

"It happens that Nik and others hunted and fished together with the dog-persons. Starting with the whale that gave itself on the very day they arrived on a *tingmisut* from the sky."

"—And?"

"When they left, Pah-nee gave this to Nik for a parting gift." Arajik also did not need to know that his younger son had played the total *soospuk* at the departure.

"And does a young hunter understand what is here?" Arajik pointed to the oddly folded bag bearing the square of color.

"*Owka,* " Nik admitted.

"An *envelope.* " The man picked it up, turned it over and around, inspecting it. "Someone fills it with the little white sheets when they have markings. Then it is sealed by wetting the shiny portion with the tongue." He laughed. "One must close the opening rapidly, before the moisture freezes. And the picture? Eh, a *stamp,* to pay for having someone take the *envelope* to your friend's *igloo.* "

Nik was astonished. He would walk a long way for a picture such as this, he supposed. Perhaps not so far as the land of the *Kalunait*, but far.

"How does Arajik *know* such things?" Once again, the boy was incredulous over his father's vast erudition. Trees, Indians, wolves—now this *stamp,* this *envelope,* their uses.

"A man traveled often in his younger days to villages so large they had names," Arajik explained simply.

Nik and Sitok agreed privately to bring up the summer accident one more time.

"A father said," Sitok opened the conversation following an evening meal and long after their mother had rolled into a robe, "that Mawena stayed in the tree for two sleeps."

"Ee-ee," Arajik agreed, "because until then, the water would not permit her husband to get close enough to help her."

Nik reflected that it was a pity that *Inuit* do not swim like fish and sea-bears and even *tuktu*.

"And after the first night, she said no words. Nor has she since." No criticism echoed in his tone, only regret and uncertainty. His voice wandered off and ceased as he mused privately. He put a snack of *muktuk* into his mouth, used the round *ulu* to sever the chunk cleanly at his lips. Then he chewed for a long time with no other sound in the *igloo.*

Nik believed Arajik, but he had trouble picturing his delicate mother clinging for so long to a rough branch in one of those *trees* that surrounded Arajik's lake. She would not have been gladdened by the experience. She must have thought herself in Paija's vicious grasp for all that time. Why, Mawena even persuaded some other woman—never she!—to accompany her husband on a long trail whenever Kiti could not go. Not of course on Arajik's treks south which took several moons by dog sled, there and back, to find markets for the village pelts. No woman went on these, nor no son either—no space, with sled stacked high! But it was not easy to envision Mawena clinging to the rough hide of a *tree* over several sleeps and the long days between. Nik shivered from thinking of the icy rainwater as it swirled and sucked at his mother's body. He winced with pain over her injured leg, felt the aching and the throb. He itched from the scratchy branchings of that stranded *tree* afloat behind her, pressing, poking and tormenting as it bobbed upon the current. Eh, his mother? No wonder his father had faltered even in describing the experience.

Nik was unwilling, however, to let the conversation drift elsewhere or sink away completely. He glanced over at his brother. Sitok seemed to be absorbed in his own thoughts.

"After two sleeps," Nik persisted on a brighter note, "someone *did* help the woman get to high ground."

Arajik shuddered to attention, raised his eyebrows, drew in breath—Yes. "But then came three or four sleeps more before it was possible to wade back across the still broad river to the camping place."

After more moments of silence, Sitok finally helped to guide the talk. "The *kayak,*" he said quietly.

"Gone," Arajik said. "No trace by the time the man and woman reached the river bank."

Nik tried. "And there on the camp side of the river now within its banks, the parents found . . . "

". . . Nothing! Eh, the travel lamp. A heavy item that water did not take. But nothing more. And the river had flooded through the shelter, although one could not say when.

For this reason, someone guessed that the others both were swept away, especially when no trace of either body could be found."

"So no sign of Urgit or Pak," Nik summarized.

Arajik blinked his eyes, kept the lashes down several moments—an emphatic *No.* No sign.

"Someone not present at the time will have difficulty imagining the power of that enormous wave which was parent to the following flood."

Nik decided that Arajik's account with Urgit's were two sides of the same flat rock. They complemented each other. Different sets of eyes and ears, that was all. Identical *kamik* on disparate feet.

While his family slept, Nik watched clouds chase each other across the moon. Tomorrow or perhaps the next day, they would be back in their village. What of Urgit? Arajik had said that he himself spent no time trying to find Pak and Urgit— Nik's father too had assumed that the other two were swept away. *How then could timid and untried Urgit be expected to search alone across what he thought of as a killing ground?*

Too, Arajik had said that he spent all of his energy for many sleeps at trying to stay alive—not going over what happened first and second and last during the day on which the river fell down the hillside. Or during the time immediately after. Arajik had, in fact, already given several versions of the catastrophe—he knew he had been inconsistent, admitted this was so: "A muddled memory of a disordered time." And his sons readily accepted the discrepancies. . . .

Yet, Nik always expected Urgit to recall every single moment and every detail of movement following the flood— right up until he left the lake to struggle home. Nik insisted that Urgit tell his recollections time and time again—then scolded bitterly when even one detail was not precisely like the last account. Nik had been totally unreasonable and even cruel, he realized now.

Sitok, though, made it clear throughout the journey back that he planned to confront Urgit in a drum duel. Arajik was surprised at his older brother's being willing to perform, for Sitok had diligently avoided such action in the past. But along the trail the last few days Sitok privately or with his brother had been humming and drumming and dancing and practicing poetry to make himself ready.

One early morning, when Arajik and Mawena still slept within the trail house built the night before, Sitok approached Nik outside. "In the village, someone wished for his elder brother to meet Urgit in the dueling ring. These days, the young hunter has little to say on the subject."

Nik did not know how to answer. He knew exactly how he himself felt. He also knew how much Sitok wanted to try out publicly his new performance skills—on this matter that he had now convinced himself was a worthy struggle.

The older brother continued. "Did the false man not say that he saw Pak's broken body? That he saw Arajik's smashed *kayak?*"

Nik sucked in cold air, Yes. "And what was more, Urgit probably *did* see what he described—some several days before Arajik and Mawena got back across the river." In fact, nothing their father had related so far meant that Urgit could *not* have seen and done exactly what he reported. Urgit never claimed to see any body other than that of his own father.

Sitok went on. "And do we not know now that the man took from *both* camps everything of value that he could carry when he left immediately—even *before* the camp itself flooded? Leaving Arajik and Mawena to die for lack of tools and therefore food and shelter?"

224

Nik raised his eyebrows, Yes—Urgit had done those things. Urgit had possibly given in to panic. What would Nik have done, given the same situation? Or even Sitok? They *both* knew what Arajik had done—concluded that the other two were swept away and then focused fully on the business of keeping Mawena and himself alive. Could Urgit be expected to be more thorough?

"Soon," his brother continued darkly, "Sitok will meet that terrible man in the dueling ring. For it is not good to have a liar live among us!"

On the last night before reaching the village, Nik went outside because he could not sleep. They had found their parents, yes. But his mother—eh, what a sad and silent woman! And the duel-to-come between Sitok and Urgit—what value lay in that?

And *Pah-nee . . . would they ever see each other again!?* Not likely, and mostly because of Nik's foolishness. How many times each day did Nik think about that dog-person? How often did he muse about her being here now, with him, with them all? And yes—he would admit it to himself and no one else—he was *glad* that this amazing young *kaluna* was a girl!

So much was on his mind these days, he realized in wonder, that he hardly ever worried anymore about whether he was to become a good hunter. He grinned in the darkness, remembering a time not long ago when he thought of little else. Until only recently, this matter of being skillful on the trail was a dilemma that smothered him with its weight.

Like his present uncertainties, one cloud above him in the sky stretched out like a seal reaching for the flippers of another, both scrambling across the moon, more creatures reeling behind. Nik decided that he must focus on one problem until he solved it, not let a mob of difficulties chase each other's tails in his head.

All right, the first puzzle. *What about Mawena?*—not that she was likely to change as a result of his effort. His mother seemed to be holding her life spirits away from her. Yet, she did not wish to die. Someone who wants quietus simply goes unclothed beyond the *igloo* and **dies.** Or in a village, someone has the loving family build a distant shelter on the prairie or on *siku* the traveler, then seal the person in.

Nik had asked his father if Mawena could walk, yet. And Arajik's response was that she *did* not. So yes, Nik decided from his emphasis, she probably could—but chose not to. And then Sitok, one night recently, had asked Arajik whether the tree which broke her leg had perhaps also injured the throat box which channels speech.

Arajik had smiled. *"Owka, ai-ee!* No indeed, the words she shouted at her husband from the tree on that first night— *Hoo-oo!* Loud and clear above the rumble of the flood! Her leg was injured, true, but her speech was in good order, both pronunciation and volume!"

Nik wished he could see into a person's mind and understand the reasoning. He chided himself sternly that a boy surely knows his mother. He has bounced along in her hood for most of three winters at least, and spent much later time there as well. What is happening here? And just as the moon emerged brilliantly with no vapor trailing across it, an answer came to him . . . a solution so simple that it already had the feel of truth. . . .

Mawena was angry! He remembered over many winters his mother's arguments with *Ananatsiak,* with Grandmother Kiti. He recalled bitter words spit out in fury when no other person was present to hear—no other than the child named Nik in Mawena's hood or playing on the *iglerk*. His mother would bring up some subject of discontent over and again. She never allowed it to be swallowed and forgotten before she had chewed it to nothing still recognizable as the earlier issue but equally unpalatable. Kiti, he had seen so often, would busy herself without responding until—having had enough—she would fix her daughter-in-law with a steady and unblinking gaze calculated to send the woman raging from the *igloo.*

His mother had a long memory and was not one to let a matter lie even when the outcome had already occurred and there was no help for it. No *pirtok* for Mawena! No "so be it" and "let it lie" for his mother. Kiti had explained to Nik at one time or another that the extremely young and spectacularly beautiful Mawena had on her tundra home been much sought after by men. She had been an orphan whom Arajik brought from inland tundra up to the ice islands prematurely. In fact, long before she had learned to be a woman.

"How many winters?" he remembered asking *Ananatsiak.*

"Perhaps eleven or twelve, no one knows—so for some several winters to come, she was but a daughter in the household." Then, regretfully, "A lovable but inexorable child who embraced sympathy and love but never training." She chuckled, then added, "At least not willingly."

Riding the sled along with Mawena's tantrums but on the other runner, Nik recalled his mother's unbounded pride where Arajik was concerned. She never seemed to tire of telling others—especially other village women—about her extraordinary man. She of course told it in the Inupiat way. "This poor excuse for a husband lies always on the sleeping ledge and snores, so what can a woman do?" Her *message,* however, was that no other man anywhere had such *silatunerk,* such shrewdness and intelligence, such strength

227

and good fortune as "her" Arajik. Why, he could accomplish . . . anything at all! He could easily fly to the moon or slide to the center of the earth like the best *angakok*, should he wish to do so. And of course such a husband was perfection that such an ugly, stupid wife did not deserve!

Nik remembered how tired he became, even as a youngster, of hearing Mawena applaud his father. So did other women of the village tire, for he had noticed the looks they exchanged. He had listened to their pale reasons for remembering a task elsewhere. For leaving the woman alone to bluster in solitude. Ever since he could recall, Nik had thought his mother's praise of her husband excessive. Compared with other fathers in the village, for example, Nik found Arajik to be short-tempered and gruff—not ever so with his wife or mother, no. But certainly with his younger son, and sometimes with the elder—and sometimes with villagers. Still, Nik also knew that Mawena *really believed* Arajik to be perfect. She considered him some kind of powerful spirit. Her tiresome praise was totally sincere.

And then last summer, Mawena learned suddenly that Arajik could *not* do all things. Or perhaps she still thought he could but *would* not. After all, he did not fly through the air to rescue her from the branches of a half-drowned tree. He did not calm angry flood waters—did not even keep the two of them warm and dry, let alone fed, at least not at first. And *well* fed? Not ever during their ordeal, at least according to Arajik's account. Nik and Sitok knew that their father had done the best he could—in fact did very well indeed just to survive, under the circumstances. But the man was no all-powerful spirit. He was *Inuk,* one human being.

And now Mawena was angry with her husband, and had been ever since the accident. Knowing his mother, Nik decided that Mawena was in fact likely to continue being angry indefinitely. . . . And his mother had shouted at Arajik from her perch in the tree? Nik giggled. Mawena was never a person to ignore her outrage. Still chortling, he decided that more than broth would bubble in the *igloo* when they returned to Kiti.

CHAPTER 17.
SORTING IT OUT
AT HOME

Nik was halfway through the porch when he heard his grandmother's deep voice within the snowhouse. Her tone did not promise delight for whomever she was talking to. He pulled himself up to the hide door and hunkered down to listen. Then a slow grin spread across his face as he realized that it was Mawena who was receiving the attention of *Ananatsiak.*

In the three sleeps since their return, Mawena had lain silent in her robes, had eaten passively whatever was given her with neither word nor look of *nakorami.* Never a thank you! And because she was delighted with the result of the inland search—the return of the parents—Kiti had held her tongue. But Nik had seen her looks darken more with each day. He had known that confrontation was coming . . . and this would be no drum feud, either, for women rarely dueled. That was mostly for men and for equals. These two were not matched—not in the hierarchy of the household and certainly not in wit. Kiti was the elder woman, and she was Arajik's mother. Her decisions within the home and family were final, largely because Mawena had never taken on or wanted the responsibility. More, Mawena never had been— never would *be!*—a match for the older woman. She did not possess the wisdom, the language, strength or the humor.

Certainly not the vitality, Nik realized suddenly—other than this unreasoning obstinacy she presently displayed. Here would be the test where Nik would learn whether his theory was correct.

"Mawena will speak!" Kiti thundered.

Silence.

"Mawena must **say** if she wishes to die!"

Continued silence.

Nik pushed up the hanging hide door slightly, rested the side of his parka on his arm so that he could see without being seen. As usual, these days, Mawena was a lump shrouded by robes on the *iglerk*. Kiti stood an arm's length from that mound, staring hard.

"—Because if a person wishes to die," she continued, "then it happens that preparations must be made."

Silence, no movement from the bundle of fur. Was his mother even awake?

Kiti's tone deepened, became more intense. Nik winced in recollection of times when she had spoken to *him* thus. "Mawena will *not* turn her face to the wall and die in this fine snowhouse!"

Yes, more silence.

"No need for all to move because a woman is too selfish to consider others." If someone dies in an unsealed snow house, everyone must abandon the village to escape restless and perhaps malicious spirits. Thus someone who expects to die—whether by choice or through physical decay—should either leave the group entirely or request to be sealed away in a tiny *igloo* built for that purpose.

No sound from Mawena, no twitch of bedding fur.

"So *speak!*"

Still nothing.

"Does the wife of Kiti's son want a small house built on the plains? Something with the opening carefully sealed after she enters?"

No response.

"Or does she prefer to be left naked on *siku* far from any shelter?"

Nik thought Mawena's stubborn silence would continue forever, but he was wrong.

His mother's face came out of her robe, and it twisted around to glare at Kiti. "This would Kiti prefer! For she has always wished to have her son and his family to herself!"

"Eh, the woman speaks!" Kiti chuckled.

"Someone nags and carps and fusses until a *stone* would speak!"

"*Ai-ee!* It would, wouldn't it!" Kiti was laughing now.

But Nik knew not to enter the snowhouse. Some problems had to be solved.

Now his grandmother asked, "And *does* Mawena wish the family to begin preparation for her death?"

"Kiti hopes so! And this one *should* say it—*ee-ee!*—and then die!—just so Arajik will be angry with his mother!"

"Words of a *soospuk!* Kiti knows well that Mawena does not intend to die."

Mawena murmured, "The woman cannot be certain."

"Wrong! This old woman knew from the start! Someone who wishes to die does not *eat* so much. Mawena devours food constantly. Already, she resembles a gravid seal cow!"

"*Owka!*" No! The younger woman blazed at her mother-in-law, and Nik wondered if she might actually strike out. But at least, Mawena was talking.

"And next, the invalid will leave her robes and stand."

Again, silence.

Kiti reached over to unwind Mawena with no great tenderness from the fur blanket in which she had rolled herself.

Nik's mother did not respond except to bring another fur around her.

Kiti picked up the corner of that one, pulled it away completely and threw it with the first into a heap at the end of the sleeping ledge.

Mawena dragged another across her.

"Hoo-oo," breathed Nik softly. "Here it comes!"

And Kiti with one motion sent that one, too, to the end of the ledge. Nik could not keep the corners of his mouth from turning up, and he had to pinch his voice box to keep from uttering sound. What followed was a progression through all the robes, Mawena grasping one and Kiti sweeping it away. At last, his mother lay on the rough ice of the ledge wearing her inner furs—her *illupak*—but having bare feet.

"S-someone is c-c-cold." Her voice trembled.

"Then someone should stand up and do some work."

"It happens that she c-c-cannot! Her leg was badly injured—broken!" A whimper in the voice.

"Was! *Ee-ee,* perhaps yes, but now is healed."

Nik could hear Mawena's chattering teeth, the unsteadiness in her voice. "It h-h-happens that a fragile woman is too c-c-cold to stand up."

Kiti turned to pick up a small stone bowl from its strap above the lamp. The contents steamed. "What will heat the woman is this hot blubber." With both hands, she held the bowl over Mawena and the sleeping ledge. "This will warm the hair and head—" She tilted the stone as she spoke.

Mawena was suddenly standing on the floor of the snowhouse. Nik saw that she did not at all resemble a seal about to produce a pup. Mawena was still so pretty. Unlike Kiti, who with dark half-moons beneath her eyes and cheekbones sharp as split stone was thinner than Nik had ever seen her. His mother, though, was in good flesh. Actually beautiful, especially for a woman having two sons nearly grown. She was well padded, had wide, high cheekbones, clear black eyes that glinted in lamplight. Chattering with chill, she picked up the bladder which contained her outdoor clothing.

"This dull old woman knows another thing," Kiti said as she helped a shivering Mawena pull furs from the bag and put them on.

Mawena did not look up.

"She knows that someone has practiced using the injured leg when no one was about."

"Ee-ee," Mawena admitted softly, "else the person would not be able to walk when she wished."

"And *ahmi,* who could know when she might wish?" Kiti smiled. "Now it is time to find work for this suddenly vital woman." She walked toward Nik at the doorway, and he held his breath. But instead of pulling back the baffle, she picked up the two somewhat stiff, still unprocessed caribou skins Arajik had brought from their inland camp.

Nik knew his grandmother had been working on the skins since their return. She had scraped them hard. She had soaked them in urine from the waste bladders, hung them in the wind, pounded them, chewed, washed, scraped some more, repeated the process. Still, because of being neglected by Mawena when fresh, they were still unyielding to the touch, not soft and rippling as caribou hides could be.

"Here!" and Kiti thrust the skins at Mawena. "These need to be softened."

"Hoo-oo!" the small woman protested. "Someone is too strict. These hides were never good."

"And did the caribou who wore them complain?" Kiti grinned. "Eh—just feel the young wife's teeth—go ahead, she must put a finger to her mouth!"

Ananatsiak waited while Mawena hesitantly brought one bare hand upward, then stopped. Kiti impatiently used her own two fingers to push Mawena's lips above and below the handsome rows of snowy enamel. With her other hand, Kiti pressed Mawena's index finger hard across the teeth.

"Hoo-oo! Is the woman not *ashamed* at her age to have such long teeth?"

Nik's mother took the *tuktu* hides with a sigh, looked over at the bare sleep ledge.

"Eh, first we arrange the robes," Kiti told her.

Mawena sat cross-legged at one end of the deeply blanketed *iglerk.* She examined the hides and took exploratory nibbles.

Nik lowered the baffle hide and squirmed around to leave as silently as he had come.

Then he heard his mother speak, and he paused. "One supposes Kiti will tell her son of his wife's foolishness?"

Kiti laughed. "One's son is fully aware of the wife's folly," she chuckled. And then with warmth, "Arajik is also aware of her tender heart, her gentle manner and her beauty—when not angered, anyway. Yes, he knows her many *good* qualities, as well."

That was it, then. Nik always knew that Kiti cared for Mawena as she would care for any troublesome child—or grandchild—of her own. He was back through the tunnel and nearly off the porch going outside when he heard Kiti's voice again, this time raised and resonant down the tunnel. She must have lifted the portal.

"And one other who knows her foolish as well as her good qualities is Mawena's younger boy!"

Having been thoroughly chilled by the ice on which he lay to listen, Nik almost welcomed the heat of embarrassment which suddenly whipped through him.

CHAPTER 18.
CIRCULAR MATTERS

Content, Nik sat by the seal oil lamp applying his pencil to another slip of Pah-nee's *paper*. Imitating Pehl-son, he had kept the writing utensil in a pocket of his *illupak*. Kiti and he were actually—for once—alone together in the snowhouse.

Before the sleep, yesterday, Nik had convinced Urgit that Urgit himself should take the trail with village men and learn from them what his father had not taught him. By promising to oil his *kayak* for him, he had bribed Atik to invite Urgit along this morning on the hunt. Last night on the *iglerk* before sleep, Nik had talked a long time with Sitok. A dueling ring having a diameter the width of two *kayaks* was already stamped out for a time following the hunt. Nik convinced his brother, finally, that personal malice between Sitok and Urgit had already collected in that circle. Nik was not certain that this was so, but the idea made sense to Sitok, who trusted his younger brother for social sensitivity. Besides, the notion promoted harmony on the trail between the two duelers-to-be.

Also yesterday, Nik had suggested to his mother that she could escape Kiti's critical eye for a time by visiting a friend on this day—any friend—in another *igloo*. Mawena had dutifully taken a *tuktu* hide to work on when she hurried out this morning. Fortunately, Aunt Saruna was midwifing for another village up the coast. She would be gone for an indeterminate time, and Nik of course had not had to arrange *that* event.

So now, with most village men hunting and with his mother and Saruna gone, Nik had *Ananatsiak* all to himself, for once. It had not been easy, and he felt much triumph and only a little embarrassment about his role in clearing out the *igloo*. He picked up his *pencil* and focused his eyes on the *paper* before him. His mind, though, was plotting courteous, inoffensive ways to elicit information from his grandmother.

While Nik sketched, Kiti worked on a lush and pale-furred hide. This pelt was from a sea-bear that a villager had stalked and caught and given her in thanks for expert medical service she had rendered in the past—not "payment," something she would refuse, but "appreciation." Already, the fleece on the huge white hide rippled softly with every move as she continued to scrape and rub oil into the skin side.

"Inupiat do not draw," Kiti told Nik.

"Inupiat do not have *pencils,*" Nik retorted.

Kiti kept on scraping with sure, firm strokes, and Nik continued his hesitant sketching.

"Someone plans to put onto this *paper* all that is round," he told her. He was proud to have finally figured out the meaning of Pah-nee's oft-repeated English syllables.

Kiti grunted to show that she heard him but was not impressed. She continued to scrape the pelt.

Nik needed most immediately to ask Kiti about Potok. What were her thoughts regarding changes in his manner since Arajik's return? Or were the differences only in Nik's imperfect perception? Other concerns in addition needed her opinion so that they would rest more easily in his head.

"Someone has matters that need discussion," he ventured.

But Kiti chatted cheerfully on about the way Inupiat art is practiced only on useful items. She did not directly criticize him, only remind him gently that he was not a *Kalunait*.

Nik wanted to discuss with her alone the strange words Nik had heard come out of Potok's mouth. He wanted her response to some peculiar behavior he had observed in these days since the boys returned with their parents.

Potok. Rather than rejoice that his long-time friend Arajik had come back unharmed, the man seemed to resent the reappearance. He lately, and previously and primarily Arajik, were the two "old" men among the village hunters, the ones sought out by others for their wisdom. Arajik had so far lived forty winters—two full men, twice all the fingers and toes on one *inuk*. Potok, five more, but without the other's broad travel experience. In the past, Potok was solicited on family matters—for all knew that not Arajik and Mawena but rather Grandmother Kiti bore most of the burden and reaped much of the joy where Arajik's family was concerned.

Not that Arajik was a *bad* family man. He was a superb provider. He always made sure that sufficient food was cached before he left on a trip. But ever since Nik could remember, his father traveled far and frequently. Nor did Mawena or any woman accompany him on his longer trips, those heavily loaded with village furs for trading in the south. The father in this household was a traveler. His *kamik* seemed best satisfied when they slapped along a trail.

So, although Potok was often deferred to by males on domestic difficulties, it was—or had been in the past— Arajik's advice that was sought on all else. When he was available, anyway. And Arajik had not been "available" for the last several moons, Nik had to remind himself.

Before, the two older men had exchanged hunting and travel tales, had enjoyed each other's company. At least, so it seemed to those who observed, including Nik. The two had discussed village matters at great length and in mutual respect for each other's opinions.

But the relationship had now changed in subtle ways. The two were visiting again—a habit of a hundred moons is not easily broken. But instead of telling tales and laughing and clasping each other on the shoulder when one or the other arrived or departed, long silences now occurred. What had previously been rich and welcome differences of opinion leading to hours of good-natured argument now resulted in Potok's loud challenges and ultimate stomping from the *igloo.* Why?

But Kiti hauled Nik back to her own subject. "Those bits of *paper* on which Nik draws have no use beneath the sun or moon—at least, not to Inupiat!"

Nik continued to sketch as he considered her words. He had drawn an *igloo* and a dueling drum. Now he was working on the likeness of an *ulu,* the sharp round utility knife.

"Potok." He threw the word out as a lure, to see whether his grandmother would seize it.

She scraped at the hide with suddenly renewed vigor but said nothing.

Nik tried again. "It may be that Potok is not so friendly since Arajik returned." A statement, not a question. She could not reproach him for a *statement,* could not say that he was rudely crowding her on a personal matter by asking such a question.

"It happens," she agreed, "that he has not been neighborly for some time."

Not behavior that began with Arajik's return? Nik certainly recalled how Potok had influenced villagers not to help the brothers with building their own snowhouse. But Nik had believed Potok's attitude then to be based on resentment over losing from his household a good hunter: Sitok. And also losing a kinsman-to-be who would—so her father hoped!—someday marry Erin. Erin hoped so, too. Nik, as well. Probably Kiti. Why not Sitok? Or did Nik's brother have her featured in some future he envisioned secretly?

Eh, there was also Potok's insistence that village-captured food be divided with no portions for non-contributing Urgit and his aunt. Also none for the two visitors, Pehl-son and his child. Yet, Nik's family had discussed those curious decisions later. Kiti suggested that the man was perhaps unsteadied by Arajik's absence, the two having stood and spoken together for so long. *But who can see into another's heart?* The family had decided to abandon their concern when Kiti proclaimed that they must build their own place, then simply wait and see. Might it be that she had waited so long now that she *saw* more than others in the family?

"Someone has wondered if Potok moved against Arajik's family while all but Kiti were gone." Not a query. Nik hoped, however, that his statement-without-demand would *function* as one.

Silence at first. Then, the busy fingers of *Ananatsiak* slowed. A frown creased three vertical lines between her sparse brows. "The man discovered the caches—first one, then another and yet one more until he found a total of seven."

"This is so?" A cache was no secret. Its content belonged to whoever built and filled the storage. But to actually *look* for the caches of others? The boys had cleared five onto their sled before going inland. What little would not fit, they had placed in the storage cellar by the *igloo.* Food remained in only two caches, when they left—food that he and Sitok had left for Kiti and their two permanent houseguests, Saruna and Urgit, who presently slept on the *iglerk* in what had been Pehl-son's attached dwelling.

And Potok troubled himself to search for even those? Nik wondered if perhaps young people like himself were not supposed to cache food? But he had never heard of any such taboo.

"Hunting and fishing here were not successful while Sitok and Nik were gone," Kiti continued.

Nik waited, sketching in a broad arc to suggest an *igloo* for backgrounding his other rounded items.

"*Angakok* was brought in to cast a spell," his grandmother continued. "An angry charlatan who spoke often and privately with Potok. At last, he returned to tell everyone that the sons of Arajik had taken all the good luck with them when they went inland off the normal season."

Nik laughed. "And if this were so, the two **needed** every bit of such fortune!"

"So then Potok said that the remaining cache food belonged to the suffering people of the village."

"*Hoo-oo!*" Nik was too shocked at first to do more than disapprove. Only someone starving and desperate may break into another's cache—and such a person is honor bound to replace at earliest opportunity whatever is taken.

"Does it happen that the people had growling bellies?" It was a question—but permitted because it was not personal, requesting general information about a past time.

"Supplies were dwindling. People became anxious when provision was no longer replaced as rapidly as it was used."

Nik frowned. Potok had overstepped. He must have gambled that the inland group would not return. No wonder he was restive over Arajik's coming back. Probably, all those in the village who had consumed food from the caches of Arajik's family were also uneasy. And resentful.

Still incredulous at what Kiti reported, Nik's next words came in tumbled phrases. "Potok . . . told villagers to take—eh, how could he justify the keeping for himself?— or the giving away!—of food stored by another and needed by that family? This is not *peeusinga*—not the Way of the People!"

Kiti had a stubborn piece of the *nanuk* pelt in her mouth, and she chewed thoughtfully while Nik tried to get his fluttering spirits to settle. The lamp burned low and smoked, but Kiti did not attend it. The frown stayed on her scrawny face, her eyes fastened on the pelt which lay across her lap. There was more to come, Nik knew. He coughed, glanced over at the lamp, rubbed with his hands to clear his eyes, hacked to rid his throat of smoke, hunkered down to get below the haze thickening in the top of the *igloo.* He sighed, then sketched half-heartedly at the paper before him while he waited for his grandmother to continue.

"Potok said that Arajik's sons—he called them *illiyardjuk,* orphans—had stolen provision from the village by taking so much food on the trail."

"Hoo-oo-oo!" Not so. Only food collected by either Nik or Sitok, or by the two brothers together, had been cached. Grandmother knew this to be so. The others would need proof to believe otherwise.

"Potok told everyone that Sitok and especially Nik captured all the food in those caches while hunting with the village group." Pent-up words came tumbling from the woman's mouth even though her voice remained calm. "To prove the veracity of his statement, he asserted that most food in caches was stored while Sitok lay wounded on the *iglerk.*

"'All know,' said the false man, 'that Nik is not yet a mature hunter so could never have found so much on his own.'"

Nik's voice was strained when he spoke. "Still, a grandmother knew well that the main hunters for this family while Sitok mended were Nik and at the first, Pah-nee." Nik did not want to reproach her—but he could not imagine Kiti keeping quiet on hearing such malicious falsehood.

"Ee-ee, two *lucky* hunters," she continued. "Creatures of both land and sea were eager to give themselves, for there was need. Potok knew all of this."

Nik spoke. "Kiti also knew that the two went out independent of villagers, occasionally with Atik. Nik and

Pah-nee went to search more frequently than others—and stayed longer on the trail even though they captured less."

The woman raised her eyebrows and sucked in a long, saturating breath. She agreed entirely. "Perhaps *too* often and *too* long." She reached over to renew the lamp, after all. Eyes twinkling, "Pehl-son suffered great anxiety."

Nik knew this to be true. He also knew that Kiti was trying to change the subject. She must feel relieved, having told him what needed to be said. But Nik was not ready to leave the knotty matter of the caches. That Potok would rob another's storage and distribute the content as if it were his own was . . . eh, beyond disrespect. It was villainous . . . not *peeusinga* . . . behavior which would—in any other village, with any other man—result in his being banished from the group forever. No drum duel—just "Go!" Or worse could happen. Food was a subject most serious.

What was occurring here? Nik felt as if he stood on a small *siku* melting beneath his feet. "And that the villagers would accept Potok's words and actions—"

"—Some did not, although all were apprehensive about the food supply. When he pointed out the whale and walrus—"

"—Whale and walrus—yes!" Nik broke in. "The share Potok declared fair and proper was given to this family, and no more—just as was given to Potok's family—but not even extra food came here for Urgit and Auntie although it was soon enough that they moved to this *igloo* and long enough that they have been staying. Nor nothing of course for the two guests. But then that meager share given was *stretched,* thanks to a prudent grandmother."

Potok knew his statement to be false—the *people* knew!

"So now the caches are empty?" Since return from inland, the family had been subsisting on food brought back on the sled and placed in the surprisingly empty storage pit near the *igloo*. Nik should have gone out with the hunters today, he realized now, if provision was so low.

"The caches have been barren for some time—although the food from them may not yet be consumed," Kiti answered. "Some remnants may be in Potok's cache or that of a villager."

Nik bit back anger and hurt. Someone—eh, Potok was storing it for his own family. And did it happen that *Ananatsiak* had gone hungry? Of course! It was hunger and not worry, as they thought, which accounted for the wizened frame and hollow eyes when they returned.

How could Potok do this thing? How could he dare? Softly, "And the villagers, Grandmother?"

"As someone said before, the people here knew better. Some would not take food."

"Eh, then Potok lost face!"

Kiti's brows raised, Yes. "Potok was angry. He with his family cleared one cache for themselves alone, took everything to their own storage place. Erin is honest, and she was of course humiliated. She came here to tell me that the cache food filled their storage pit to overflowing. So much was in the cache that it became necessary to keep some in their *igloo.*"

"Where it would go bad if not consumed soon," Nik mused aloud, "and so be wasted."

"*Ee-ee,* a boy speaks accurately! But for any loss, Potok will find a way somehow to blame Arajik and his sons. Still, when a grandmother says the villagers would not take from the caches, she means **directly**."

"Eh?" Nik gave up completely on his drawing. All of this Kiti said was distressing—not good information to receive about a man *or* a village.

"Believing this *igloo* of Arajik to have great plenty,

almost all the people who did not partake from the caches visited here—to eat, of course—with Kiti, also Saruna and Urgit. Every day. It is unknown whether Potok suggested that they do this thing."

"Grandmother—who else knows about all this?" Nik was positive that Sitok did not. Had Kiti told Arajik?

"Those present at the time—"

"—Arajik?"

"*Owka,* No. He was not present then."

"And when the father and elder son learn now that the caches were plundered . . . " Nik's voice trailed off. He realized that he had not lived enough winters to predict what would happen.

His grandmother ignored the thought he had voiced. "Thus, with the many guests coming to the *igloo* and consuming food, the storage pit supply decreased. When Kiti realized that the onslaught was deliberate, she contrived with Saruna and Urgit not to be home when people came to call."

"But where did the three go?"

"Eh, onto the ice—fishing."

"Grandmother!"

She cackled. "When only fish were brought out to share with visitors, people discovered other activities with which to occupy themselves."

Nik laughed. Who but Kiti would dare to play so loosely with the laws of hospitality! "And are people now angry?"

"*Owka,* only ashamed and embarrassed. They knew their actions were dishonorable. And they may now be frightened of Arajik should he learn about what happened."

"Potok, too?"

"Embarrassed also—which is worse for the soul than anger." Her voice softened almost to a whisper, and she glanced at the baffle hanging in the doorway. "Potok was certain that Arajik and Mawena were dead. *Also* convinced by his own desire that Kiti's grandsons were lost. He did not expect ever to face the men of this family."

Nik sighed. "It is possible that Potok envisioned himself taking over this household when the three males did not return."

Kiti's eyebrows rose slowly, Yes.

Nik rearranged the white sheets on his lap, went back to sketching on a clean surface. He said slowly, "So with Saruna, Potok wished for two **more** women to feed? And Urgit, who does not hunt? The old man does not think clearly!"

On the *paper* before him, Potok's head and upper body emerged, his thick right arm carrying a spear raised and ready. Then behind and beside him appeared his wife and the three daughters. Would the visage of Kiti form next, then Saruna . . . Urgit, too?

Kiti sucked in breath to emphasize her next words. "The greedy man looked forward to owning the contents of caches and storage racks, household equipment, the *umiak* and remaining dog sled—all. Now, he is disappointed."

Nik looked at his sketch, showed it to his grandmother. "It might have happened that the people here in Arajik's *igloo* could not eat after the caches were empty," he murmured.

Silence.

Ridiculous idea, Nik decided. Kiti was not feeble—and not likely to be silent. "One person of this household would have proved too troublesome." He smiled.

"Two old women and an untried young man? Not troublesome for long. Much can happen to old women and inexperienced youngsters."

Nik doubled his fists hard, the pencil rolling off the paper and onto the ice. Can happen especially fast when someone does not expect ever to face the men of the family. Nik wanted to go find the hunting group *now*, tell his father and brother what had happened, join with them to confront Potok.

"What will Arajik say?" Nik wondered aloud.

"He will not believe. Nik is only hearing Kiti's guess."

"Based on experience! One need not fall in headlong, to know the sea is wet."

She smiled, cocked her head. "Arajik would laugh. . . . 'Potok? Not possible!' Anyway, the men of this household *did* return. So the problem has disappeared."

"Only a dilemma of spirit remains," Nik responded with deep pain. "These have been friends."

"Ee-ee." He could barely hear his grandmother's voice. She was working on the bear pelt once again. Her dark eyes glistened with collecting moisture as she lowered them to her task.

Nik too was troubled, but outrage pushed away the sadness. He went back to the sketches, quickly put the features of Potok and his clan to the bottom of the stack. Two other matters bubbled in his brain. He hesitated . . . but so rarely did he have Kiti all to himself! "Pah-nee, Grandmother . . . will she return?"

The woman looked up from her work, startled. She said nothing, only looked at him.

"The dog-person took a part of her companion when she flew away." Kiti might ridicule him, and he deserved her derision; but the boy also knew that his words would never go beyond the ears of *Ananatsiak.*

The woman continued to watch him. Then she raised her eyebrows and returned to the white bearskin. *"Ahmi.* Who can say the future?"

"Someday—" would his grandmother now make fun of him? "—it may happen Nik will wish to find her."

"Like the caribou and the musk ox?" She did not look up.

247

Nik thought about her words. The antlered one was mild in temper, useful to Inupiat. The muskox was a mystery—wild, unpredictable, fascinating, probably of great value, but strange and independent—turned in upon itself. The two creatures were unlike as permafrost and spirit lights. Nik and Pah-nee, an imponderable combination? Eh, Kiti's words provided matter for reflection in idle moments, only not now.

"One thing more?" he asked. "Arajik. May someone speak?"

Kiti stopped scraping hide and looked over at him again. "Will a son criticize his father?"

"Owka, No—only share an observation."

She raised her eyebrows, returned to scraping. He could continue.

But given leave to speak about a parent, Nik hesitated. Then, "It happens that one's observation must start with a question."

"Naturally," she smiled.

"Might Arajik's mother note a change in the man?"

"Ee-ee."

"Does she find him less . . . well, more—eh, a pleasing difference?"

She looked up.

"Does Kiti find him perhaps less haughty than before?"

"Yes."

"Perhaps—more patient now?" Nik prompted.

She sucked in breath, Yes. Nik waited a long time for Kiti to put her thought into words. "He is more humble now," she said finally, "for he has learned that even Arajik is mortal."

"And learned perhaps that he needs others—needs his sons, even the younger one—in order to survive?" Nik added eagerly.

She sucked in breath long and slowly, Yes. "One hopes that this perception does not affect him on the hunt."

"How, grandmother?" Nik asked.

Kiti scraped hard as she collected her thoughts. Then, "When someone knows he can jump over the crack in ice which has suddenly opened—then he *can!* But when someone is uncertain—then the foot may falter, the leap might have some slight hesitation . . . resulting perhaps in less distance by the length of a few ice crystals—so *disaster!"*

"A son cares more for Arajik *now,*" he said. Then came one final suspicion to explore with the old woman sitting on the *iglerk*. "If Arajik were to challenge Potok on this matter of the caches, and if their talent were equal, then whom would the village be likely to choose as winner?" He was asking a question about politics, he knew.

Kiti stared at him long and hard, said not a word.

He realized at last that he already knew the answer to his question. And so did she.

CHAPTER 19.
A BROTHER IS MISSING!

Nik found Sitok working with the team on a rise behind their snowhouse in moonlight so bright it created sharp shadows. The boy stared at the scene before him and tried to imagine how it would look in sunshine. No one had seen even the south glow of sunlight for nearly two moons. Even though he like most *Inupiat* preferred winter time, Nik sometimes missed that blinding ball.

"Someone has news," he told Sitok when he caught his attention.

Sitok of course did not respond other than to look up.

"A mother now speaks. And walks." He chuckled. "And works."

"Ee-ee, Kiti?"

Nik was disappointed that Sitok was not surprised. "Yes—someone overheard all of it." He was eager to relay the tale.

Nik accompanied his brother down the hill with the dogs. He wanted Sitok to demand details. But his brother did not speak again until they had finished staking the team, and even then not about Mawena.

"Sitok also has news. He will duel with Urgit in two sleeps from now."

"Ai-ee!" Nik said as brightly as he could. Although he wanted Sitok to try out his new performance skills in public,

he was very definitely not in favor of this duel. Why not wait for a feast, when anyone was permitted to perform? And with a larger, less critical audience, as well—every person in the village, young and old.

"Urgit has agreed," Sitok added when Nik made no further comment.

Urgit was *obliged* to agree, Nik thought to himself, but that didn't mean he would be pleased to meet Sitok in the dueling ring. Nik put his *kamik* into step with his brother, listened to the dry crunch of their joined footsteps, admired the bright moonlight and the foreshortened shadows that preceded them.

"It also happens that the team goes onto ice after one more sleep," Sitok was telling him, "if Nik would wish to hunt."

"Yes, perhaps." Nik found himself ambivalent. . . . He needed the experience of the hunt to sharpen his skills in the company of experts—and would Arajik also be going? Yet, Nik was still weary of the trail. The inland trip had been especially burdensome, so filled with anxiety—Sitok injured and before the parents were found. Too, he had set several tasks for himself here in the village, jobs that must be done at home with a degree of privacy not possible when others were around—in fact, not likely even with village men gone because Saruna and probably Urgit would continue to be present in the *igloo*. He sighed with frustration. "The men go for seal?"

"They go for whatever should wish to give itself," Sitok answered. "Remember Koogee-Kahgee?"

Both boys laughed. Sitok especially was restless, Nik knew, and probably Arajik as well. Neither had gone out since returning home. Hunting, Nik reflected, was a great deal more than simply finding food. It was something which a man needed to do in order to sharpen his skill and test his luck—and so be happy.

On the ice in dazzling moonlight the next morning, Nik had reason to remember his grandmother's words about confidence. Sitok ran ahead of the team by a couple of sled lengths. He flowed like strong wind and paced the dogs. Fully healed, with only a few scars remaining from both accidents, Sitok appeared to be making up for time lost in mending.

Above the hiss of well-packed runners and the groan and grind of late winter ice, occasional notes of melody fell on Nik's ears. He knew that his brother was practicing for the drum duel to come. The second team of dogs took the sled and Nik straight over a fair-sized ridge of ice, perhaps in an effort to catch up with Sitok and his team. And for this reason, Nik was able suddenly to see from above what Sitok could not. Even though they were deep on the shelf, ice was breaking off ahead of his brother. A crack widened even as Nik took in the scene.

He bellowed a warning to Sitok, told his own team, "Drop!" Here was an order that could not be obeyed immediately because of momentum. But Nik yanked down and held the drag-anchor with all his strength to keep the sled from overrunning the dogs.

Whether Sitok heard his shout, Nik did not know. As if in a dream, the younger boy saw his brother's team jump the widening rift and Sitok himself suddenly leap high and far to land safely on the separated ice. But he also watched helplessly as Sitok's hunting bag bounced up on impact and flew half an arc back into the sea.

Nik's team and sled were stopped, and the sled stayed put, did not injure any dog. But Nuko as Nik's lead went into the water, dangling below the surface, restricted by her harness. Nik ran forward and hauled her out dripping. She shuddered with cold and shock. He slipped her harness from the work collar so that he could hold her freely, then looked across at Sitok. The stranded young man was less than a sled's length away, but stood on moving *siku* looking back across a widening breach already too great to jump with safety.

"Get robes!" Sitok shouted.

Of course. Some coverings were on Nik's sled. Still clutching Nuko, the boy ran back. There, he pushed the dog down and yanked three furs from under the strapping. At the channel, he rolled each robe separately and heaved it across with success, even as he listened to his brother's instructions on what else was needed. Sitok knew by now that his hunting bag was gone.

He wanted a snow knife, and he needed sinew for fishing. By good fortune, he had been carrying his spear. The handy *ulu,* as always, was in his parka pocket. Could Nik get food across?

Nik glanced at the slowly widening breach as he raced back to the sled. Nuko perched shivering on the sled where Nik had dropped her. The wet fur now encased her in ice, and shudders quaked through her body. With one hand, Nik pushed her down on one robe, pulled out the last one to draw over her. With the other hand, he pulled from under the tie straps the only packet of food he had brought for this short trip. *Muktuk.* Good. Nik yanked up Sitok's snow knife and on impulse took his own hunting bag. Everything his brother needed for the trip to come would be there . . . except warmth and light, solid land and his loving family.

The ice island on which Sitok was stranded had by now moved to almost a sled length's distance. But Nik still had no difficulty in throwing supplies across. Nothing fell into the sea.

"Someone will find help!" he shouted. "A man must go to a hummock or a pressure ridge—something high where he can be seen!"

Sitok probably did not hear him, by now, for wind was gusting. But then, his elder brother would doubtless realize that he had to make himself visible for would-be rescuers. Many unattached and wandering ice packs, large and small, were in the water. Nik tried not to think about how much they looked alike, especially in winter gloom—all these *siku,* these orphans of the pack ice.

He harnessed another dog to lead the team. Even in discomfort, Nuko growled her disagreement. "Pah-nee should be here," Nik told her as he wiped her down hard with the tails of his tunic and then the edges of the robes.

"Someone's brother will be displeased by the smell of wet dog in this fur," he warned Nuko. Then as they continued rapidly back to the village, "But at least two people in this world think Nuko smells like fresh berries in sunshine." He chuckled as he loped along beside the sled, the catastrophe forgotten for a moment. "And one of these is a grandmother." He did not need to tell the dog who the other person was, even though that one was gone forever. . . .

It was mid-day when Nik and the team skimmed into the village. Only Potok and the harpooner Tukla were visible outside, the latter with his team and freshly back from the hunt.

"Arajik is where?" Nik inquired. "It happens, trouble on the ice!"

"That person has taken the trail," Potok said. And then insolently, "Perhaps to visit one of his many caches."

"What's needed?" Tukla asked at the same time.

Nik told about the accident as he drew the sturdy harpooner and his sled along with him to his own snowhouse. There, he pulled shivering Nuko from between the robes and put her on her feet. She stood shuddering, uncertain, eyes dull. *"Ananatsiak! Ai-ee!"*

"She fell in?" Tukla asked. "That's the trouble?" He was unimpressed.

Nik raised his eyebrows. "And Sitok is moving away, on *siku.*"

The older man scooped up the big dog easily in his arms, re-wrapped her in a dry robe from his own sled. "Tukla's *kayak* needs repair, ever since the walrus hunt. But Nik should go round the village to inquire of paddlers. This dog will be cared for." He brought Nuko up and spoke soothingly to her, headed for the porch and for Kiti, who was just now emerging from the tunnel.

"Try also to borrow a *kayak* for Tukla," he urged as he bent down, still carrying the dog, to go inside.

In less time than is required to eat a meal—time which for Nik dragged out like a full dozen sleeps—four villagers including Tukla himself trotted with the bulky *umiak* across ice to the lead. Surprisingly, Urgit was one of the volunteers. The other two were paddlers who had brought news of the whale, Kotil and the tough little man named Poona. He with his wife Akini and their baby had recently followed bachelor Kotil in requesting permission to join the village. They had built their snowhouses while Nik and Sitok were inland. Two more villagers, Posi and Wutik, trotted along beside the *umiak,* their *kayaks* on their shoulders. Nik even drove his dog team, less Nuko, for Kiti had insisted on putting robes and food onto the sled to be transferred to the big boat when it was on the water.

In spite of danger from more ice splitting off, Nik took his sled to the water's edge with *kayaks* and *umiak.* It was no surprise that the floe on which Sitok landed was no longer distinguishable. Nik had tried unsuccessfully to borrow a *kayak* for *Tukla.* But never mind, it was the *umiak,* after all, which would receive Sitok if—no, **when** he was found. The seven went onto the water.

After a time, Arajik appeared with a third *kayak,* having returned from the hunt to hear of the catastrophe. He pulled alongside the *umiak* to speak with Nik. "Not easy, to borrow a boat in the village these days," he said simply, but pain and confusion echoed in his voice.

"Potok's *kayak?"* Nik asked.

"Owka, No—Atik's. He went to visit caches, today. Now he waits upon the ice"—the man pointed behind Nik, east and slightly north, up the coast—"for Nik and the *umiak* to collect him."

The boy had wondered earlier where loyal Atik was, for he would normally be first to offer help. He spoke to Arajik of Urgit's helping to carry the big boat. Both were glad Nik had sent the ignorant young man back with the team and empty sled. He was quite certain Urgit was relieved, as well. The awkward man was twice lucky on this day; for with Sitok floating off, no drum duel was likely to take place tomorrow. And now, no risk for Urgit by being on the *umiak* among shifting isles of ice. Still, timid Urgit had actually volunteered to help with the search.

And Potok had **not.** . . . Again, Nik wondered what was happening to his village. He would feel better with skilled little Atik in the *umiak,* though, and he signaled a turnabout to the three other paddlers.

After the remainder of that day plus one full sleep and another day, and in spite of Nik's sharing the food Kiti had sent—Posi and Wutik turned their *kayaks* back to land. Both murmured about other tasks awaiting them. Both said that they would probably return, but Nik did not expect them. Nik reflected that they had not stayed to search for a missing *Inuk* even for as long as they would normally stand above a seal hole.

In the *umiak,* Kotil and Poona both grumbled when they saw first one and then a second *kayak* depart. But Atik and Tukla teased them by giving ridiculous reasons for going home themselves—"*someone must feed* kringmerk," and *"It happens that an* igloo *needs new chinking"*—so Kotil and Poona stayed with the *umiak* peaceably enough although silent. Now only Arajik darted skillfully among the floes by *kayak* like some slender, curious bird, up channels so narrow that he risked being squeezed and held fast or popped out like an eyeball if the lead closed in before he found open water.

Floating ice all looked the same, Nik decided. If Sitok stayed by the edge to be easily visible should a paddler go by, he risked having the ice on which he stood break off, possibly sink beneath his weight. And if he left the edge without climbing a tall ridge, he reduced the chance of being seen. Nik could not settle on a solution—other than to trust Sitok.

As he paddled and searched, Nik thought of ways to tease Sitok when he was safe—yes, *when* he was safe once more. Now the younger brother would have rescued him not once or twice but *three* times! How often Sitok had come to *his* rescue over the years including this very winter—well, these efforts need not be mentioned. Nik projected himself forward in time, say ten sleeps? Sitok would be safely found, the family all together once again. Because Nik *needed* an older brother! Poor Sitok himself, not to have one . . . eh, poor Urgit . . . poor Pah-nee! *Pirtok!*

After time equal to three sleeps, and even with careful managing, the food Kiti sent was gone. Nik was discouraged—not that he would stop looking. But he saw *only* search in his future—hour after hungry hour, day after day of quest until life spirits left all of them. Arajik and Atik were still hopeful. Tukla was subdued, especially after the food was gone, but Nik knew that the man would stay. Kotil and Poona were sullen and silent, but they kept paddling the *umiak*.

Still, conditions could have been worse. No storm

buffeted the water or filled the air with needling granules. And the sky stayed clear, too, often with bright moonlight. Low fog normal on the water for this season did not occur. Also, with the robes Kiti sent, everyone was warm. Even Arajik had a big fur wrapped around his legs below the hatch of Atik's *kayak.*

On the day following what would have been the fourth sleep, Nik saw a glow of fire upon a floe. At first, he could not believe what his eyes told him was there. Could this be a wild reflection on smooth ice, perhaps from mischievous spirit lights that flickered unseen in the sky? Or had the search somehow got turned around in direction? Did Nik see light from some unfamiliar village on the shore? But no. The fire gleamed steadily on the hummock of an ice floe, right there on the upturned face of *siku* the traveler. And anyone knows that ice will not burn. Their search was finally finished!

Sitok was in good spirits. No, he had not worried. Nik inspired him. *Nik?!* Certainly. Remember the time when Nik and Pah-nee set up camp in the blizzard after Sitok was injured by the white bear? They had built a small lamp from thick layers of walrus hide bound from the outside with ice. Sitok took a wide strip of Nik's whale skin with blubber attached, his *muktuk,* and made from that a bowl. Sitok's "lamp" had fuel built in! He bound sinew on leather strips to form wicks. He used flint and dry moss from Nik's hunting bag to start a fire which slowly melted and burned the blubber lining. He ate nothing but fish he caught while on the floe, for he wanted to burn *muktuk* as lamps.

Sitok had, in fact, been more comfortable than his rescuers. Certainly better fed, he and his dogs, for fish had been most generous in giving themselves, he said with nose wrinkled in distaste. And Sitok told Arajik that he knew **absolutely** that Nik would find him because Nik was not an *inuk* to give up. At these words, Nik exchanged glances with his father. Did Sitok have any idea how many of the pack ice wanderers, those *siku,* clogged the lead and cobbled the sea beyond? And how very similar they all looked? Once more, theirs had been the search for one particular lemming among countless lemmings that scuttled among tundra grasses. Sitok, Nik decided, *should* have worried a great deal.

CHAPTER 20.
ARCS OF THE ARCTIC

The drum duel that had been postponed was set for the day after Sitok's return. The original circle now obliterated by strong wind and blowing snow, a new one was neatly heeled out, and the two young men were about to begin when Nik reluctantly joined the villagers. Urgit held the big drum as he walked to the middle of the ring. When Nik told his brother about Urgit's volunteering to go with the search party, the older boy only looked thoughtful. Would Nik ever know the meaning of Sitok's great silences? Kiti once observed that Sitok's *quiet* carried far more meaning than his sparse speech ever did. Not to Nik, it didn't. Not yet.

Urgit looked around and smiled hesitantly. He lifted the drum high on its sturdy stick and started the beat as his feet moved to match the rhythm. He did not race toward Sitok in mock threat, as was customary. In fact, he did not race *anywhere.* But then at last, he did open his mouth and begin.

> "On the land and on the ice
> One finds no bolder or more fortunate hunter
> Than mighty Sitok."

"Hoo--oo--oo!" came from the assembled villagers. What kind of start was this?

Urgit went on for a while to enumerate Sitok's additional virtues, beginning with fantastic but imaginary feats accomplished while still in his mother's hood. Puzzled, silent, people looked around at each other. Urgit's drumming and dance were surprisingly good. His poetry was pleasant enough, the rhythm pleasing. His voice, outstanding. But what was his *point?*

"Son of Arajik the traveler,
Elder brother of distinguished Nik,
Child hunter of proven great fortune—
Grandson to the wise woman of the village—

One beseeches all of them:
Adopt!

"Take this unskilled, unqualified
Lump of graceless, bumbling Inupiat!"

Uncertain laughter came from those who watched. Humor was here—for only orphaned babies and young children were adopted—so *what was Urgit's meaning?* More of this proposal came from Urgit's lips, and with no sign of an unexpected twist or turn that people expected. Urgit praised Sitok and all those in Sitok's family, one by one. Those in the past, those present and all yet to come. Then the slender man with sharp features handed the drum to his adversary.

Nik's brother did as he had planned. He reviewed the tale of last summer's incidents. But a duel must occur between two opponents, and Urgit had not so far established himself as a foe. Therefore, Sitok sparred with the wind—and a mild zephyr, at that. The quality of Sitok's dance and drumming surprised the audience, for none but his family had seen him perform. They smiled at each other and raised their eyebrows. They coughed politely to show that they approved of what they saw . . . but the words he sang increasingly lacked *passion.* More and more of his early zeal melted away.

Back and forth went the drum between the two young men. Urgit continued to describe faultless Sitok and his many virtues—some real, many fanciful. Sitok continued to be mildly critical and arguably humorous.

But nothing was there. Here was a hollow dispute—for a quarrel requires adversaries—and the audience became listless from the slow pace and lack of fervor, the one-sidedness of the debate. Here was not a *duel* but a *duet!* Some walked away, and others chatted and laughed together about other matters. And when both young men were exhausted—Sitok by the empty dispute and Urgit by his nature—only a handful of spectators remained. Sitok was last to perform. But as he left the circle, Urgit grasped his shoulder and walked off with him. The drum duel was over. Actually, no duel had occurred.

Muttering came from those few villagers still present, the ones who must decide the outcome. But disciplined by tradition, they huddled to discuss the result. Should not be difficult to decide, Nik muttered to himself, but to what purpose?

Arajik sat with his sons by the food bowl. Kiti sat at her station on the *iglerk* where she could tend the lamp. Beside her, still wearing her outside furs, Saruna sobbed into her *nuilak*, the rough of her hood. On the other side of Auntie Saruna, also sitting on the ledge and virtuously chewing at one of the caribou hides brought from inland, was Mawena. Urgit had walked out onto the plains after he heard the verdict of the villagers.

Arajik swallowed a bite noisily, did not replace it with more food, sat staring across the sober circle at Sitok. "Someone drums and dances well."

The elder son smiled faintly, raised his eyebrows only a little to acknowledge the compliment. He did not have the heart to disparage his performance in the customary manner.

"And Sitok's voice was clear and echoing," Nik added.

Kiti's bristling tones came from the ledge. *"The older boy will duel outstandingly in all respects when he has a genuine dispute."*

Everyone in Nik's family was unsettled by the outcome of the duel. Not only had Urgit lost the competition—if one could call it a contest at all—but he was *banished,* ordered to leave the village forever. The decision was unfair. The punishment far exceeded the crime. In fact, what exactly *was* the crime? Nik knew that people were tired of seeing Urgit around when he contributed so little to the village. So was Nik. So was Sitok. But one did not properly handle that problem in this way! And now Urgit's Aunt Saruna would go with him out onto the ice prairie to die. Not because she was sent away but because she loved and was loyal to her only relative. Likely, she considered herself in part to blame for his growing up unskilled. And in part, she probably was! She might have influenced her brother but did not. Or did Pak disregard her counsel?

In the silence following Kiti's outburst, Arajik eyed Sitok gravely. "We need to know the feeling of the elder son on this matter."

Sitok said nothing, only gazed back steadily into his father's eyes.

"Here is no time for the famous Sitok *silence!*" Arajik stormed. "Here is a time for **speech,** so talk!"

"Someone's feeling?" Sitok said hesitantly, then laughed. "It happens that someone realized, in that time out on the ice before the duel began, that Sitok's quarrel with Urgit had no substance."

Arajik turned his gaze onto Nik, who was moving about restlessly. "Another son has something to say?"

Nik held himself in check. His *feelings* were that this whole village should be banished in a blizzard! "The younger feels the same as his elder brother."

"Ee-ee, only he felt it a whole lot sooner!" Sitok declared. "Nik knew on the inland trail that a drum duel would serve no purpose—" he glanced over at Saruna—"or change Urgit's actions. Nik *knew,* and he said so when asked. Yet the elder brother took no heed!"

Arajik pursed his lips, then blew air out. *"Pirtok!"* What's happened has happened and cannot be changed! He turned.

"Mawena? Does she have thought about the drum duel and its outcome?"

Nik's mother put the hide into her lap and looked up. "This one believes that Saruna should not be permitted to accompany her nephew." She picked up the hide once more, began to work industriously.

"Saruna is free to do as she wishes," Arajik snorted. "Now Kiti? A mother's further comments are welcomed."

Kiti laughed. "This one has only questions! And she will now perform the discourtesy of *asking* them! Going back only a little in time, did Arajik easily borrow a *kayak* to search for his son lost on ice? Eh, and did Nik easily find *and keep* volunteers for the quest? And does this village, in spirit as well as action, respect the caches of another?"

"Answers are all *'No,'"* Arajik said quietly. He had learned about the empty caches from Atik, then had to press Kiti closely to get facts. But although he had by now discussed the matter within the family and digested the information, he had not yet approached the taciturn and evasive Potok. Arajik explained to his sons that he must wait for his rage to soften.

"And did this village," Kiti continued, "after a drum duel in the past, decide on the basis of what was right—or of what was **convenient?"** She spat out the final word as she considered the duel between tiny Atik and big Unipak.

A shiver went through Nik, although he was not cold. These were strong words, even for his outspoken grandmother. Following that duel so wrongly judged, the mighty spirits of the hunt had to step in later to right the grievous wrong. Those and of course Sedna herself.

"What of the father?" Nik asked Arajik, glad to hear questions permitted in this family council "What might his thoughts—his *feelings* be?"

"His thoughts," Arajik said slowly, "are that his family has good sense. . . . also that this village has become too large in some ways, remaining too small in others. Will Nik go out now to find Urgit as he prepares to leave?"

Nik found the frightened young man in the first place he looked. Following his walk in solitude, Urgit had gone to the snowhouse of bachelor Atik. The order to leave was effective tomorrow following tonight's sleep. When Nik told Urgit that Arajik wanted to speak with him, Atik asked to go along.

"And does a person still wish to be *adopted?"* Arajik asked Urgit when he stood up and pushed back his hood after coming through the tunnel.

Urgit looked down at his ragged boots and said nothing. But color came to the tips of his ears.

"One has thought for some time," Arajik continued, "that a person may be clumsy because he has never been trained to be otherwise."

Urgit's head came up slowly. "A great man such as Arajik would consider adopting someone?"

Arajik laughed. *"Owka,* No, for Urgit will not fit into Mawena's hood!" All laughed. "But a hunter would consider *training* someone who has never had that opportunity. Taking on a *student."*

Kiti sucked air in sharply to express her approval. So did Sitok and Nik. Saruna ceased sobbing, her face emerging from her parka.

Urgit again dropped his eyes, and the life had gone from his voice when he spoke. "These are useless words. After the sleep, this one insignificant man will be gone forever."

Arajik chuckled, nodding. "And what if—after the sleep—a *number* of the villagers should *all* be gone forever?"

Urgit raised his eyes to peer steadily at this man whom—as it turned out—he had left to die near an inland lake. His face lit up. "Arajik would do this thing?" Banished, Urgit *had* to go after the sleep. But villagers anywhere were always *free* to go.

Nik's father motioned both newcomers including Atik to sit with the family on the floor robe. "This father poured his knowledge of the hunt into his elder son. He ignored the younger—or worse, spent little time with him, then ridiculed the child for not knowing more. How splendid it was for Nik when his father was gone!"

"Owka! No!" the boy said amid several *"Hoo-oo's"* of disagreement from others.

"Only when Arajik went away was the elder brother enabled to have time with the younger. At last came opportunity for a boy to become a hunter! Eh—" he sighed, "—what parent wants to admit such a shameful thing?"

Kiti's shining eyes fixed on this person she had raised, her youngest brother who thought himself her son, and Arajik's eyes fastened steadily on hers. The others deliberately avoided *all* eyes by looking around the snowhouse. They were confused by Arajik's words. What trail was he following?

266

"The father's treatment of his younger son was a grave error that cannot now be remedied. *Pirtok.* The elder brother filled in, so disaster did not result. But Arajik *owes!*"

Uncomfortable with his parent's confession, Nik stood up and turned as if to go outside, but his father gave him the hard stare which forced him back to his seat.

"Pak's failure to train his son was also an error. Nor can Pak now make amends."

"Hoo-oo!" Someone does not criticize those whose spirits have fled. Still, all knew that Arajik spoke truth, and they settled back.

"Urgit has no elder brother."

Nik had not ever before heard Arajik say serious words critical of himself. And he suddenly understood where the words were going.

"Would Arajik be allowed by Urgit to step in?"

Silence.

Nik's father continued to look at the banished man. "If someone is willing to be taught and trained—perhaps by *three* hunters?—"and he looked first at Sitok, then at Nik before returning his level gaze to Urgit—"then everyone shall work through the sleep period and be ready to go in the morning."

"Ai-ee-ee!" breathed Urgit, still not quite daring to hope. A few moments ago, he was looking at certain death for frail Saruna and of course for not only himself but any line that might have someday come—all condemned. Now, did he dare to anticipate a life richer than he had ever known?

"Ai-ee!" Saruna echoed.

"How about *four* hunters?" Atik asked.

"Does someone else wish to join the travelers?" Arajik inquired.

"Ee-ee!" Atik looked around the group. "And perhaps some others also from this place."

267

"Understand, it is expected that the group will wander for some distance, start a new village somewhere? Those who leave are not likely to return."

Atik raised his eyebrows and held them up. "This man is not closely attached to many people here." He smiled.

The others laughed. How Atik must have fretted over the decision that followed his drum duel. Yet, none heard him complain.

Suddenly, Nik slid back from the circle around the food bowl and slipped outside without explaining. He walked over to the snowhouse of Potok, where he coughed politely to let them know he would like to come in. Maleet bid him enter.

"A message for Erin," he told Potok, who raised an arm to indicate that the boy was free to speak as he liked. Nik fixed the pretty girl with a stare, then ducked back through the baffle, down the tunnel to the porch outside. She knew to follow.

Erin appeared within a few moments, still fastening her parka. Nik told her what was happening. Impulsively, she reached over and hugged him, rubbed her nose against his inner cheek in what Nik considered to be a sisterly manner. Then she followed him to Arajik and made her request for permission to go along.

"A young woman will miss her family," Arajik observed.

"*Ee-ee,* but she will miss even more those who go away!" she declared.

Everyone but Sitok laughed.

"And do any here object?" Arajik looked around.

Sitok's ears turned reddish-purple, but he did not oppose.

They worked through the night. Seven others in the village would accompany them, as it turned out, all with sleds, most with a *kayak* or *umiak,* one with both. Potok was at first astonished and disbelieving, finally angry in that early morning of departure. But then advantages occurred to him, not least of which was having in his own household one mouth fewer to feed. He took down from the rack behind his *igloo* a small sled which he had not used in a long time. He cheerfully packed and iced the runners for his daughter.

"It happens that one has miserable old dogs extra, none worthy of receiving a single meal upon the trail," he announced. Then he brought out four *kringmerk* along with harness, and he hitched them to the sled. Three were among the best in his team; the fourth really *was* a poor mutt, rotten toothed, half starved and craven. Potok's wife Maleet caught up with Erin on one of the girl's trips back and forth from prairie caches and storage pits of others going from the village. She piled onto her daughter's sled three sleeping robes, a small travel lamp and some of Potok's old weapons. She also gave her eldest daughter a beautiful set of underfurs, *illupak*—shirt, leggings and socks beautifully made from the softest parts of snowshoe hares. They must have come from her Big Feed.

"These worthless, ugly bits of apparel clutter the *igloo,"* Maleet told her. "An eldest daughter would perform a favor for her mother to help relieve disorder in the home." And then the two women hugged each other, both knowing they were unlikely to see each other again from this day on.

Potok hated watching so much food leave the village as it disappeared into bags packed onto sleds. If Erin had been engaged to Sitok, with a formal understanding that they would marry, then the man could have demanded and received a substantial food gift, regardless of past circumstance. But the two were not promised, so he could request nothing. In fact, Arajik would be reasonable to require—although he did not do so—that Potok provide food and good tools as payment for protecting his daughter on the trail. So Potok stood there motionless physically and off balance in his thinking amid the bustle of the exodus.

Kiti took time from packing to go over to him privately.

"Arajik says that Potok may have the snowhouse for his own, after the family is gone," she told him. The very *igloo* that he had forced her grandsons to build alone.

"And perhaps provision in the storage igloo?" he asked hopefully.

"Oh no," she told him, "for that bit is already packed. But Potok *may have the contents of all the caches,*" she continued, and waited for his eyes to light up with thought that the family had other cairns which he had not found so had not raided.

"And he has previously collected all of these," she finished, then walked away.

While others did a last-time check on supplies, Nik drove a team and highly stacked sled east to the sea and out onto ice. There, he commanded the team to drop and stay. He unharnessed Nuko from the lead, told her to come along. Now he pulled his hunting bag from its place in front of the handles and lugged it over his shoulder out farther until he found and climbed a tall hummock. He dug into his bag to retrieve Pah-nee's *paper.*

"Nuko is well again," he muttered to pictures Pah-nee had drawn, "although she sorely misses the dog-person."

He smiled. Pah-nee's circles were everywhere in the pictures he had done. But some circles could not be drawn, for they were not visible. The search inland. His spiraling thoughts about Pah-nee herself.

He had decided lately on a different sort of circle he would make following a few more winters. He knew that he could not bear to part with the incredible square of color Arajik called a *stamp*. But what he *could* do was take that *envelope,* when he was older, and start south—perhaps with Nuko—and deliver the *papers* from it to Pah-nee in person. Yes, he could probably do this thing. Making the trip was of course not an important matter, since it happened that Pah-nee turned out to be only a girl—except that by doing so he could then keep the *stamp.*

Arajik crawled up onto the hummock. Sitok and Atik stood below. "The younger son is one who has the instinct for fortunate direction," Arajik told him. "Point a way for us."

Nik was pleased—although this was a terrible responsibility, too. He lifted his left arm, and it pointed south and slightly west. "Are all agreed to stay by the coast?"

"*Ee-ee,* except of course in summer when tides would wash the people away." Arajik was smiling.

"And could it happen," Nik continued, "that the wanderers might go so far south as the first trees?"

"*Tall* ones!" Sitok added from below, as he remembered Nik's pleasure, inland, when they finally got to some trees which put the promised creak in his neck while he stood at the base and looked toward the top.

Arajik laughed aloud. "A boy must remember that trees can keep Inupiat from seeing far. But we can visit trees."

Nik stood up and collected the fur on which he sat, stuffed it into his hunting bag, then rolled the *paper* slips into their hide and snugged them with sinew. There would be plenty of time to consider his father's words as the group made its way down the coast. To see far is important. *And to see all around.*

Arajik was looking at him as he straightened up, the smile on his face now hesitant.

"The *Inupiat* story," Nik told him so softly that those at the base of the hummock could not hear. "The strong people who travel, settle for a while, then travel again."

"Until they come around fully," Arajik agreed cheerfully, his eyes narrowing in fun.

Nik smiled back. Perhaps someday he would tell his father about Pah-nee's circles. Eh, he and the whole group were excited about adventure to come. Nik half slid, half clambered down the hummock, Nuko beside him with tail wagging. She too was eager to start.

As Nik reharnessed his lead dog and got his team up and ready, he considered the future. Uncertainty, yes, moving into the unknown—but with the people and the life he loved. Inupiat travel—that's what they *do,* he reflected. But he had no particular sense of completion to come—*nor did he want one!*

Appendix A

KOOGEE-KAHGEE
THE BOY WHO WOULD
BECOME A CARIBOU

A Tale Told at a Whale Feast[1]

This all happened long ago, before the moon was placed securely in the sky. A small *Inupiat*[2] boy spent much of his time in tears. The reason? All the other children, even those still naked in their mothers' hoods, poked fun at him. In age, he was eight winters—and making no progress at all toward becoming a hunter.

His loving father carved him a bow. He also fashioned him ten arrows. Each arrow was cleverly trimmed with an eider duck feather to help it fly true.

But Koogee-Kahgee, for that was his name, managed in one day to lose every arrow. And he broke the bow, besides. No, no, he didn't *mean* to. In fact, he set out proudly that first morning with his shining weapons. He planned on that day to become the mighty hunter of his dreams. But you see, he had to test the ice in the bay to see whether it would hold his weight. It would not, and there went his bow!

And he did need help inland with getting up the slippery bluffs and down the rock-strewn slopes. So there went his delicate arrows, one by one—for none was made to be a staff, and many low hills and shallow valleys were in that place.

---

1   A freely adapted version of the traditional Inupiat tale of "The Boy Who Would Be a Caribou"
2   Arctic Inuit (Arctic Eskimo of tradition)

The same occurred not once but fully five times with the small harpoons his five uncles had made for him. One was thrown at the shadow of a flying snow goose when it passed across a valley so sunken and so vertical that no descent was possible. Another was used to feel ever more deeply and broadly into a seal's breathing hole—until *nathek*, that mellow and sweet-tempered mother, lost all patience and with her mouth took the harpoon right down through the ice hole for breathing, down through the *aglu,* and buried its tip in the floor of the sea.

And a third—ah, why take time to recount calamities? But oh, the fishing sinew . . . one needs to know that the moon above was brilliant blue as dancing lights in a northern sky before Koogee-Kahgee snarled his line on it, tipped it slantwise and drained out all its color. Only remember that this boy destroyed without spite or intention more weapons and implements of the hunt than any ordinary *inuk* could need in three lifetimes. But Koogee-Kahgee's parents, his older brothers and many relatives were loving ones, and patient—as someone may by now have guessed.

But all this love and patience around him could not heal the pain poor Koogee-Kahgee suffered from his own embarrassment and from teasing by other children often led, sadly, by his older brothers. Their mocking made him all the more determined, though. No more experienced than before, unfortunately, and not the least bit sensible.

Koogee-Kahgee went to hunt
For seal on ice one winter day.
Instead, a walrus gave itself
To this important hunter.
"No!" said he, "one comes for **seal**—
So safely go away!"

Koogee-Kahgee found
The mighty whale at peace
In shallow depths awaiting him.
"Out to sea where whales belong!"
Said he, the lusty hunter,
"For today, this person goes for *fish*—
If only one's long sinew
Were not wrapped
Around an iceberg"

"Take me, Koogee-Kahgee!"
Said the circling muskox,
Coming forward.
"Sink the spear . . . or . . .
Whatever weapon one would choose—
Within this flank,
For one grows weary digging
At the tundra, nibbling lichen.
Take this creature,
That *oomingmak,* the tired muskox
May have some value
As food and sleeping robes
For mighty *Inuk,* man."

But Koogee-Kahgee scolded her
For shirking in the
Muskox way of life.
"Now go!" he did command,
"For Koogee-Kahgee needs
To find a caribou!"

"How will the hunter capture
Long-legs?" asked the Muskox.
"Where's the killing spear?"
Said Koogee-Kahgee,

"Certainly one will seize a caribou!
Strong *inuk* needs no spear.
This speedy hunter plans to
Run the antlered one to ground—
So tire him, he's winded."

Of course none of this worked out, and Koogee-Kahgee was now desperate. He left his warm and loving family, put his prosperous village behind him to go out upon the frozen tundra to seek new kin among creatures for whom hunting and the skill of wielding weapons was not vital.

He came first upon a great white snowshoe hare.

"Sir or Madam," said Koogee-Kahgee, since he never could distinguish between the male and female rabbit, "this human wants to join your clan."

"And why would someone wish to be a rabbit? Oh— you tell me you're unskilled at hunting? You think the hare-y life is full of ease?"

"That, one cannot say," the boy responded. "But *human* life's beyond this child, that's certain. And someone needs to find a family where weapons are not used."

The snowshoe regarded Koogee-Kahgee thoughtfully. "It's not so easy being a Big Foot. Wolves, foxes, even ravening bears all prey on us. . . . Oh well, a human boy may stay through the sleep with us, and then we'll see."

The hares gave Koogee-Kahgee a thick white robe on which to lie. And they covered him with two more furry hides provided by their own ancestors. The boy curled up cozily and slept the sleep time . . . but then woke up in the morning *sh-sh-shiv-ver-ing!*

You see, the hares had talked about the matter while the boy slept.

"Too big for our warrens—and getting bigger! He'll never be a rabbit," they decided. So carefully, they rolled him from the coverings, which they of course took with them when they left.

Koogee-Kahgee clapped his hands together, slapped his legs and hopped about to get himself warm. Then he sighed and—eyes dripping tears that froze before they reached his jaw—walked off in search of some new clan.

At length, he met a family of ptarmigan. "Please," said he, "could this young *Inuk* join your flock?"

"But why on earth and sky would a human child wish to do that?" inquired the plump white bird.

"Because someone is no good as a hunter," said Koogee-Kahgee.

"Of course *not!* The boy is far from fully grown!" the ptarmigan observed.

"Still, one knows," said Koogee-Kahgee sadly, "and this one wishes instead to become one of the most beautiful birds of the north."

"Well, *nakorami,* thank you, certainly. But the young *inuk* should know that not only do creatures of the land prey on us," warned the ptarmigan, "but also the cousins from the air, the other birds. One is continually running about, trying to keep from being eaten, or from having one's offspring devoured, or from having one's eggs stolen—and that's not even mentioning the continual search to find food for ourselves. . . . Has Koogee-Kahgee given thought to how much a bird needs to eat between each sleep?"

"Just let this traveler stay the night," Koogee-Kahgee begged, "and the ptarmigan family will see how nicely everything works out."

The ptarmigans were not so sure. But they made their guest warm and comfortable, then discussed the situation while the tired boy slept.

"He's too big for our nests, that's certain," some complained.

"And although his size would mean that only wolf and bear would prey on *him*—"

"—*All* would notice him, then come to capture *us.*"

Everyone agreed. And in the very early morning, they gently rolled Koogee-Kahgee onto tundra ice, picked up their robes and flew away. As before, the boy awakened *freezing cold,* leaped up to clap his hands and slap his thighs and race for warmth around the deserted camp. Then, he trudged ever further inland to search for a new family.

Now Koogee-Kahgee came to caribou—there, stretched across the high plain and spilling into the valley beyond, grazed a magnificent herd.

The boy walked up to the first adult he saw. "Madame, this youngster wishes to join the fine group of caribou."

"Oh my goodness!" exclaimed the caribou, who was not accustomed to making decisions. "One must locate the leader, bring him here! Oh dear, oh dear . . ." and the creature galloped off.

The herd chief was a wise and grizzled ancient with antlers that poked many fingers at the sky. "It is said—but hard to credit—that this young *inuk* standing here wants to join the herd."

"Oh yes!" Koogee-Kahgee assured him. "Someone *needs* to join a family that does not find its food with weaponry."

"Umm-mm-mm," mused the chief caribou. "This grandfather will speak with other elders," and he did and then returned. "You may sleep here on these skin robes for this night," he announced—and Koogee-Kahgee's hope plunged. For had he not spent the last nights with two different species, each morning waking up to find himself abandoned in the cold?

"No, don't weep, for someone's eyes will freeze,"

the old one cautioned kindly. "And then how can he see the predator who tries to take him?"

The boy blinked back his tears. "What did the mighty chief and his elders decide?" he sniffled.

The patriarch only smiled. "Be sure to use the covers," he instructed. "Stay with every part of you between the robes set out here—and by morning, a surprise!"

The boy did as bid, and he awakened early on the following day. For one thing he still *had* warm robes—a big improvement over the last two mornings. And for another—discovered when he tried to scratch his nose—he found a hoof attached to what had been his arms and was now two hairy legs.

"What's happening!?" he demanded, trying to rise. Much effort was required to manage all those legs . . . *and such a heavy head!*

But at length, he staggered to his feet and looked around. The caribou were grazing across the snow-covered valley by digging down with their sharp hooves to find moss and lichen beneath the snow. Koogee-Kahgee copied them—awkwardly, at first. The taste was unfamiliar, not to his liking, definitely not seal blubber or *muktuk,* no whale skin with fat. But in short time, he got on well enough.

In fact, this new-formed caribou got on very well for ten sleeps or so. But then one morning he was homesick—for his human parents, his aunts and uncles, and especially his two older brothers—even though they had led the village children in teasing him.

The wise old chief did not have to be told. He *knew,* just as soon as he saw the eyes of their most recently acquired herd member.

"Go back to the village, youngster. The small boy who stands here will someday do well as *Inuit* and" —he sighed— "as hunter."

"But one's antlers!" wailed the boy, "and one's hooves and tail and ears and furry legs!"

The old caribou chuckled. "This chief tells a child to return to his family," he commanded not too severely, "and promises all will be well."

The boy trotted back to his home village—and those four hooves served him well on the long trip! Approaching he saw his two brothers . . . hunting . . . together fitting their arrows and drawing back their mighty bow strings—

"—*Owka!* Don't shoot this creature!" he shouted, "for the prey is not as it seems!"

"That's certain," the eldest agreed, "for never before has this hunter heard *tuktu* speak."

"Come closer," the other brother instructed, "and two fine hunters will see what they can see."

The three got together. The two older brothers pulled off the antlers of Koogee-Kahgee. Next, the furry head, the hoofed legs. All came away in their hands to reveal their young brother furless in his *illupak*, unhoofed and unhurt. Everyone had thought him lost forever after he wandered away. The older boys could hardly wait to take him back to the grieving family. And every person may be sure that the feast for rejoicing was a long and tasty one!

But this does not end the tale. Until that time, Inupiat lived only inland on permafrost and tundra where the short summers had much food. But the long winters were a time when hunger scourged the dark land. Koogee-Kahgee insisted, on his return, that the whole family move to the seacoast during winter. "Some of the people will learn to hunt walrus," he insisted, "and also seal and whale. *But this one Inuk at least will never hunt for caribou."*

Because his family loved him so strongly, and because they were so glad he was not lost after all, they agreed and moved in time for the next winter. They were surprised at how much more food could be captured on the coast during the cold season, and they built a village of *igloos* there. They would stay in that place always except in the summer season of dangerous tide and treacherous ice along with unending light. That move and that decision, as all know, accounts for the existence of coastal-dwelling Inupiat.

And Koogee-Kahgee did grow up broad and muscular. He *did* learn gradually to become a hunter who used weapons skillfully and brought back plenty of food for his family. Although he went out during inland summers to capture prey including ptarmigan and giant hare, he always held firm about not hunting caribou. However, he never would reveal the reason, and his family always wondered.

All who knew, in fact, were Koogee-Kahgee as well as his two brothers—who were never *absolutely* certain—and of course the caribou themselves. And these were all who needed to know.

APPENDIX B

SEDNA, QUEEN OF THE ICY SEA
A LEGEND OF THE ARCTIC INUIT

Retold by Phyl Manning

Long ago in the Far North, where a crackling sky can glow and flow with color even to this day, creatures walked and crawled and flew above the treeless land. But nothing ever swam. Ice-bound oceans were salty tubs of emptiness. Inuit, the true people, used this water to get from where they were to where they wished to be—in winter as frozen trails for sleds and in summer as liquid trails for boats. . . .

An aging man and his wife lived with their three grown daughters in a tiny village close to water but far from other settlements. There lay the problem: how were the girls to marry? All must be wed—but in order of their ages, for that was *peeusinga*, the Way of the People in this place. But the eldest one, Sedna, refused every proposal.

The father searched the land to find bachelors willing to come and consider her. And in fact, she had an offer from every man who took the trouble to find her. Each was anxious to marry after he saw and spoke with this bright and witty woman. For Sedna was beautiful. She had strong teeth. She had broad, well-padded cheeks, a delicate nose, a stocky, sturdy frame. Her long black hair looked like swirls within deep summer seas.

With each passing season, the father grew more angry. He had worked too long, he complained, as the only hunter in his family of four hungry women. For too long, he had traveled the frozen tundra, he reminded them. Too often was he alone with his team and his terrible responsibility. He was weary, now—too old for such obligation. His joints ached on the trail, and a chill deep in his bones refused to warm even in summer.

So men were willing, but Sedna was not. Her reasons for refusal were original and endless. . . .

"That Oodlvak? Far too heavy! The extra dogs required to pull his sled all must be fed."

And again, "*Owka,* No, the one called Kanuq is far too old for this young girl." Sedna's tone was respectful, but her words were not the ones her father wished to hear.

Or, "Litunik smells so bad!" Sedna clawed her nose and shivered. "The good food oils lie restless on his skin."

"Kumun? Most unlucky in the hunt, from the look of him. Slim as a stem! A wife would starve in his care, and any child."

"Panituk? *Ai, namunilunga!* This ignorant young woman is not good enough. The handsome hunter deserves someone more worthy."

But in time, Sedna's *atatak,* her father, lost all patience. **"Come here!"** he thundered. **"Wed then *Kringmerk*, the lead dog of my team!"**

"*Hoo-oo!*" said Sedna, stepping back. A human marry a dog! Who was this stern man? What had he done with her mild father?

The parent tucked his top lip beneath the bottom one. "The dog is handsome in his ice white coat, willing to wed a human, always quick to obey my commands, so excellent in thought."

"*Owka—No!*" echoed the shocked mother and both younger sisters.

"A clever creature, he's earned his place at the tip of the team by wit and strength."

"*Ai-ee! Hoo-oo!*" the women mourned.

"It happens that noble Kringmerk may make for a daughter the best husband of the lot."

"Oo-oo-oo!" came spirit wailing from the arching walls of the snowhouse.

Kringmerk the dog seemed at the wedding feast to be pleasant and funny. He appeared attentive to his bride. He did of course gobble his meat without first clipping it off at his lips, but everyone forgave him. After all, what does a dog know of meal manners and how could he handle the sharp little *ulu* for cutting?

Then Kringmerk took his bride far north and east to a permanent ice island otherwise deserted and unknown. There, he threw off all appearance of grace. He became a tyrant who made impossible demands—and then punished Sedna brutally when she was unable to fulfill them.

"Design a sled," he growled, "that one strong dog can hitch and unhitch by himself."

"How can that be, Husband?" Sedna asked. Experienced, she could fashion a graceful sled and lines from hide and bone and braided thong. But devising harness to be manipulated without hands and agile fingers was beyond her. She tried and tried, but nothing worked.

"It happens," Kringmerk told her, "that the useless woman shall live in a snowdrift for the next three sleeps."

Sedna pleaded for mercy, as a storm was battering their *igloo*; but her husband pushed her out into the wind with only her furs and a narrow snow knife for digging.

Over and again, the woman was given tasks no one could do. "Make wings to permit mighty Kringmerk to fly through air above the water and hunt at will on other islands," he commanded. Or, "Bring the fleet caribou and meaty muskox closer to this place. A hunter becomes weary on the long and lonely trail." But the wings Sedna devised would not permit flight. And her coaxing calls to prey animals brought only a hoarse voice for herself and one ptarmigan curious about the noise.

Her punishment for failure was severe. She was scolded continually, insulted, threatened. In first rage at some new flaw observed in his wife, Kringmerk would apply those strong front teeth to bite. Then Sedna would run out onto the prairie until his wrath abated. In winter, she would be banished without food to a far cave for half a moon. In summer, she might be lashed unclothed and defenseless to a rock as bait for the ravening white sea bear.

But Sedna survived, and hardships made her strong. Babies were born, as babies *are* born—but hers with Kringmerk arrived in litters, six and eight little ones at a time, all to be loved and tended and trained before the next birthing. Too many, too often. Pale, hairy little dog-children everywhere! The small island became crowded. The hungry mouths exceeded the food supply.

"Get rid of them," Kringmerk commanded his wife, giving to her his sharp killing knife. He saw the horror on her face and for once relented slightly. "Or drown them, if you prefer."

Heartbroken, Sedna gently placed her children three and four litters at once into giant *kamiks* she devised, those sturdy waterproof boots worn by *Inuit*. She packed food and sent her babies south with the tide. She put them into the care of *Ooangniktook,* the sturdy north wind who was going that direction anyway.

Time and again as years passed, the mother was forced to bid farewell forever to her children. Only centuries later did she learn that they had landed safely in the warmer south and gradually formed their own alien civilization of pale dog-people, the hairy *kablunait,* "the ones with heavy eyebrows."

Always strong minded, Sedna became ever more solid and enduring as the fiery pain of her lonely life tempered her. She knew that her situation was impossible, but she had no way to improve it, no means to get away. Kringmerk refused to build a boat—and who knew where to go? Where was safety? The woman sent messages telling her parents that the dog husband was not as he had appeared in the village. She burned pictures into scraps of hide and begged her *ananak* and *atatak* to come and rescue her. She gave these messages to the birds, the only creatures which could take them across water to her homeland south and west.

But no communication was ever delivered. Kringmerk had performed special service for beasts and birds—remember, nothing lived within the sea—to bind and obligate them, should he ever need their help. A whistling swan with an infected leg where waves drove her onto sharp rocks knew to find Kringmerk. His licking tongue had healing powers, as does the tongue of any canine. During times of storm and high wind, when birds could not find food, Kringmerk fed them—even if his own family must go hungry. Thus, even had they wanted to—which they did *not*—the creatures Sedna charged with carrying her requests were powerless to help.

So Sedna's parents heard nothing at all from their eldest married daughter. Perhaps *because* they didn't, over many years, they at last decided on their own to make a visit. They went in summer when the air was mild, and open water permitted passage with their boat among the floating ice islands of the northern sea. They came paddling their *umiak,* the rounded, hide-covered whaling boat, still rudderless and without a keel—but larger and more stable than a *kayak.*

On the island, they found their daughter wretched, ragged, hungry, cold, childless—and skinny as a wind-sucked caribou leg. They agreed to take her home.

But Kringmerk said *No.*

So one morning, they waited for the dog to go on the trail, then smuggled Sedna into their boat and paddled toward their own village far away on the mainland.

When Kringmerk returned from his hunt and found Sedna gone, he knew exactly what had happened. So he called in favors from the creatures on earth most savage and unfeeling—his friends, the birds. "Force them back!" he commanded. "Do what must be done. The human woman is not to go from this place."

Over the sea, birds large and small collected above the little boat bobbing on waves far below.

"Gah-o-gah-o-gah-o back!" warned Thayer's gull as he swooped down. His brown bead of an eye was fixed on them unblinking. The fuschia eye-ring emphasized the bloody threat.

"Sker-rr!" screamed the chunky skua, her hooked bill clattering as she swung low. "You should be sker-rr-rrd!"

But the parents refused the commands, and the boat moved homeward.

"Turr-rr-rn!" moaned five small eider ducks.

"Na-wo, na-wo!" sang Ross's gull as he rode air eddies and flicked his tail wedge up and down as further warning.

But the *umiak* kept its course.

And when birds attacked the fleeing family, battering with their wings and slashing with their beaks, the three people were at first able to beat them off.

Then a silhouette of the merciless gyrfalcon showed against the sky. "Bahck! Bahck-ack!" her harsh tones menaced.

"Gah-o-gah-o back!" Thayer's gull repeated.

"Ke-yah! Ke-yah!" squealed three herring gulls, coming so close that the boat party could see the red spot on each lower bill. "Or we will ke-ee-eel yah!"

Suddenly, the gyrfalcon folded her wings against her sides and streaked down toward defenseless heads.

Sedna's parents dove beneath a robe on the floor of the craft. Sedna lifted one of the fire-hardened bone paddles from the water, held each end tightly and at the last moment raised it high and horizontal to break the force of the death dive. The weight of the bird shattered the sturdy implement. If that hooked beak had connected with headflesh, as was this aerial killer's design, no life spirit could have remained.

The parents crawled out from under the fur robe thoroughly frightened. Sedna's mother pointed into the sky where more gyrfalcons were assembling with jaegers and the largest gulls.

The man peered up, then at his wife.

They both avoided Sedna's eyes, and the daughter knew that surrender was near. *"Atatak! Ananak!* Father! Mother! Please, no!"

Any diving jaeger could split a skull in a single dive—and *would,* if the puny humans did not turn their craft around.

The father stopped paddling, undecided.

"Owka, No!" Sedna begged. Then, "It happens that this woman refuses to return."

A shadow darkened the vessel as birds flocked densely above.

A drifting swan whistled, "Rr-rr-rree-ady?" and Sedna's mother whimpered. A few of those mean-spirited giants afloat beside the *umiak* could flail the occupants with broad wings while they pierced the stretched hide of the craft with their black bills. Boat and people alike would sag and flutter downward to the bottom of the sea. Even in those ancient days, all including birds knew that *Inuit* do not swim.

The father examined Sedna's broken paddle, then threw it away. "Some other way to take a daughter home will surely present itself," he decided aloud. He picked up the remaining paddle and, heedless of his daughter's pleas, headed back the other way.

As they went, Sedna tried to reason with them. Terrified and ashamed, neither parent would meet her eye or speak. They were determined to save their lives by obeying the fowl that threatened overhead.

When the island of Kringmerk came to view, Sedna was desperate. She flung herself off the side of the craft and into the sea. She clung to the gunwale to stay afloat.

"Get back in!" her father commanded, offering the paddle to help her climb.

But Sedna refused. Years of toil and strain from a difficult survival had made Sedna stronger in spirit than both her parents together.

"Come, girl! It may be possible to reason with someone's husband," her mother said.

But Sedna knew that no amount of talk would change the mind of Kringmerk. Although numb with cold and fighting for each breath, she made no move to come aboard.

When the boat continued to delay, down came the birds once more! Wings beat all about the three humans. Sharp beaks tore *Inuit* flesh. Birds shrieked and people howled as the *umiak* crashed and tumbled on the waves.

After a time, Sedna saw her father's face bend to hers. He bled from eyes and ears, a deep gash reddening his cheek. "Drop away!" he gasped.

"*Owka,* No!" she told him, dodging the talons of a peregrine falcon.

"Kiee-kiee-kee-ill!" it shrilled as it swooped up to try again.

291

Suddenly, Sedna's father took his sharp little *ulu* from his tunic, the round utility knife used when eating to nip meat away at the lips. *Atatak* raised it high with both arms. "Death may be the daughter's choice . . . but she cannot choose it for her parents as well!"

Down came the *ulu* and off went the fingertips of both Sedna's hands, up to the first joints. *These fell into the churning water to become the first fish in Arctic seas.* The cold enveloping Sedna was surpassed by her great dismay at the prospect of returning to a hated existence on the island. She felt no pain, only changed her grip to grasp the boat tightly with what parts of her hands remained.

"Dig-a-dig-dig!" promised the parasitic jaeger as he picked his human target and zoomed down.

"Which-uh-which-which-which-uh-you?" squealed his even larger cousin, the pomarine jaeger descending with beak extended.

And following these two strikes, all birds renewed their attacks.

Now once again the *ulu* descended. This time, the knife chopped away Sedna's fingers to the second joint. *These larger pieces of her hand became the first seals and walruses that today inhabit the icy ocean.*

But Sedna had learned during ghastly seasons as wife of a sled dog to accomplish what must be done by using whatever was available. Now she moved her hands higher to clasp the gunwale with the last segment of her fingers.

And one last time the knife came down, this time to slash away the final bit of every finger to the knuckle. *And these, swirling in saltwater, became the very largest fish and mammals—the big sharks and mighty whales.*

Now unable to grip the *umiak,* Sedna disappeared beneath the waves and sank slowly to settle at last on the bottom far below. And there she lives today. She retains the courage, the great strength tempered with compassion that she gained in her bleak life on land. And with the wisdom born of these, she rules all creatures of the Arctic seas. . . .

Which shall come to the surface and give itself for human use? Where is the more patient hunter? The most deserving fisherman? Sedna weighs such matters. And who among the people who crave food found only in her kingdom has obeyed the Sea Queen's law to honor the spirit of every creature taken from the water? Sedna decides. And finally, who among those intruders on the upper border of her kingdom—those who dare to ride their flimsy craft upon the surface of the sea—*who* among these few, these *Inuit,* is worthy to join her in the deep?

AUTHOR'S NOTES

The *Inupiat* lived for about five thousand years in what is surely one of the least hospitable environments our planet has to offer. The bodies of these originally Asiatic people adapted to the harsh climate by becoming more compact—with somewhat short arms and legs, small ears, noses having hardly any bridge. The pad of fat on cheekbones—that chubby-cheeked look associated with *Inuit*—also helps to protect from frostbite. Even the clattering (to our ears) consonants of their speech originate mainly far back in the mouth, "away from the cold," as Nik describes it, either by chance or by design. The name *Eskimo,* which means "eater of raw meat" was given these Arctic dwellers by historically hostile Algonquin Indians and was meant to be an insult.

"So?" asked *Inuk*—for the diet traditionally consists of at least ninety per cent *meat* including fish and *is* usually eaten raw because the land offers nothing much to burn.

The very name *Inuit,* which these people call themselves, has the same meaning as the meaning of the name most indigenous groups in an isolated place give to themselves: "human beings," the *people.* They refer to a single individual as *Inuk.* And those *Inuit* in the very farthest north (Greenland, Canada, Alaska and Siberia) refer to themselves as *Inupiat,* which means "man[kind] pre-eminent." Then they are broken down according to where they spend winter as *inland* or *coastal,* sometimes further designating themselves (or being designated by others) according to some landform in a particular location.

Traditional Inupiat recognized no *authority* other than that within the basic, sometimes slightly extended, family unit. No head man or chief existed, and therefore no tribe or even clan. Remember that the Arctic cannot support many people in one place. Every Inuk *did* recognize the power and control exercised by environment—by weather and geographical conditions. Any person in the Arctic was attuned to the environment, saw himself and herself as organizers of chaotic nature. *Inuk* lived on and with what (little) was available and made from this scant provision an often joyful existence.

In a harsh land which rarely gives a second chance for error and demands great strength, courage and persistence for mere survival, the traditional *Inupiat* was nevertheless gentle, forgiving, non-violent in relations with other people. He solved major disagreement, for example, with a *duel*—and the duel consisted of drumming, dance, clever and usually humorous poetry with song. The winner was decided by the audience on the basis not only of issue(s) but also and largely of excellence in performance.

Inuit loved to *wrestle.* But a wrestling match lasted only until one or the other wrestler was thrown off balance. That was it. The "losing" opponent didn't need to fall, only lurch a little . . . end of match!

No traditional *Inupiat* would strike a child for any reason. And physical force was used on another adult human only in the most desperate circumstance. In the severe and unremitting cold of a dark, extended winter, *Inuit* were warm and loving with each other, unfailingly hospitable to guests. They freely shared what little they had with friends *and strangers.*

In a land with few available resources—fish and game, short-season berries, herbs and bird eggs, plus virtually unlimited stone, permafrost, ice, snow and water fresh or salt—these people managed a robust and vigorous existence. Food, clothing, shelter, warmth and light came from these resources, as did weapons, tools and transportation.

The sled dog, historically, became an integral part of *Inupiat* life. Vast distances are involved in the Arctic. The traditional and fairly nomadic Inuit could not have existed, at least not as we know him, without his canine helpers.

In the very far north beyond trees and shrubs, where most of the *Inupiat* lived, nothing broke the emptiness. No natural points of visual reference occurred permanently in any direction. Yet, a healthy *Inuk* never or very rarely got lost. That is, he may not have known exactly where he *was,* but he could always get home. ***And*** he or she could get back to the place where he was (and didn't know exactly the location of at the time) many years later.

The view—when weather and daylight permit a view—is monochromatic: earth and sky often indistinguishable from each other, bland as this page without print. But *Inupiat* lived life with joy. They loved to travel. They loved to entertain guests at home. They laughed frequently. They drummed and sang, danced and told bright tales. One word for *breathe* in the language *(Inupiaq)* is the same as their word for *creating poetry.* While traditional *Inupiat* did not have a visual art as we usually define it—an aesthetic, independent effort—they did decorate amulets and domestic tools and weapons as well as (for example) the hide skins forming a lean-to or tent for summer. Using stone or even rare and precious driftwood, they would *release* what they perceived to be within the material—say a walrus from a piece of soapstone. Once the form emerged, however, it was (traditionally) thrown away as worthless. For the traditional Inupiat, value lay in the *process* (the actual carving), not the *product* (the resulting statue). The *Inupiaq* language (unwritten, traditionally) is built basically around **verbs** (process?) whereas English (as an example) is built basically around **nouns** (product?). The inner life of the traditional *Inuk* was as colorful, as creative, and as imaginative as the outer world was featureless.

Do the *Inupiat* of tradition still exist? No, at least not on the American continent, possibly a few in Northeast Greenland and (more likely) Siberia. If anyone officially knew of isolated groups, you may be sure that governments would soon or late step in to require that they "become civilized." They would need to obey their country's laws, pay taxes, and send their children to school at city centers. Commercial interests would hurry along to introduce firearms and stainless steel sled runners (even though these are known to snap like pretzels in extreme cold), then snowmobiles (nicely dependent on petrol so that the owner is then dependent on currency). Suppliers would be sure to send in plenty of sugar (Now we need dentists!), coffee, tobacco and liquor, as well. The traditional *Inupiat* knew nothing of these cultivated amenities. In fact, the traditional *Inupiat* is one of the few peoples known (back when they *lived* traditionally) to use no mind-altering substance whatever.

Those who study different cultures say that traditional *Inupiat* were among the healthiest and happiest people ever known to exist on this earth . . . and surely—by our civilized standards—with the least reason to be so.

Phyl Manning

GLOSSARY

(INUPIAT to ENGLISH)

aagii .... no definitely, emphatically not!

aglu .... breathing hole for seal; see *natchiagruk*

agviq .... **bowhead whale**

ahmi .... cannot be known in advance

Aleut .... Inuit people and language on and near Aleutian Islands

amarok .... **wolf**

amoutik .... Women's parka having double hood (one to hold baby)

ananak .... Mother (female parent)

ananatsiak .... Grandmother (Kiti)

angakok .... shaman, medicine man, magician, herbalist healer)

atatak .... Father (male parent)

avik .... **walrus**

Big Feed .... woman's private cache in household: edible, wearable treasures and useful tools

bladder .... animal part: elastic-walled sack-like container (use);

Blink of Eye .... no (length of eyelid closure indicates emphasis)

blubber .... edible fat of whales, seals, walruses (sea mammals: *puyee*) various sizes/sources

breath sucked in .... yes (non-verbal)

cache .... storage of food rock-covered to protect from predators dog-people .... descendants of Sedna: non-Inuit from south (and about everywhere is "south")

ee-ee........................... yes [Also non-verbal yes:
(1) raising of eyebrows,
(2) sucking in breath]

Eskimo .... means "eater of raw meat"; uncomplimentary name given by North American (Algonquin) Indians

eyebrows raised .... yes (non-verbal)

floe .... large mass of floating ice

hummock .... mound or ridge (not necessarily high)

idjak........................... spectacles slitted to prevent snow blindness (usually made from bone or wood)

iglerk.......................... sleeping ledge inside snow house

igloo .... any human shelter: wood, sod, hide (tent), snow, reinforced concrete, fiberglass

illiyardjuk................... orphan (among traditional Inuit, there were many orphans and widows)

illupak........................ underwear: lightweight fur and hide

Inuit (plural) .... the human beings (plural)

Inuk (singular) .... a human being (singular)

Inupiaq....................... language of the Inupiat Inuit

Inupiat .... The People ("man pre-eminent"), of NE Canada, N.Alaska, Greenland, N.Siberia

Irkrelrete.................... means "Lice"; uncomplimentary name for Algonquin Indians given by Inuit

kabloona .... (singular) any non-*Inuk*; literally: person with "heavy (or big) eyebrows"; dog-people

kaluna .... same meaning as above; more often used

kalunait (plural).......... (plural) same meaning as above; dog-people *kamik*........................fur boot, usually lined with grasses or (better) muskox fur (quviut) collected in summer

kapvik........................**wolverine**

kayak........................small, maneuverable, hide-skinned boat with hatch that fits around waist(s) of paddler(s)

koolitak........................men's parka for outdoors

kringmerk........................**sled dog(s)** [no other dog is known to traditional Inupiat]

kussuyok........................coward, cowardly

lead........................channel of saltwater between coastal ice and floating ice islands

muktuk........................whale skin with layer of blubber attached (food)

mumuktopaluk........................delicious, "It tastes good!"

nakorami........................thank you!

nanuk........................**white (Polar) sea bear**—largest of all bears on this planet

natchiagruk........................baby seal on ledge at aglu

nathek........................**seal** (relatively small "true" [earless] seal and delicious)

Nigitook........................name for south wind

nuilak........................fur trim for a parka hood

Nuliajuk........................young girl; also refers to the legendary Sedna, Queen of the Sea

Ooangniktook........................name for north wind

oomingmak........................**musk oxen**

owka........................no [Also non-verbal blink of eyes; time lid down indicates emphasis]

Paija........................evil spirit-woman with no good qualities: totally malignant

pantomime........................communication/entertainment by facial expression and body movement alone *peeusinga* .... customary, the way we do things here

pelt .... mammal hide with (usually) fur still attached

permafrost .... permanently frozen soil (can be a few feet to 1/3 mile deep)

pirtok .... what's happened has happened and cannot be changed or undone: so be it

pressure ridge .... mounding where incoming ice (tidal) builds against grounded coastal ice

ptarmigan .... largish, **grouselike bird** with feathered feet; color changes with seasons

puyee .... creatures of the sea (usually means the big mammals)

Sedna .... woman who rules the sea and all creatures (puyee) within it

siku .... ice island (floating, not grounded)

sila .... internal condition (of person) and external condition (environment, weather)

silapak .... outer garment for wearing outdoors

silatunerk .... clever, intelligent, and shrewd

soospuk .... nitwit, bungler

tingmisut .... airplane

Tornarssuk .... spirit of the land

Tornraksoak .... moon spirit (or Takkuk)

tuktu .... **caribou**

tullugak .... **raven**

tuwawi! .... Hurry up!

ulu .... utility knife: very sharp, small, crescent-shaped

umiak .... women's or/and whale boat; large, traditionally rounded and rudderless; carries much

Yup'ik .... people and language of Inuit in W. Alaska, Bering Sea islands, south tip of Siberia

ACKNOWLEDGEMENTS

Many thanks to Jenny Kay especially, and to Willa Perrine and Doug Bratten for proofing and editing. Also to <u>every</u> member of 6Meet for patience and suggestions. Also to Claire Braz-Valentine's Monday Group as well as the UC Chico O.L.L.I.s.

I am most grateful to Mary Awa for running with the ball—promotion past, present and future.

Thanks also to Karol and Sultana Saritaş, as well as to Kent Brisby for tech support and, with Mah'mut Saritaş, their unfailing encouragement.

And thank you John Lescroart for giving me confidence and counsel that I "not write another word" before doing some serious marketing. I waited a while to heed counsel.

And appreciated certainly is publisher Pamela Marin-Kingsley for "taking a chance."

As always, where tales of the *Inupiat* are involved, my gratitude goes to Edmund Carpenter for his dreams *(Eskimo Realities)* and to Barry Lopez for his realities *(Arctic Dreams)*.

Phyl Manning

ABOUT THE AUTHOR

Originally from Nebraska, author Phyl Manning worked as an educator while living overseas much of her adult life—the West Pacific, Southeast Asia, Europe—and has traveled to large extent along "paths not often taken." Focused on the traditional Inupiat in conjunction with doctoral studies in Anthropology, she was determined to give these remarkable people literary breath, thought, and action after her scholarly writing was concluded.

Ms. Manning presently lives in New Hampshire.

Breinigsville, PA USA
12 December 2010
251236BV00001B/1/P